WISTERIA WOVEN

Wisteria Witches Mysteries

BOOK #11

ANGELA PEPPER

CHAPTER 1

Monday

28 Days to Halloween

Something tapped politely on my bedroom window.

"Now what?" I asked wearily. "Shouldn't you still be getting your beauty sleep?"

I closed the book I had been reading and climbed out of bed. I expected to see the scaled face of our resident wyvern on the other side of the glass.

"What are you up to now, you overfed parrot? Have you lost track of all your secret entrances, you walnut-brained, duck-footed syrup sucker?"

Ribbons loved my insults. It was our thing. The pint-sized creature regularly threatened to eviscerate my entrails, but he secretly adored me. I was, after all, the person who kept him supplied with maple syrup.

Plus coleslaw.

And cat food.

He had eclectic tastes.

I lobbed a few more pet names his way as I lifted the window, but I wasn't greeted by his usual telepathic response. It wasn't Ribbons at my second-story window.

Shame on me. I should have guessed by how polite the tapping had been.

A winged creature I'd never seen before hovered outside. It was unable to get in through the defenses, so I cast a modifier, opening the house's protective envelope at the window.

I prepared a battle spell, letting it pool in my palm at the ready. *Zara is a good witch. Zara does not fireball first and ask questions later.*

My visitor landed on the inner portion of the windowsill with a metallic TINK. Its gleaming wings folded down, metallic feathers of gold and silver sliding over each other with precision. There was a soft hum, and the audible ticking of clockwork.

The creature—it didn't feel like a machine—cocked its shiny metallic head and stared at me with the blackest of eyes. They were like two camera lenses.

"You'd better not be taking photos of me in my pajamas," I said. "At least let me know if you are, and I'll try to find something matching." I straightened my top, which was polka-dotted, and did not match the striped bottoms.

The lens-eyed thing, Clockbird, preened a feather as though nervously stalling for time. Was it a drama queen sort of bird? Some shirttail relative to the notoriously histrionic harpies?

The beak opened, and there was a metallic sound, like a throat being cleared, followed by the grinding of gears. The beak snapped shut. Clockbird went back to preening.

I asked, "Are you here on your own behalf?"

Clockbird shook its head.

"Delivering a message?"

Clockbird nodded. A tiny screw fell out of the side of its head.

"That explains it," I said. "You've got a screw loose. It's on the windowsill, next to your claw."

The bird snatched up the screw and proceeded to fix itself, using a specialized talon as a screwdriver.

"No rush," I said flatly, shifting from one bare foot to the other. "I've got at least an hour before I have to be at work. Sure, I woke up early to tackle my to-be-read list, but who needs fiction when reality is so much stranger?"

Clockbird lifted one wing and raised a feather. *One moment, please.* More whirring.

Who sent this messenger? I waited, mentally scrolling through a list of the usual suspects. At the top of my list was my mother. She had spied on me before using birds— though never mechanized ones. Spy cameras were the domain of people like Vincent Wick.

I was only halfway down my list of suspects when the bird's beak opened with a snap, and it began to speak.

"ZARA RIDDLE," Clockbird said, not shouting, but not speaking quietly, either. It seemed to be talking in all-caps.

"That's my name," I said. "Don't wear it out."

"YOU ARE CORDIALLY INVITED TO..." The bird trailed off. Its eye lenses were no longer trained on me, but on a spot near my feet.

Clockbird and I had been joined by my furkid, Boa, a fluffy white cat with no powers.

Boa stepped around me, moving silently and steadily toward the windowsill. Her body seemed to float, as though drawn on an invisible thread. I'd seen this before. *Stalking mode activated.*

The clockwork creature on the windowsill trembled and rattled like an old car.

"Don't mind Boa," I said to Clockbird. "She can barely catch a spider without help. You were saying? Something about a cordial invitation?"

The bird restarted. "YOU ARE... CHEEP!" It jumped backward several inches.

Boa had drawn closer.

3

"I'm not cheap. I'm frugal," I said. Cue the laugh track!

Clockbird chattered and clicked, too nervous to resume the message.

I scooped up the cat. Boa wriggled in protest, but I held her tight while I waved for the bird to carry on.

"ZARA RIDDLE," Clockbird said again. "YOU ARE CORDIALLY INVITED TO ATTEND THE—"

It was interrupted this time by another flying creature. Our resident wyvern had landed on the windowsill behind Clockbird.

"What am I missing, Zed?" Ribbons asked telepathically. "What is this? It does not smell like prey, but it looks like prey, Zed. Is it a chicken? Are you luring tasty chicken to your quarters without me?"

Clockbird turned, saw the wyvern, and took to the air inside the room with a panicked clanging of metallic wings.

That was when the white fluffball in my arms kicked off from my chest. Boa soared through the air with the grace of a predator. A predator who didn't get the majority of her calories from lightly-microwaved canned cat food.

Boa caught the bird mid-air. She bit its head clean off before landing gracefully on all four paws.

I was both horrified and proud. "Boa! Bad girl!"

The headless mechanical bird was limp on the floor. Boa buried her face in its workings, ripped out a mouthful of internal clockwork, flashed me a defiant look, and ran from the bedroom.

I turned to Ribbons for assistance.

He wasn't on the windowsill, but on the floor, gobbling up the rest of the clockwork creature.

"It's delicious, Zed," Ribbons said in his charming Count Chocula accent. "Here. I saved you the liver."

He jumped in the air, dropped something in my palm, and was out the window in three wingbeats. The wyvern's scales shimmered in the dawn's early light as he disappeared from view.

I looked down at the object in my hand. The *liver*? It was hard and green with glittering facets, like a jelly bean made of emerald. It was warm.

My daughter appeared in the bedroom doorway, rubbing her eyes. She was wearing the reverse of my mismatched pajamas: stripes on top, polka-dot bottoms.

"What's going on, Mom?"

"A clockwork bird arrived to cordially invite me to something, but I don't know what. Boa ate the messenger before it could finish."

Zoey frowned. "Boa can't catch a spider without help." She turned and walked away, calling back over her shoulder, "It's too early in the morning for you to be this weird."

As she shuffled away, another redheaded family member came toward me from the other direction.

It was my aunt, Zinnia Riddle. She had her own perfectly good house, but she had wanted to sleep over after dinner the night before. She had something on her mind, but two glasses of wine hadn't done the job of breaking it loose. Zinnia had extremely rigid boundaries, magical and otherwise. It was a wonder that oxygen could get through her lungs.

"Good morning, Aunt Zinnia."

She tucked a lock of long, red hair behind one ear. "I heard a commotion," she said. "Did you see a ghost?"

"No. Just a clockwork bird who wanted to invite me to something. Boa ate it. Well, most of it. Ribbons ate the rest."

"The ghost took the form of a bird?"

"There's no ghost," I said.

She cast her hazel eyes down and pulled the guest bathrobe tight around herself. "No ghost," she said, almost whispering. "That's odd. I thought surely it would have followed me here."

5

CHAPTER 2

Zinnia didn't want to talk about the ghost she may or may not have brought to my house.

She promised she would come clean and explain everything, but only after she'd had a cup of tea and heard about my early morning visitor.

We went downstairs to the kitchen, where I put on the kettle and prepared a gourmet breakfast of Pop Tarts.

I told her about the arrival of Clockbird, its truncated message, and its sudden demise.

Zinnia's first question was, "You wake up before your alarm clock so that you can read magic books?"

"Not magic books. Just regular fiction."

"But why?" She blew over her hot tea. "Never mind. That's irrelevant, and, besides, we all have our coping methods." She glanced around. "We ought to check on your feline companion. Fetch her for me."

Boa was already in the room, positioned in the middle of the kitchen work triangle—all the better to trip me and send food flying. She was ever the optimist. No matter how many times I'd used magic to keep from spilling food, Boa remained hopeful. And good for her. It was that never-give-up attitude that had enabled her to gobble the choice bits of Clockbird.

I scooped up the cat. Out of the corner of my eye, I saw Zinnia drop something from the palm of her hand into her tea. My curiosity was piqued, but she hadn't dosed my tea, so I didn't ask.

I put Boa on the table, and we checked her for signs of distress. Zinnia put one finger in each of the cat's ears while casting a diagnostic spell. Boa squirmed and made a fuss, but she allowed it.

Zinnia released the cat and sat back in her chair. "She'll be fine. There is nothing indigestible inside her system. The bird must have only appeared to be made of metal. I suspect it was chitin, or enamel and dentin, like fish scales or teeth."

"Or maybe Boa already, you know, *expelled* the clockwork gears. Check your shoes before you put them on."

"I always do." My aunt grimaced as she sipped her tea.

"Any idea who sent the messenger bird?"

She looked pensive for a moment, then asked, "Is your relationship with Detective Bentley nearing a benchmark?"

"Like an anniversary?" I counted on my fingers. "We've been official for about five weeks, so yes. That might not be a benchmark for other women my age, but you can color me surprised. Five whole weeks and I haven't scared him off yet. Do you think it was him?" I clutched my heart. "Bentley sent me a love-o-gram?"

"I am not the party to whom you ought to be directing that question."

"Maybe my new sister sent it. Persephone Rose could be planning a fancy dinner party. Do you think it was her?"

"Again, I am not the party who would have that answer."

"Fine." I stared pointedly at her empty teacup. "Your time's up. You haven't touched your Pop Tart, but your tea's gone down the hatch." I grabbed her toaster pastry for myself. "Now tell me about this ghost you dragged into my house without so much as a warning."

She pursed her lips and looked down into the empty cup. "There's no ghost."

"Oh, no, you don't. Upstairs, you told me there was one. You're not the little boy who cries wolf. Spill it before I embarrass both of us by casting spells on you. I brushed my teeth with gargoyle butter this morning, so I'm ready for anything."

She sighed wearily. "I *thought* something had been following me these past few days, but it appears I was mistaken."

"You saw a ghost?"

"Not exactly. I sensed an energy. That was all. Staying here last night was a test. You are the one who is Spirit Charmed. You can see spirits. If you didn't see anything, that means there is nothing to see. I was mistaken."

"Since when are you mistaken about anything, let alone witch enough to admit it?"

She blinked three times. "Oh, Zara. It's too early in the morning for your verbal combat."

I was about to remind her that it had been *her* idea to bring a ghost for a sleepover when we were interrupted by another voice.

The voice said, "Ham?"

Zinnia and I looked around. We appeared to be alone in the kitchen. From the sound of the water running upstairs, the home's other human occupant, my daughter, was still using the shower.

I looked into Zinnia's hazel eyes, which gave me the uncanny feeling I was looking into a mirror that was out of sync with reality. We looked so similar, and her eyes were the same as mine and my daughter's, except with a few extra lines at the edges.

The query came again. "Ham?"

Maintaining eye contact with Zinnia, watching for signs of deception, I said, "Your ghost talks."

"There is no ghost," she said.

The voice spoke a third time. "Ham?"

Zinnia's gaze went to the floor. I whipped my head in time to see Boa's mouth closing.

I turned back to Zinnia. "Stop trying to change the subject. I know it's you."

"Me?" Her hands, which had been resting on the edge of the table, curled into partial fists.

"What witcher-i-doo are you up to? A ventriloquist spell? Nice way to change the subject away from your ghost."

"Whatever is happening right now, it isn't my doing." She took slow, deep breaths, then asked through clenched teeth, "Do I look like someone who pretends to be a talking cat?"

"How should I know? You *look* like a nice middle-aged lady who works for some boring municipal department. You don't *look* like someone who boils potions, travels through time, and creates mayonnaise-based weapons for the military."

"I suppose you are correct." Her jaw unclenched, and she arched one eyebrow. "One might say that *you* look like an ordinary librarian."

"I've been called worse."

We both nodded. I'd offended her with my suspicion, but she'd gotten over it quickly. Our relationship was stronger than ever. Zinnia got on my nerves as frequently as I got on hers, but I loved my aunt. I would rather spend one hour bickering with her than two hours with someone who agreed with everything I said. Family keeps you on your toes.

She turned her attention to the fluffy white feline on the floor and asked, "Has the cat ever spoken before?"

"Not that I know of. Do you think Fatima Nix did something to her at the vet clinic? Some pet whisperer thing?"

"Fatima communicates with animals, but not by making them speak."

"Hmm." I tapped my fingers on the table. "Ribbons is always threatening to make Boa talk, but he wouldn't dare. Or, actually, he *would* dare, because heaven knows that flying snakeskin cowboy boot doesn't listen to a word I say." More tapping. "But I don't think he has the supplies, or he would have done it long before now."

"The bird," Zinnia said, thrusting one finger in the air excitedly.

"Clockbird?"

"When the cat consumed its vital organs, that must have given her the ability to speak."

"That's..." I paused. "I was going to say that's crazy, but it's not. That is exactly the sort of thing that happens around here. Why am I even surprised anymore? My father's a fox, my mother's a vampire, my best friend is a gorgon, and now I've got a talking cat. Perfect. Where's my Hollywood agent? My life is a wacky sitcom."

My aunt leaned across the table and picked up the green gem that had been part of Clockbird. "May I take this? I shall ask around and see if I can determine its origin."

"Be my guest."

"Did you say this was the liver?"

"That's what Ribbons told me."

"Fascinating." She rolled the bean in her hand.

The pipes above us clanged as Zoey turned off the shower upstairs.

A moment passed in comfortable silence.

Zoey yelled down the stairwell, "Mom! Someone ate my deodorant! It was a new stick, too!" She stomped around above our heads, muttering about how the new coconut-based beauty products were too good to be true.

"Ribbons," I said to my aunt, shaking my head. "First he ate all our tubes of lipstick, and now this."

She wrinkled her nose. "That doesn't sound like the work of a wyvern." She looked up and gestured at the ceiling. "I thought all those cobwebs were the result of your housekeeping skills, but it appears you may have an invisible spider problem."

"Great." My forearms prickled. "Wait. Do you mean the *problem* is invisible, like with termites, or that the spiders are invisible?"

"The spiders." Her forehead wrinkled. "Which is good. They're basically harmless, unless you were to actually see them." She jerked her arms inward and hugged herself. "Some secrets ought not be revealed."

"If they're eating makeup, they're not harmless. I've already got enough mouths to feed around here."

"I'll get you something that should clear them right up. Don't worry yourself." She glanced up at the corners of my kitchen ceiling in a wild-eyed manner that did not put me at ease. "They're harmless."

"How big are they?"

"No one knows. No one whose testimony is reliable."

"I'm starting to put things together. This energy you've been sensing, it was the spiders, wasn't it? How generous of you to bring them over here, to my house. Thanks. Thanks a lot."

She frowned. "I don't believe it was my doing. It's simply the time of year. Spiders move indoors before winter. You should be flattered. They only move into homes with positive energy. Not like invisible bees."

"When you put it like that..." I looked up at the ceiling, which was covered in cobwebs that hadn't been there the day before. "Nope. I'm not going to be flattered into running a hotel for invisible anything, let alone spiders."

"I'll bring over some traps. In the meantime, whatever you do, don't conjure any forced-visibility spells for a while."

I agreed to be cautious, and asked her to tell me more about the extermination process.

After another cup of tea, when all the spider talk had died down, my thoughts returned to the reason for my aunt's overnight stay. I wasn't giving up on getting through her rigid boundaries.

I pretended to be startled by something behind her. "A ghost," I exclaimed breathlessly. "Standing right behind you, Aunt Zinnia. It must be the one who followed you over here."

She pursed her lips and gave me a skeptical look. "Describe its appearance."

"It's wearing a white bed sheet with eye holes," I said. "It must be one of those shy ghosts."

She wasn't buying it. "I told you, Zara. There is no ghost. I must have been mistaken."

"So you insist." I sat back and crossed my arms. "It's probably for the best there's no ghost. Between the talking cat and the invisible spiders, we've got enough shenanigans to keep things weird until Halloween."

"Halloween," she said hollowly, staring ahead blankly. "I suppose it is that time again."

"Could you sound any less excited? What kind of witch doesn't love Halloween?"

She continued staring at nothing, as though she was in some other time and place where she couldn't hear me.

Boa brushed up against my shin. "Ham?"

Ah, the irony. My aunt wouldn't talk, and my cat wouldn't stop.

CHAPTER 3

When I walked in the staff entrance to the library, my coworkers, who were standing near the sink in the staff lounge, immediately started talking loudly about the weather.

"Don't stop the gossip on my account," I said. "What were you two talking about before I walked in?"

The head librarian, Kathy Carmichael, answered in a sing-song voice, "Just how nice it is that September is over, with all its dreary rain." She patted her dark ringlets. "The humidity makes my hair so tight."

"Humidity is the worst," said the pink-haired children's librarian, Frank Wonder. He grinned at me the way he did when he was plotting something, which basically all the time.

"Right," I said flatly. "Humidity. That's all you two were talking about."

Frank asked, "What's new with you, Zara? Did you have a nice visit with your father over the weekend?"

"Nobody got bitten hard enough to leave a scar, if that's what you mean."

"That's good," Frank said.

Ruefully, Kathy said, "I can't say the same for most of my family gatherings."

We all nodded knowingly at each other.

Silence filled the staff lounge. Sweet, beautiful silence. There was nothing quite like a library in the hours before opening.

I was curious about what they'd been discussing, but I hadn't had much luck that morning getting intel out of others. Did everyone but me have a screw loose?

Using magic, I pulled my favorite mug from the cupboard and floated it lazily through the air. Casually, I said, "Something curious happened at my house this morning."

They exchanged a look. A *knowing* look. They were clearly up to something.

My stomach burned around my breakfast. The two of them were conspiring now? I did not care for this new dynamic. Kathy claimed the public was our boss, but she was still the head librarian. Frank was supposed to share secrets with me, not her. It was the two of us against Kathy and her authority. How could we enjoy letting off steam through childish behavior if nobody was willing to play the adult?

I did not like this new development at all.

Kathy asked sweetly, "What happened at your house this morning?" Her light-brown eyes glowed orange next to her dark skin. She blinked innocently behind her round glasses.

"Never mind," I said, raising my nose in the air.

"Zara, don't be a pill," Frank said. "Tell us what happened at your house."

"Tell us," Kathy implored.

As much as I wanted to treat them with a dose of their own medicine, I couldn't keep the morning's events to myself. Since learning of each other's powers, I had been telling my coworkers most of my adventures. Seeing their reactions made even the most gruesome disasters seem worth it.

"It all started when something tapped on my window," I said, then relayed the whole adventure.

They were horrified. Not about the possible ghost, the invisible spiders, or the cat being able to speak. They thought all those things sounded fun. They couldn't get past the idea of Boa eating a talking bird.

"No, you didn't," Kathy said, exhaling the words with disgust. "You let your cat attack a defenseless bird?"

"I didn't *let* her do anything. Do you know nothing about cats?"

"Whooo would do such a thing to a magical creature?" Kathy, who reminded me of a hooting owl even though she was a sprite, had a soft spot for birds of all kinds, except chickens—for obvious reasons.

"You monster," Frank said. "I can't even look at you." He turned away in what I hoped was fake disgust. Frank and I joked around a lot, but he was even more of a bird enthusiast than Kathy.

Frank Wonder was a winged shifter, like his sister. She was a swan and he was a flamingo. Two of Frank's best friends, Knox and Rob, were also bird shifters. Like Kathy, he still ate chicken, but turkey was off the table.

"Easy now," I said. "Boa acted alone. I'm a good witch, I swear. Look! I brought donuts. Would a bird murderer bring everyone nice jelly donuts?"

Frank's small, hooded eyes narrowed. His crooked chin twitched from side to side, like a comma being repositioned on a line of text. "Those donuts are from last week."

"Yes. And I'm the one who brought them in for Fresh Pastry Friday." I held out the box as a not-too-stale-to-eat peace offering.

Frank reached for a donut, blindly grasping around because his eyes were so narrowed at me in accusation that he couldn't see what he was doing.

After Frank had manhandled every pastry, Kathy used her whip-like sprite tongue to grab two donuts at once. As

I caught a whiff of the sticky saliva on her tongue, I longed for the good ol' days. Ah, how much more hygienic the staff lounge had been, back when Kathy hid her identity—and freaky sprite tongue—from us.

Frank licked the icing sugar from his fingers and relaxed visibly. He shot another knowing look at Kathy and asked, "Should we tell her?"

Kathy smirked and gave him a coy shrug.

"Tell me what?" I demanded.

They snickered.

I stamped my foot and cracked off a blast of pink sparkles. "Listen, you two. I am all out of patience for secrets this morning. If you don't tell me right now what you're snickering about, I'm going to summon every conspiracy nut within a hundred-mile radius and bring them here to request your librarian services personally." The air filled with more pink sparkles as I picked up speed. "And I'll put a disguise glamour on all of them, so you won't know who you're dealing with until it's too late, and you're deep into research about aluminum headgear that deflects brain-control rays."

They snickered some more.

I asked, "Did you two send that clockwork bird?"

"No," Frank said. "We didn't send it." He flashed his eyes at me playfully. "If you keep asking the wrong questions, you won't get your answers."

"You two," I said, shaking my head. "Ever since the Goblin Hordes cleared out, you two have been just bored enough to cause trouble." I gave Frank a thumbs up. "Good prank. You got me." All my blustery sparkles and fireworks fizzled out.

"It wasn't Franker the Pranker," Frank said. "I wish I could take the credit, but I didn't do anything. In fact, both of us received the same invitation."

"We did," Kathy said excitedly. "Early this morning. Like you." Her head bobbed, sending her dark ringlets swinging and her round glasses sliding down her narrow nose.

"Both of you got a talking bird invitation?"

Frank smirked and gave an apologetic shrug. "That's what we were talking about when you got here. We didn't know if you'd gotten one, since you're..."

"A witch," Kathy finished.

"Exactly," Frank said. "We didn't know if witches were getting invited."

"We didn't know, because this has never happened before," Kathy said, gushing now. "Not to regular people like us. I've been to the event before, but always as a plus one. I've never gotten my own personal invitation."

"This is all new to me," Frank said. "Rob and Knox have been telling me stories, but I've never even been as a plus one."

"Been to what? You're killing me."

In unison, they said, "To the Halloween Costume Ball at Castle Wyvern!"

"That's it? A costume party?"

"Not just any costume party," Kathy said rapturously. "It's very exclusive." She did a flourish with both hands, as though framing a brightly-lit marquee. "For supernaturals only."

"Oh." I scratched my head. "So what? Supernaturals are kind of a dime a dozen in Wisteria."

They stared at me like I was the one with a screw loose.

I talked it through like a game show contestant. "So, it's a Halloween costume ball, with shifters, and vampires, and half-demons, and they're all dressed up... as each other?"

Frank and Kathy nodded excitedly.

"Okay," I said slowly. "I'm starting to see the appeal. But who sent the invitations? And am I still invited, even after my cat ate the messenger?"

"I'm sure it's fine," Kathy said with another sweeping hand wave. "If they're going to send things to the houses of witches, they've got to expect some casualties. I'm sure they factor it into the budget."

"Who's *they*?" I asked, even though I already knew the answer. *They* had to be our friendly neighborhood "good guys." The ones who kept all of us civilians safe from harm by wiping our minds and lying to us with cover stories about deaths, disappearances, and other strange events—many of which their own employees were behind.

They worked deep underground when they weren't driving around in Department of Water vans. People in the know called them the DWM. The Department of Water and Magic.

Frank said, "It was Non-Human Resources at the DWM that sent the invitations. They pay for the party, since it's basically a staff event, with mostly their own agents and a few guests." He giggled. "Plus whatever musicians they hoodwink into risking their lives playing for the party. Rob and Knox told me that last year, they had a big band, the kind with an orchestra. The trumpet player, who didn't know any better, got a little handsy at the water tank with what he thought was a girl in a mermaid costume. Boy, was he in for a surprise. It took half the Department's medical team to put him back together again. On the positive side, I hear he plays trumpet better than ever... with his new bionic mouth."

"Back it up." I swirled my finger in front of Frank's nose. "Did you say the invites came from *Non-Human* Resources?"

He batted his eyelashes. "They can't exactly call themselves *Human* Resources, can they?"

"Fair enough." I shrugged. "So what are you two going dressed as? What costumes?"

Kathy, who'd been bouncing on the balls of her feet, came back down to earth.

Frank made a long, low croaking sound.

Together, they both said, "Costumes?"

"It *is* a costume ball," I said.

My coworkers exchanged a frown. Frank ran one hand through his pink hair. Kathy took off her glasses and began cleaning them.

"You don't know yet?" I jabbed one thumb at the calendar. "Halloween is in twenty-eight days. We need to get cracking."

"Fluffernuts," Kathy said.

"Double fluffernuts," Frank agreed.

I asked, "Kathy, what did you go as in previous years? When you were a plus-one?"

"It was never a costume ball before now," she said. "Just formal dress. Gowns and tuxedos. A few people had eye masks, but that was it."

"I'd prefer formal dress," Frank said. "I have some vintage tuxedos I'd love to bring out of storage."

Kathy grumbled, "Now the pressure's on." She rubbed her glasses hard, making them squeak.

Both muttered about getting to work and opening the library's front doors to the public.

It was that time, so I washed down a stale cruller with hot coffee—the breakfast of champions—and we all got to work.

CHAPTER 4

The first patron in the door that Monday morning was one of our regular conspiracy enthusiasts.

Frank elbowed me. "That one's all yours."

I hissed back, "You're so generous, Mr. Wonderful."

"Don't give me that attitude. You and I both know you brought this on yourself, Little Miss Jinx. You summoned him, with your pink sparkly thunderstorm and your not-so-empty threats."

I pretended to kick him in the shin. He wasn't wrong. I'd been developing more control over my magic, but it wasn't really mine to control. Magic had a mind of its own. Supernaturals like us had to be careful not to give it any ideas.

The conspiracy enthusiast stepped up to the counter.

Dorian Dabrowski was about eighty, average height, and in excellent shape for any age. He dressed in dark wool suits with dusty-rose shirts and bright yellow cravats. His bowler hat, which looked normal on the outside, was lined with three types of foil.

What made Mr. Dabrowski a conspiracy *enthusiast* rather than a conspiracy *nut* was his net worth, rumored to be upward of five million dollars.

"Hello, Mr. Dabrowski," I said warmly.

He tipped his bowler hat at me. "Good day, Agent Red." He winked twice.

"Mr. Dabrowski, I'm not a secret agent," I said. "Just a librarian."

"Oh, I know." More winking. "*They* wouldn't hire someone like you, someone who thinks for herself. I would imagine they tried to recruit you, but you escaped their underground labyrinth before they could wipe your mind." He leaned over the counter and whispered, "They have gorgons down there."

I breathed out the words, "No way." I leaned in, close enough to smell his expensive aftershave. "Actual gorgons?"

"The ones that turn you to stone with their eyes. Horrible creatures."

"What if these gorgons only used their powers for good? Would they be so horrible?"

He stared at me a moment, his blue eyes widening with wonder, then giggled with genuine pleasure. The giggles turned into loud laughter. Another thing that made Dorian Dabrowski an enthusiast rather than a nut was the fact that he *loved* the idea of a secret underground organization. At least someone with a plan was running things, he often said. Anyone with actual power would be better than politicians, in his opinion.

"Imagine that," he wheezed mirthfully. "A *good* gorgon." He used a silk handkerchief, yellow like his cravat, to wipe the tears from his eyes. "Agent Red, you truly are one of a kind."

"If you knew my family, you'd see I'm more of a variation on a theme, but I appreciate the compliment. What can I do for you today?"

"There are two things. You have already given me the pleasure of your smile, so all that's left is..." The wrinkles around his features deepened.

"Do you need help with the town's archives? More research into the notorious Wakeful family?"

"Not today. My concern currently is a little girl who's lost."

"An actual missing person? Mr. Dabrowski, you need to talk to the police if a child is in danger. I'm serious."

"Agent Red, you and I both know the local police don't believe a word I say. They're pleasant enough. They humor me, because I'm old and I pay a good deal of taxes on my properties, but they're not like us. They're not believers."

"How about you tell me more about this little girl, and I'll pass it along? I know a few open-minded people at the WPD."

"All I know is that she's lost." His tone was dead serious. "She can't find her way home."

A tingle went up my spine. "That's worrying. It's every parent's worst nightmare. How old is she?"

"I don't know. She doesn't speak."

"Where is she right now?" *Please tell me she's not locked up in your mansion.*

"She's not locked up in my mansion." He forced an awkward chuckle. "Trust me, I know how this sounds. I do. And I truly appreciate that you and your coworkers have always treated me with kindness and respect."

"A library is for everyone."

"Of course. But I wouldn't want to take up all of your time. If you'll just direct me to your section about the worlds on the other side of mirrors, I can take care of the rest myself."

"Do you mean portals?"

He smiled. "Yes! Portals. Direct me to the materials about portals."

"Those books are on the fiction shelves. Fantasy and science fiction."

He winked at me. "Fiction it is, then. Point me in the general direction."

"I'll take you there." I came around the counter and escorted the eccentric gentleman to the science fiction and fantasy hardcovers. I pointed out several popular titles in the portal subgenre.

He pulled down a slim volume and read out the title. "*Through the Looking Glass, and What Alice Found There.*"

"It's the sequel to *Alice's Adventures in Wonderland.*"

He gave me a dumbfounded look. "Why would she ever go back?"

I held out both hands. "Why do any of us keep doing the things we do?"

He clutched the book to his chest. "This is exactly what I was looking for. Put it on my tab. I don't care about the cost."

"Mr. Dabrowski, are we really doing this again? I keep telling you, this isn't a book store. You can take books home, as long as you promise to bring them back."

"I don't know how you people stay in business with that revenue model." He winked again.

CHAPTER 5

After Mr. Dabrowski left, the library got busy. I promptly forgot about his lost little girl because it was only the latest in dozens of things he'd come to research, and the man was wrong about things far more often than he was right.

The library wasn't loud, exactly, but it was teeming with life and humming with quiet conversations.

Now that it was October, everyone was in the mood for all things Halloween.

While some towns specialized in Christmas, or summer celebrations, Wisteria put everything it had into Halloween. There would be multiple corn mazes in the farm fields outside town limits, plus pick-your-own-pumpkin patches, horse-drawn hay rides, barn dances, and more. Each weekend leading up to the big day had its own parade, starting with the upcoming March of the Scarecrows.

That year, there had been some talk of officially including zombies, since a few people always showed up in zombie makeup anyway. The mayor herself decreed that zombies could only participate if they made an effort to resemble the scarecrows the parade was supposed to be for. All zombies had to display a minimum of seventeen stalks of straw poking out of their clothing. Most people agreed that was fair enough. And besides, the zombie trend was waning. After a few shivery parades in tattered clothes, the zombified participants were eager to trade in their shredded businesswear for comfy flannel shirts and denim coveralls, not to mention the insulating layer of straw.

By lunch time, we had checked out a number of books about costumes and entertaining, and had heard many opinions on the scarecrows versus zombies debate, among other things.

"Tradition is important to uphold," some folks said.

"But traditions must evolve with the times," others insisted.

"The old ways are the best ways."

"Once upon a time, the old ways were the new ways."

"Kids these days need to respect the wisdom of their elders."

"Kids these days have a lot to teach us all."

"All of the holidays have gotten too commercial, and they start way too early."

"I wish it could be Halloween all year long."

"What's with all the pumpkin-spice-flavored everything? Pumpkin is a gourd. Nobody likes the taste of gourds. That's why, if you've got nothing better to make a pie with due to crop failure or wartime rations, we dilute the gourd taste with heaps of sugar and cinnamon. And what about all these pumpkin spice lattes? It should be called what it is: sugar-and-cinnamon hot milk, assuming it's even made with milk and not that white gruel they extract from tofu, or oats, or heaven knows what else. You can't milk an oat! People have lost their minds!"

Through it all, I smiled and nodded, which everyone took to mean I agreed with them.

In between daily tasks, Frank and I strung up the Halloween decorations while Kathy replenished our seasonal feature table with more Halloween books for all ages.

The upcoming costume ball hadn't left our minds. When our after-school part-timers came in to help, the three of us actively brainstormed ideas for costumes. There was no shortage of research materials nearby. It was nice to work at a place known for its selection of books about, oh, everything.

Kathy took her inspiration from the morning's metallic messenger birds. She gathered illustrations of clockwork creatures from various art and sculpture books. She was leaning toward dressing as a clockwork owl, thanks to a strong push from yours truly.

Frank, who was still fixated on breaking some vintage tuxedos out of storage, wanted to dress as tap-dancing Gene Kelly from the classic movie *Singin' in the Rain*.

"But it's just a man in a suit," Kathy said, looking perplexed. "You'd look like yourself, at a formal event."

He replied airily, "What's wrong with that?"

"It's not a costume." The crafting-obsessed head librarian's face and fingers twitched in anguish. "The point of a costume ball is to wear a costume, and the whole point of wearing a costume is*making* a costume. If there's nothing to make, what good is it?"

"I'll make my hair different. I'll color it dark, like Gene Kelly's. You can help."

Kathy snorted. "You're completely missing the point."

"Am I? I'll still be in disguise. Nobody will know it's me without my pink hair."

"Maybe so, but they won't know who you're supposed to be," she said sourly. "And they won't be able to compliment your work, because how much work is it to put on a suit?"

"Not everything worth doing has to involve a hot glue gun."

"A hot glue gun?" She sputtered. "How dare you? I rarely use something as undiscriminating and scattershot as a hot glue gun. Do you take me for some sort of amateur?"

He raised an eyebrow. "Kathy, you're not a *professional* crafter. You're a hobbyist."

"My pine cone creation won first prize at last year's wreath toss."

"Only because you had Becky Anderson chucking it across the sinkhole."

"The woman's considerable muscularity was key to my victory, but that wreath was ten times more aerodynamic than any of my competitors' creations. And the key," she waved a finger for emphasis, "*the key* was its hot-glue-gun-free construction."

"Glue-guns schmoo-guns," Frank said. "You partnered with Becky Anderson because you knew she could throw a refrigerator across the sinkhole without breaking a sweat."

"At least I made an effort. I didn't just drag any old thing out of a trunk filled with mothballs."

Frank clutched his hands to his chest. "Mothballs?" He shook his head in disbelief. "You think I would store my clothing in mothballs? It's like you don't even know me."

"You know what I meant. The key to a good costume isn't so much the idea as the execution."

"I respectfully disagree with you completely. The key is the idea."

"The execution."

"The idea."

"The execution."

"The—"

I waved my hands and interjected, "That's enough already."

They looked up from the art books they'd been poring over while bickering. Kathy had removed her glasses, and as she stared at me, I noticed she had round circles around her eyes. The lines gave her a startled goldfish look. She was one of those people who looked better—more like herself—with her glasses on.

"Oh, good," Kathy said. "Zara, you can finish this. Tell Frank that the execution of a Halloween costume is far more important than the idea."

Frank rolled his eyes and said, "Tell Kathy that nobody cares about beadwork, or lamination, or the tensile stretch of a cape. It's all about the idea."

"You're both right," I said.

They snorted at me and then faced off, ready to continue the argument.

"I have an idea with a nifty execution," I said teasingly.

They slowly turned to face me again.

"What's your idea?" Frank asked.

"It's for you, Frank," I said. "You could actually sing in the rain. There's a fountain spell I could modify."

Frank's eyes widened. "Magic? As part of my costume?"

Kathy frowned, deepening the circular lines around her eyes. "Is that allowed?"

I gestured for them to follow me to a private area of the library—over near Harry's chair.

Using a water bottle plus an umbrella from the Lost and Found, I demonstrated how the magic would work. The fountain spell required a small amount of liquid, which could be circulated in a circuit of any design. I showed them how I could create a curtain of droplets off the edge of the umbrella, then capture them before anyone got wet.

"Or," Kathy said, putting her glasses back on while she bounced on the balls of her feet, "we could do the same basic idea using Christmas tinsel and high-quality craft glue. No magic required."

Slowly, I said, "Tinsel would work."

"It simply won't do," Frank said, crossing his arms. "No cheap tinsel. I want Zara's magic."

Kathy let out a triumphant laugh. "Hah! Now who cares about execution?"

"This is different," Frank said. "Zara offered to do a spell. How can I say no to that? What good is it being friends with a witch if you don't get a few perks?"

I raised an eyebrow. "Perks?"

Without missing a beat, he said, "And I'll color my face gray, so I look like I've stepped out of a black and white movie."

"Bad idea," Kathy said, shaking her head. "You can't change your skin color for a costume. People will get offended."

Frank groaned. "At grayface? Who's going to be offended about grayface?"

Kathy said, "You heard the fine print on the invitation. All costumes must be culturally sensitive and inoffensive to all types of beings."

"What?" I hadn't heard the fine print until then, thanks to Her Royal Fluffiness the Huntress, so my jaw dropped at the news. "Are you kidding me? Our costumes have to be inoffensive?" I laughed hollowly. "What else? Do we need to submit a costume proposal to Human, I mean, Non-Human Resources for approval?"

My coworkers stared back at me.

After a few slow blinks, Frank said, "Yes, Zara. That's exactly what we have to do. It was in the fine print."

"It was at the end of the message," Kathy said. "The bird was very specific. Your costume must be inoffensive to any being, living or dead."

I shook my head. A person could expect that sort of nonsense from a corporation with a regular*Human* Resources Department, but not from a secret underground organization that dealt with apocalypses and interdimensional vermin on a daily basis.

I grumbled a curse under my breath.

Over the course of the day, I'd come up with a number of fantastic costume ideas for myself. I'd assumed the challenge would be narrowing it down to just one. But now my excitement was turning to dread.

My costume had to be inoffensive to any being, living or dead?

I had a sinking feeling that not a single one of my ideas would get through the approval process. Heck, they'd probably send me home for some of the outfits I wore to work, or to pick up groceries, let alone to their fancy ball.

"Well, the joke's on them," I said. "I'm not doing it. I take a lot of flack over my personal style, but I draw the line here. I will not submit my creativity for their corporate judgment."

"You have to," Frank said.

"No, I don't."

Kathy sighed. "Zara, you do have to. Just because your cat ate the invitation doesn't mean the rules and regulations don't apply to you."

"They don't apply to me," I said. "They don't apply, because I'm not going to the ball."

In unison, Frank and Kathy cried, "You're not going?"

"Nope." I crossed my arms. "I'll stay home."

Together, they said, "You can't stay home on Halloween."

"Someone has to," I said. "I'll stay home with my talking cat, and I'll hand out candy."

For the rest of the day, they tried to change my mind, but I wouldn't budge.

Maybe it was all the years my mother had nixed my costume ideas at the last minute and made me change into whatever she wanted me to be.

Maybe it was all the endless complaining from townspeople about pumpkin spice coffee and the old ways versus the new ways.

Or maybe it was the fact that this Halloween would be my first one in my very own house, with its very own front door and its very own doorbell, and how, deep down, I really wanted to stay in and hand out candy.

Probably it was a combination of all three.

Frank and Kathy could go to the castle on their own, have a wonderful time, and tell me all about it.

I would be staying in and having a nice, quiet, nonviolent evening.

Or so I thought.

CHAPTER 6

Even though I refused to attend the ball at Castle Wyvern on principle, all the talk about costumes did put me in a shopping mood.

After my shift at the library, I paid a visit to one of my favorite haunts.

Mia's Kit and Kaboodle was a secondhand store, but minus the bad lighting and smell of mothballs. I thought of Mia's as less of a thrift shop and more of a boutique of treasures with history. All of the items, ranging from clothes to household goods, had plenty of life left in them. The owner, Mia Gianna, had high standards—much higher than my own. Even Frank shopped there on occasion.

I'd actually invited him along, but he'd declined. His nose was out of joint about me not going to the ball. "People will be offended," he'd said, meaning himself. But, as I'd told him when we'd clocked out, I didn't care who was offended. I didn't work for the DWM, and I didn't owe them anything. *Not my zoo, not my monkeys.*

More importantly, I didn't need a costume ball to have fun, let alone to buy fun clothes.

"Hello, Zara," Mia called out cheerily as I entered her shop.

She looked glamorous that day, with wings of iridescent blue eye shadow and white lipstick sparkling in contrast with her dark skin. Her curly hair was a shade of pale gray that might have been natural but probably wasn't, judging by how youthful and unlined her face was. I hadn't yet figured out Mia's age, and didn't mind. It was fun to guess.

The place was buzzing with activity. Over two dozen people were shopping, shifting hangers back and forth on rolling racks. That particular sound of metal on metal created the comfortable, steady din that was specific to warehouse sales and thrift shops—and music to my ears. The crowd included at least three mother-daughter pairings.

I let out a low whistle and commented to Mia, "It's really hopping in here tonight. I half expected to have the place to myself on a Monday at dinner time."

"Not this month. Only twenty-eight days until Halloween." She pointed to a large countdown calendar on the tall wall above the cash register. "This is my busiest time of the year."

I smacked my forehead. "I should have known."

"Are you going to any big parties? We have some gowns with crinolines that would be perfect for a fancy event."

"I do like crinolines."

She leaned on the counter and rested her chin on her hands. Dreamily, she said, "Some of my customers are going to a costume ball at that castle up in Westwyrd. I hear it's very exclusive." She sighed. "A real ball in an actual ballroom. Doesn't that sound wonderful?"

I scrunched my nose. "Castle Wyvern? It's not that wonderful. It's just a spa for rich ladies who get a kick out of terrorizing bus boys. I would know. My mother loves it up there."

Mia pouted her full, frosty white lips. "Either way, I sure wouldn't turn down an invite if I got one. A person would have to be crazy to pass up an opportunity like that."

I gave her a cagey look. Was she messing with me?

One great thing about being a witch was getting the answers to questions rather than being stuck wondering forever.

I cast one of my bread and butter spells, the one that increased my ability to bluff. It wasn't exactly a lie detection spell, but it really opened up people. Mia Gianna was, as far as I knew, a regular lady with no powers.

When the spell took hold, I asked, "What do you know about this costume ball?"

The air between us shimmered, and Mia's pupils enlarged as the spell enthralled her.

I added, "Specifically, what sort of things do you know that most people wouldn't?"

"All I know is that my cousin, the trumpet player, played the event with his big band. He claims it was the most wonderful night of his life, even though he has zero memory of what happened."

"A trumpet player?" That sounded like the story Frank heard from Rob and Knox. "Did your cousin happen to mention anything about trying to kiss a mermaid?"

She laughed. "You are really something, Zara. He's been obsessed with mermaids ever since."

"How's his trumpet playing?"

"Better than ever!" She stared at me in awe. I sensed the spell breaking. She batted her false eyelashes. "How did you know?"

"I *didn't* know." I swirled a bit more magic. "We never discussed this."

"We didn't?"

"I just got here. I'm walking in now."

She nodded, looked down at the cash register for a moment, then looked up at me.

"Hello, Zara," she said, rebooting before my eyes.

"Hi, Mia. It's busy tonight."

"It sure is. Only twenty-eight days until Halloween." She pointed at the calendar again. "Do you have any plans for the big night? We have princess gowns with crinolines."

I smiled and grabbed a shopping basket. "I'll be at my house, handing out candy and frightening the neighborhood children like a responsible adult."

"I hear some people are going to a fancy costume party at an actual castle. Can you imagine?"

"Sounds drafty," I said, and I headed off to the women's clothing section.

* * *

I was happy to see that Mia's business was booming, but not exactly thrilled when I saw the long lineup for the changing rooms.

Mia's voice came on over the sound system: "Attention all customers wishing to use the changing rooms. Priority will be given to those willing to share a stall with a family member. The Kit and Kaboodle policy of one person per change room is hereby suspended until the end of October."

The mother-daughter pairings in line murmured happily. The front-most duo made a rush forward when the first available door opened, bypassing all the singles.

I stood frowning with my armload of clothes. Alone. Thinking about what spell I might use to get through this predicament. Create a distraction to clear the store? Too extreme. Disguise myself using a glamour? No good. My human glamours were glitchy, and people might question the sudden appearance of a leafy bush.

Someone tapped me on the shoulder. "Zara, you can share with me."

I turned to see Carrot Greyson. Her breath smelled of hummus and bean sprouts. The twenty-something rune mage wore a scoop-necked top that displayed her many tattoos of colorful flowers and butterflies. A cougar on her chest reached out a paw as though scratching her collarbone. The ink on her otherwise pale skin was perfectly balanced by her orange dyed hair and buggy blue eyes.

"Thanks," I said. "But didn't Mia say only family members could share a change room?"

She grinned. "We're family."

We were family? Carrot and I did have several connections. She used to work at the Permits Department with my aunt. Her great-uncle lived across the street from me. And she was currently dating my daughter's father, the genie. If they married, she would technically become Zoey's stepmother. That probably did make us close enough to family to jump the line for a change room.

"You're right," I said. "We are family."

Two minutes later, Carrot and I were bumping nude body parts in the change room.

Don't get too excited.

It was mostly elbows.

Carrot wriggled her tattooed body out of her clothes and asked, "This is your first year, right?"

"My first year for what?"

She caught my eye in the mirror and smiled sweetly. "You know that I know that we both know. All the invitations went out this morning, and it's all anyone's talking about."

"Oh?" I smiled with equal sweetness.

"I happen to know all the witches got invited this year. Rumor has it, this is going to be the biggest, craziest Monster Mash ever."

"Monster Mash?"

Her bright blue eyes bugged out as she giggled, then whispered, "That's what everyone in the know calls it, unofficially."

Of course they did. The Monster Mash. I wish I'd thought of it first.

I cast the sound bubble spell so we didn't have to whisper, then informed Carrot we could speak freely without being overheard. "But we'd better keep our feet moving so we don't incur the wrath of the lonely singles in the line."

Carrot did a little tap dance to show she understood. There was more accidental bumping of nude body parts. The change room seemed to shrink. It probably hadn't *actually* changed size, but I lived in a house that regularly moved walls around, so keeping an eye open for rooms closing in around me had become part of my reality.

My elbow hit something soft. "Sorry," I said. Carrot felt squishier than she looked. "It sure is busy in here tonight." I tried to pull off my clothes with minimal elbowing. "How are you doing these days?"

She took in a sharp inhale. "It's been a tough year, but I'm looking forward to this costume ball," she said. "It'll be nice to have at least one good night before... *you know*."

"One good night before what?"

"You know."

I didn't know, and I almost hated to ask. "One good night before interdimensional timewyrms burst out of the ground and eat the whole town?"

"Timewyrms?" She started laughing. Soon she was snorting, and then, suddenly, she was making choking noises.

I turned around to see that she was crying. Tears streamed down her cheeks. "Oh, Zara. It's just so tragic!"

I waited, standing there in nothing but my underwear, for the poor girl to compose herself.

She didn't.

She flung herself against my bare bosom and sobbed tears all over me.

"There, there," I said, patting her inky back. "I understand. It has been a tough year for you."

Carrot had lost a coworker to a murderous ex-boyfriend in January, and then her next boyfriend had killed her brother during the summer. She'd had a tough year when it came to men. Now she was dating my daughter's father, the genie. Had she broken her streak? I didn't know Archer Caine very well, so I had no idea. Zoey assured me her father was trying to be a good person, and at least trying was something.

"It's been lousy," Carrot sobbed. "I can't wait for this year to be over."

"At least you have Archer now. He's a good guy, I'm told, and things are going to get better." As I tried to reassure her, I found myself believing my own words. "Better and better. You know what? Since we're family, we should do a big Christmas together with all of us. My daughter would love it."

Carrot pulled away and stared at me with enormous eyes. "Christmas?" Her lower lip wobbled. "He didn't tell you?"

"What? He'll be away at the time? Smart guy. Maybe we could all do something together in January. Ice skating, perhaps."

"He won't be here in January," Carrot said gravely.

"Oh. He didn't tell me he was... going on a trip?"

"He's going soon. I feel so bad for you and Zoey."

"Don't worry about us. Riddles are tougher than they look." I grabbed some makeup-removal tissues from the holder inside the change room door and wiped the tears from my chest. "Our family has a long tradition of fathers being absent for major holidays. Zoey will get over it."

"He's dying," Carrot said.

I snorted and kept dabbing with my tissue. "What's that? It sounded like you said Archer was dying."

"He is."

"You must be mistaken. He's a genie. Genies don't die. At least not without the right combination of hard-to-source poisons."

"He's dying, Zara."

I looked up as a fresh tsunami of tears washed over Carrot's cheeks.

As the tang of her salty tears filled the sound bubble, I started to feel very foolish. Saliva filled my mouth, and I had to swallow several times. Who had earned herself a C- in female friendship that day? Me. I really needed to work on my listening skills.

"I'm so sorry," I said. "Are you sure he's not faking?"

Carrot wailed.

I opened my arms and invited the poor girl in for an unrestrained sob.

My mind was reeling. Carrot was a sweet kid, and she was honest. I believed her. I believed that Carrot believed Archer Caine was dying, but *was he* dying? Really?

My daughter's father had only been part of our lives for a short time. He couldn't go away now. It was too soon. It wasn't fair. It had to be a mistake. He couldn't abandon Zoey. And he couldn't leave poor little unlucky-in-love Carrot Greyson.

CHAPTER 7

On the drive home, I imagined a future without Archer Caine in it.

My body was cold, and the world outside my car looked heavy and gray.

I switched on Foxy Pumpkin's heaters to full blast.

The autumn surroundings took on a blurry quality, and my eyes felt gummy.

Although Archer had caused me trouble since his arrival, he had also rounded out our family. Zoey had gained a father. I'd gained a coparent.

For sixteen years, I'd done just fine raising my daughter on my own, but this new reality of having another parent to talk to was, to my surprise, better. I liked knowing he was around, with all his time-bending genie powers, just in case. Having him on our side had lessened some of my worries. Even the way I talked about Zoey had changed; I enjoyed saying a new-to-me phrase: *our* daughter.

If Archer went away—*when* Archer went away— things wouldn't just revert to how they had been before him.

His participation in our lives had set this up. The jerk. In the future, I would have to feel his absence. I would have to mourn him.

A visual came to mind: me, wearing a black veil, sobbing graveside at a funeral.

Where had that come from? I would not be his widow. We shared a child, but I was not his wife nor had I ever been. So why was part of my mind already planning my all-black widow's wardrobe?

Carrot Greyson would be the closest thing to a wife left behind.

Poor thing. The girl really couldn't catch a break.

The music playing on the car radio was particularly melancholy. I switched it off as I turned onto Beacon Street, preferring the soundtrack of the dashboard heaters. My mouth felt sticky, and my stomach was a cauldron of acid, yet I wasn't hungry. Is it always like this? My memories seized up, and I couldn't imagine a time I hadn't felt exactly how I felt at that moment, with every joint tense, and my skin too tight, like it had shrunk in the dryer, or was someone else's.

This feeling—this preemptive grieving—might last a while. I would need to pace myself. Or accept it. Or find a distraction.

I slowed the car as I rolled past the Moore residence. The blue house next to mine was still empty.

Empty.

I suddenly missed my former neighbors with a sharp pointedness that was almost unbearable.

Why did people have to go away, just when things were getting good?

They're not dead, I told myself. *The Moores continue to exist. Deep breaths, Zara. Keep it together. What kind of witch are you?*

They *were* alive. I forced myself to consider how the Moores might be settling into London.

Was Corvin pounding the streets with a dog walker who had no idea the big black pooch at the end of her leash was a hell hound?

Was Chessa free of her past and the pitying looks people gave her?

Was Chet somewhere he could finally relax, or, conversely, was his chronic discomfort helping him fit in better with the English? Sure, it was a stereotype that I pictured all men in London as the handsome yet awkward British actors in romantic comedies, but the stereotype had to be based on *some* truth.

Making fun of Chet in my imagination cheered me up.

I pulled up to the curb in front of my house and parked.

There were lights on. The house should have been empty. My daughter was away for the evening, setting up a fake haunting with her new witch friend.

Who was in my home? Had the invisible spiders started messing with the electrical wires in addition to eating deodorant and making cobwebs? Had my mother returned from her global gallivanting earlier than planned?

It couldn't be anything too bad. I could count on the protective wards to keep out most evil—though it didn't work on Ribbons. Whoever or whatever was inside was probably benign.

I cast some detection spells from the porch. There were no alarming clouds indicating bad juju. I was cleared for access.

I stepped inside. By the sound of it, someone was in the kitchen. By the smell of it, they were cooking something wonderful. That ruled out my mother. Zirconia Riddle could throw together a few things, but nothing that smelled wonderful.

That left my aunt. Had she returned for a second sleepover, this time with an actual ghost?

I called out, "If you keep showing up here, I'm going to start charging you rent."

A male voice called back, "Worth it!"

I skipped happily to the kitchen to find my vampire boyfriend stirring a pot full of fragrant, dark red sauce.

Detective Theodore Dean Bentley. Forty-two, divorced, but, like all the merchandise at Mia's Kit and Kaboodle, still in excellent condition and probably better than I deserved. He'd always been handsome, but I hadn't been able to see it until he saved my life by losing his.

Becoming a vampire had made his face more square, his dark hair thicker, his cheeks more strikingly hollowed, and his imperfect nose perfect. Or maybe it was becoming my boyfriend that had improved his looks. Who could say?

He greeted me with glinting silver-gray eyes and the slight curve to his thin lips that passed for a smile.

"Bentley! Why are you here? I thought you were working late."

"I was," he said, sounding weary. "Then I got all your text messages."

I had been going in to hug him, but now I took a step back. "*All* my text messages? I only sent three or four."

He raised an eyebrow. "Three or four dozen."

"What?"

"You were blowing up my phone."

"Was not." I pulled out my phone and did a quick review. "This isn't *blowing up*," I said indignantly. "When you send a bunch together, they're not individual messages. They're separate paragraphs of the same message."

"But there's a message alert on each one."

"Well, there shouldn't be. It's just good grammar to separate thoughts into paragraphs instead of a big wall of text. No need to get mad about it. Excuse me for being a thoughtful communicator."

"I'm not mad," he said. "I like that you're a thoughtful communicator."

"Then why bring it up?"

"I didn't. You asked me why I was here and I told you."

I scowled at my phone, scrolling back, reviewing what I'd sent. "I never once requested that you come over to my house. I specifically told you to have fun solving all your cases tonight."

"Exactly," he said. "I know how sarcasm works. You meant the opposite of the words you sent."

"No. This isn't sarcasm. I didn't put the sarcasm emoji on it."

"The lack of an emoji is what makes it even more sarcastic."

"But I didn't mean it like that, and you can't prove I did. Let's break it down, word by word. *'Have fun solving all your cases tonight.'* No sarcasm whatsoever. I can't think of anything more fun—not to mention satisfying— for a detective than solving all of his cases in a single evening."

"All my cases?" He spoke neutrally, as though testifying. "At any given time, I might have two dozen cases open."

"But if you ignore all of Old Man Wheelie's complaints about kids moving around his garden gnomes, how many actual cases do you have?"

He gave me one of his steelier looks and said nothing.

"Let's round up and call it twenty," I said. "I still can't think of anything more fun than solving twenty cases in a single night of overtime."

He turned his back to me, looked into the pot on the stove, and stirred in silence.

"That smells good," I said.

"Thanks." He didn't look at me.

"I'm glad you decided to come over, of your own volition."

He turned his head, but didn't meet my eyes. "It sounded like you were having a rough day."

"Apparently, I was. The evidence is at hand, after all. A girl doesn't blow up her boyfriend's phone with a million messages over nothing. Not unless she's crazy."

He said nothing.

"Okay," I said, one finger in the air. "I think I heard the tiniest touch of sarcasm in there."

More pot stirring.

"I *was* having a bad day," I said. "But I can handle it."

"Zara," he said gently—just gently enough to put my teeth on edge. I'd heard him use that same tone when talking with agitated suspects. He was *managing* me.

"I can handle it," I repeated. "I've handled a lot of things on my own. Just because my mother groomed you to take care of me doesn't mean you have to come rushing in like a white knight at the slightest hint of trouble."

He took a sidelong look at me, one eyebrow raised.

Here we go. I could have kicked myself for bringing up my mother. Discussions about Bentley's true loyalties and motivations never went anywhere good—not the discussions we'd had, and not the thousands more I'd conducted in my head.

I sheepishly looked down at my feet. *Oh, good*, I thought. *Shoes.*

We didn't wear shoes inside the house, but I'd rushed in and forgotten to take mine off. For the moment, I was glad to have something to do. I lifted one foot, cast the shoe removal spell, then the other one. Perfect execution. I was getting good at the spell. I only sent myself flying butt over teakettle about once a week, at most.

Without looking up, I said, "Whatever you've got bubbling in that pot, it really does smell wonderful."

"I used a recipe," he said.

"From a book?"

"Something like that."

I rubbed my hands together. "What can I do to help? Set the table?"

"Already done. You can put out the fancy napkins." He gave me a hint of a smile.

"I'm on it, Detective." I grabbed the roll of paper towel, separated two rectangles, then folded them to be fancy.

"I was going to put out candles, but all I found in the candle drawer were bare wicks."

"We have invisible spiders," I said. "They eat waxy things."

"Invisible spiders? Should I be concerned?"

"Nope. I can handle it."

"So you say."

Firmly, I said, "I can handle it."

He took in a deep breath, as though preparing to say something, then he glanced over at the window and exhaled audibly. The exhale was so powerful, the spiders' cobwebs on the window frame and ceiling fluttered.

I grabbed a broom and quickly swept the day's new cobwebs into the garbage. Then I took a seat, picked up the wine bottle, and pretended to read the label.

"It's already open," Bentley said.

"Couldn't wait for me, huh?"

His back was to me again. "The sauce recipe called for wine."

"Then my body must also be a sauce recipe, because it is *calling for wine!*"

He let out an amused snort. One of Bentley's better qualities was that he acknowledged my bad jokes but didn't encourage them.

"Pour yourself a glass," he said. "I'll be ready to serve this in a minute."

I poured a glass for myself and one for him.

When he joined me at the table with the food, I gave him the speech I'd been mentally preparing.

"Sorry I'm so difficult." It was a short speech.

He said nothing.

"Long day," I said.

"Long day," he agreed.

I took a bite of the red sauce he'd dished up for me. It was too spicy. My sinuses tingled and my eyes watered.

"Perfect," I lied.

He chewed slowly, then washed it down with wine. "You don't think it's too spicy?"

"Not at all. Curry is supposed to be hot."

"It's not curry."

I nodded and sipped the wine. "The wine is good."

"Wine is always good." He offered his glass in a toast. "To wine," he said.

"To wine," I agreed.

I ate as much of the spicy stew as I dared. My stomach could handle a lot of abuse—it always had, even before my witch powers had kicked in, but I didn't have much of an appetite. I'd been in a daze since my talk with Carrot Greyson. I didn't even remember sending half the text messages to Bentley that I did.

Archer Caine would be leaving this world.

It kept hitting me in waves. I'd forget for a moment, distracted by Bentley's terrible cooking, then it would hit me. Archer was dying.

I'd dealt with plenty of death and loss that year. Even moving to a new town was a type of death—a loss of one's old life. But a friend—a family member—dying in front of my eyes was different. It brought back all the complicated feelings I had about my mother's death—feelings that had only become more tangled after the discovery it had been fake.

"You don't have to force it down," Bentley said of the food.

I hadn't given up yet, and swirled my fork over the chunks. "I did have a big lunch."

"I tried," he said.

"That does count for something," I said.

"At the end of the day, it's the only thing that counts."

"It's not the only thing that counts. Outcomes do matter."

"Not as much as you'd think," he said. "Win or lose, it's how you play the game."

I pointed my fork at him playfully. "Says the detective with dozens of open cases at any given time."

"That's different." He frowned. "Actually, no. It's not that different." His eyes lost focus, and I got the impression he was having another one of his internal tribunals about the meaning of phrases, and which rules might be applied to which life situations.

He and I were different in that he thought about things a lot more before acting, whereas I was always trying to retroactively figure out what the heck I'd been thinking after the fact. It was probably for the best, since he carried a gun. If my defensive fireballs had been bullets, I'd probably be enjoying dinner that night in a prison cell.

Bentley cocked his head and frowned at me. "What were we talking about?"

"The fact that you get an A for effort on this meal." I stuffed another forkful into my mouth, which had thankfully gone numb. "Yummy."

"You didn't have any smoked paprika, so I used cayenne pepper." He blinked. "They're the same color."

"That's... kind of brilliant. And it sounds exactly like something I would do."

"We must be rubbing off on each other," he said solemnly.

"Like those old married couples who finish each other's stories and wear matching ski jackets." I grimaced in horror. "Yikes."

"We need to be careful. Soon I may lose the ability to read a menu on my own, and I won't be able to remember what I like or don't like at my favorite restaurant. I'll turn into my father, and you'll..."

I shot him a warning look. *Turn into my mother?*

He picked up our plates and stood. "Let's move on to the next course."

He scraped the red stuff into the compost bin, and we finished up our wine with some cheese, salami, and crackers.

As we cleared the dishes, I asked Bentley about his day. I had to ask three times to get anywhere.

It turned out he'd spent most of the day in meetings and doing paperwork.

"It was kind of a boring day," he said. "Nobody tried to resurrect any ancient gods or start an apocalypse with flying monkeys."

"That you know of."

He nodded. "That I know of."

"Boring can be nice. It beats the alternative."

He flipped the tea towel over his shoulder, and leaned against the counter next to the sink where I was washing the pot.

He watched for a moment, then said, "You don't have to talk about the business with Zoey's father if you don't feel up to it."

"I know," I said.

"But it might help to talk about it."

I scrubbed the pot with gusto. I found myself pressing my lips together in what usually passed for my hilarious impression of Zinnia.

Why wasn't I talking about my feelings? Talking was one of my favorite activities, along with eating. Talking while eating was the best.

But I usually did the end-of-day recap with my daughter. What made her different from Bentley was the fact that our relationship was permanent. I could speak freely, and embarrass myself with her. She had already seen me at my worst. No matter what I said, she wasn't going to stop being my daughter and leave me.

Bentley, however, could wise up. He could see my flaws. He could shrug off my mother's grooming and hit the bricks. Even though he was supposed to be my protector, the woman's glamours didn't last forever. I'd been unable to say the word *vampire* for ages, and now I said it all the time.

I looked up from the pot, fixing my gaze on a spot just below his eyes.

"Penny for your thoughts," he said.

One came to me: *I wish you were Zoey's father.*

He ducked his head so that I was looking into his eye. "Well?"

I shrugged. "My mind is blank."

Why couldn't you be her dad? Why couldn't I have met you sixteen years ago instead of a genie who was just coming of age and didn't know he was destined to break my heart at least twice?

"Tell me what you want," he said.

"A time machine."

"We can try. I have the keys for City Hall." He reached into his pocket and jingled some keys theatrically. "Not literally, because these are my personal keys, but I can get them."

"Just stop," I said.

"Stop what?"

"Stop being such a striver. Can you just, I don't know, relax? Stop trying so hard. Not everything bad that happens is a puzzle to get solved."

"That's not true at all. Your belief is incorrect."

My jaw dropped. "Are you serious?"

"Everything is a puzzle. That doesn't mean there's a perfect solution that everyone is going to love, but there is always an answer, even if the answer is acceptance."

His words made sense.

No.

His words were nonsense that only sounded good.

I shook my head. "Are you trying to trick me? Don't even think about doing one of your vampire mind control glamours on me. You'll be sorry."

He flipped the tea towel off his shoulder and snapped it at my butt. "What are you going to do about it?"

"I'll cast a spell on every bakery in town so that they refuse your business. You'll never taste a rainbow-sprinkle donut again, my friend."

He looked up and rubbed his chin. "Would that be so bad?"

"It would be torture. When you can't have something, it only makes you want it more."

He looked me up and down, then said huskily, "I want you."

"You can't have me. There's a ban in effect."

He gave his head a slow shake. "I want you," he said, growling.

"You can't always get what you want."

He moved with vampire speed, and was suddenly embracing me.

He said it again.

"I believe I've made my point," I said, melting into him as we both knew I would. "The ban is now lifted."

CHAPTER 8

A while later, Bentley and I reversed our steps, making the bed and then putting on the clothes that had been strewn between floors.

When we reached the starting point, in the kitchen, I realized something was missing. I'd taken several steps within the work triangle without tripping on anything furry.

I looked around and asked, "Have you seen Boa?"

Bentley put his hands in his pockets and looked sheepish. "I saw her earlier. She might be napping."

"What's that spell people use for magically summoning felines from even the deepest slumber? Oh, right. *Here, kitty kitty.*"

Boa did not come running.

"That's suspicious," I said. "I summoned the kitty, but there is no kitty. And the giant fruit bat isn't here, either."

Bentley kicked at something on the floor. Could he see the invisible spiders? According to my aunt, he'd be shrieking in terror if he could. He had to be avoiding eye contact with me for some reason.

"You *know* something," I said. "No. It's worse. You *did* something."

His shoulders shrugged up to his ears. "You know how I am with cute animals. They're my weakness."

I knew exactly how he was. The man kept peanuts in his suit pockets for feeding wild birds and Petey the Squirrel.

I stared him down. "What did you do?"

Reluctantly, he said, "I may have given you-know-who some H-A-M."

I tsk-tsked and shook my head. "You gave in to her demands? We don't negotiate with the house pests. You know better. Was it the talking?"

"That must have been it." He nodded. "I know you warned me, but nothing could have prepared me for the reality." He held both fists under his chin cutely. "That adorable face looking up at me. The soft pink mouth opening, and then, in the cutest little voice, *ham?* You should have seen it. I had no choice."

"You always have a choice."

He met my gaze briefly then looked away in shame. "She finished off a three-pound ham."

"By herself? She's going to explode."

"She didn't eat it all. Your dragon helped."

"He's a wyvern."

"He probably ate most of it, but she held her own."

"You're a sucker. I'm going to buy that cat a cell phone, teach her how to use it, and have her call you directly when her next craving hits."

"I wouldn't mind."

I rolled my eyes.

He finished buttoning and tucking in his shirt. "Anything good to watch on TV tonight?"

"Does it have to be good to be watched?"

"I'll go warm up the couch."

"Give me a minute. I'm going to check on the orchestrators of the ham-pocalypse."

I found both the fluffy white cat and her scaly partner in crime on Zoey's bed, swirled up together like peanut butter and chocolate. Neither showed any ill effects from eating the ham, let alone the morning's clockwork bird.

I returned to the living room and joined Bentley on the couch. I flopped down with a sigh. He sighed right back.

It was a bit weird how comfortable the relationship could feel, at a variety of heat levels. One minute, we were like two teenagers pawing at each other, then the next minute we'd switch into our old-married-couple routine.

I asked, "Did I tell you about the whole Clockbird thing?"

Without pulling his gaze from the TV, he answered, "The cat ate a clockwork bird and now she talks."

That had been part of my text message tsunami. "But did I tell you the bird was an invitation to a costume ball at Castle Wyvern?"

"Yes. And you're not going because nobody tells Zara Riddle what she can or can't wear."

"Also because it's going to be stupid and corporate."

"Sure."

"*Sure,* as in you agree with me?"

"It will, indeed, be a corporate event."

"Are you saying you *want to* go to the ball?"

He changed the channels and didn't answer.

A promo spot for the upcoming Wicked Wives reboot came on, and I lost track of what I'd been getting worked up about, which was probably for the best.

Bentley's ex-wife was one of the stars of the show. Seeing her on the screen now probably deserved some sort of comment, but what?

"Good production values," I said.

"Big budget," he agreed.

"I am going to watch the heck out of that show," I said. "Right here on this couch, with the gorgons."

"I won't be here."

"Who said you were invited?"

"I won't be watching, because I don't want to see Lana..."

I finished for him. "Kissing hot actors?"

"Acting," he said.

"Because she's so bad at it?" She wasn't.

"Because when I see her in something, it breaks my reality. My mind keeps asking this question: *Why is Lana on a film set talking in a fake accent to these other people who are speaking normally?* It's like I'm in a Twilight Zone episode, where I can clearly see that Lana Lang is the one element that doesn't belong there, but nobody else gets it. Then it carries over to other films and TV shows, even the ones she's not in. I can imagine the cameras, the lights, the caterers, and the whole crew standing there, just outside of the frame. I keep waiting for the camera to accidentally shift and give me a glimpse of what's behind the veil of illusion. Do you know that feeling?"

I pondered the question a moment. "It's like when you're a little kid and you see your favorite teacher at the grocery store in flip-flops. She's there with some scruffy guy in a sleeveless T-shirt, and he's touching her back. And you run up to say hi, and she looks embarrassed, like you caught her. Then your mother drags you away, and you get really quiet for the rest of the day, because, deep down, you're worried that you've ruined a veil of illusion that was there for your own protection, and now nothing will ever be the same again. Do you mean it's a feeling like that?"

"Kind of." He tilted his head thoughtfully. "What would you call that feeling?"

I shrugged. "You wouldn't be able to call it anything. There are way too many emotions that don't have any words in the English language."

"But there must be some easy combination of words."

"Take it from a spell caster: the easy combinations of words aren't as effective. They become clichés, and lose all their power. My strongest spells have what Margaret

Mills would call *stank* on them. That's where I throw in a few ugly bits that don't belong, because, in the end, all the wrongs make a right."

He nodded, seemingly satisfied by my explanation. Bentley was a good listener. I felt heard by him, even if he didn't like what I was saying. Few people were as present and focused as he was. Sometimes I felt exposed, which was both intoxicating and terrifying.

The TV promo switched to a sitcom that was a spin-off of another sitcom, featuring a former child star who was blossoming into a spectacularly awkward phase. Say what you will about Hollywood's brutal expiration date on actresses, they've got nothing on formerly-adorable child actors.

I stretched out on the sofa and put my head on Bentley's lap. He traced the edge of my ear then stroked my hair.

The advertisements ended and a show came on. It was one of those new shows about superheroes that claimed they weren't like all the other shows about superheroes. It was exactly like those other shows, but it was still good, because it did have superheroes.

Bentley asked, "Are witches superheroes?"

"No," I said. "But librarians are."

"What about vampires?"

"No," I said. "But detectives might be, if they're really good at their job."

"I see."

He kept stroking my hair as I rested my head on his legs. I was being petted. I understood why Boa enjoyed the activity so much.

When the show we were watching reached a dramatic yet dialog-free scene, Bentley asked, "How long?"

I knew exactly what he meant. How long did Archer Caine have until his death? I knew what Bentley was thinking, not because of magic or psychic powers, but because the superhero character on the show was dying from some incurable alien infection. The character was standing in the rain on top of a building, being super dramatic while also being shirtless to show off his physique.

"Carrot doesn't know how long," I said, still staring at the TV. The character on the screen slowed time enough to stop the rain briefly. *Come on, superhero show. Try a little harder to take my mind off my everyday worries.*

"Are we talking years? Months?"

"Based on his decline they think it could be months, or it could be days. He's lost his genie powers already. He can't do any of that freaky time-bending stuff."

"That's not necessarily bad. He tripped me up a lot at the castle this summer, and he's gotten me a few times since."

"Archer's been messing with you?" I pulled my head off Bentley's lap and sat up. "Why didn't you tell me?"

"It was harmless stuff. Mostly involving donuts. He kept placing them in my hands while I was interviewing people. I actually thought it was you the first few times."

"That does sound like me."

"So, I started popping up where he wasn't expecting me. Let's just say the donut games are over, and I won."

"Of course you did."

He raised his eyebrows. "I did. He told me I won."

"Of course you won, *dear*."

He snorted. "Are they sure he's actually dying? Losing your powers isn't the same as dying."

"Carrot said that Dr. Monkey-Finger-Toes at the DWM said the loss of his powers is a sign he's about to get, um, recycled."

"Recycled?"

I waved a hand. "Reincarnated."

Bentley lowered the volume on the TV. "How does that work?"

"The body he's in now dies, then he gets born as a baby somewhere else in the world. The time frame varies.

It could be a year or two. His existence is cloven with his sister's, so it will be near wherever she wound up."

"Did you say his existence is *woven* with hers? Like soul mates?"

"Cloven," I said. "C-L-O-V-E-N."

"Like a hoof? A cloven hoof?"

"Like the past participle of cleave." I found myself speaking more quickly, and waving my hands. Talking about the English language was much easier than talking about anything else. "Cleave is both a verb and an adjective, and it's one of the special ones."

"Like the exception to a rule?"

"Even better." I was practically breathless. "It's an *auto antonym*, because it can mean two opposite things. It is its *own* antonym. When you cleave something, you might be splitting it in two, or you might be joining two parts. It could mean either thing." I bounced on the couch. "Gotta love auto antonyms. Such tricksy words."

"That sort of word would be terrible in a witness statement." He frowned. "It wouldn't hold up in court. The point of words is that they mean something. Why would a word also mean its opposite? It's not right."

"Words change over time. The word *terrific* used to mean something that inspired terror. Now we use it to describe something good."

"But it doesn't still mean something bad. It doesn't mean both things. It changed. It..." He leaned back and eyed me warily. "Are all the words constantly changing meanings on us?"

"Yes."

He blinked slowly.

"They believe it's the work of teen girls," I said. "Those who use the language the most, change it the most. Fun fact: Shakespeare probably stole most of his clever lines from the teenagers of his day."

He tilted up his chin. "What about witches? They use language to cast magic. If the words are changing, that must affect spells."

"Good observation, Detective. You're absolutely right. Sometimes we blame clichés, but we don't really know why some of the oldest spells, which used to be so reliable, don't always work for us modern witches."

He rubbed his chin. "Casting spells must be a *terrific endeavor.*"

"Was that a pun?" I grinned. "That was so good." I patted him on the arm.

"We must be rubbing off on each other."

"Would you like to know some other auto antonyms? There's *sanction*, and *dust*, and—oh, I've got a book about linguistics that you should read." I jumped up to get the book.

The vampire moved with lightning speed. He stood between me and the bookshelf, solid as a wall.

"Not so fast," he said. "We were talking about Archer Caine. You said he's going to get reincarnated into a new body. Is it always as a baby?"

"It's supposed to be a baby. Not a full-grown stolen body, like he did with the clone of Chet Moore. That whole thing only happened because Archer's essence was powering the gross machine in the Pressman attic when Chet was embedded in it. You know about that."

"I was still in the dark at the time, but I did read the reports."

"The doctor figures that's why he's breaking down already. The cloned body was unstable. His catabolic and anabolic states aren't in balance. I guess you can't cheat nature." I leaned to the side, scanning the bookshelf with my eyes. I had a whole section about linguistics.

Bentley leaned over, blocking my search. "So, he's not really dying. He's just changing form."

"I guess you could say that."

"I also died and changed form."

"It's nothing like what happened to you," I said.

"Then explain it to me like I'm an idiot." There was a sharp edge to his voice.

"How would you like to go to sleep tonight, and wake up tomorrow morning a baby with zero memory of who you are? That's how it works. They don't remember their genie lives until they're teenagers."

"So, it's a fresh start." His steely eyes glinted, like someone who suspected he was being tricked into feeling sorry for someone who shouldn't be felt sorry for.

"What are you getting at?"

"Zara, he's not dying."

I took a step back, repelled by an energy I didn't like. "Are you saying we shouldn't feel bad about a family member dying because he may or may not technically be dying?"

"Feel how you want to feel." His nostrils flared. "I'm not going to lie to you. He's a bad influence on Zoey."

I scoffed. "That kid is impermeable to bad influence. She grew up under my care, so she's got full immunity."

"She's been drinking alcohol. Her and Ambrosia Abernathy. Up at the Inn."

"You must be mistaken. Zoey would tell me if she was drinking."

"I heard it from Persephone Rose, who heard it from her mother. They wanted to tell you, but I said I'd talk to you about it first."

"And now you have. Thanks. Is that all?"

Bentley didn't speak. His facial expression was so intense, I had no choice but to laugh.

"This is ridiculous," I said. "You know what probably happened? I bet Ambrosia cast the inebriation spell on her. That little witch didn't get ridiculously good at that spell overnight. She's probably been casting it on her teenaged friends for ages. Did Persephone's mom give you details? Did she see any empty liquor bottles?"

"I'll find out."

"Or don't," I said. "I'll talk to Zoey myself. She's my daughter, not yours."

"I know," he said. "You're always reminding me."

"Is that what this is about? Are you jealous of Archer? Are you happy about him dying because it means that Zoey will lose the parent you're in competition with?"

His eyes closed, as though he'd been stung by my words.

Later, after he'd left the house and I'd been alone with my thoughts for a while, I would realize that he *had* been stung by my words.

Words—even the ones outside a spell—had power.

I looked at the empty spot on the couch next to me, and the empty spot by the bookshelf where we'd argued up until the point he'd stormed off.

I missed him, and I was mad at him for making me miss him.

And the chill I'd felt earlier was back.

I reached for a blanket, catching a glimpse of movement in the reflection of a glass photo frame. My skin prickled and my hearing amplified. I noted that, given the angle of the frame, it shouldn't have caught anything.

I recreated the reaching movement, watching the frame. Nothing moved in the reflection, but perhaps I hadn't gotten the motion quite right.

A person who wasn't aware of the supernatural might have shrugged off such a phenomenon, but not this witch. This witch suddenly remembered her conversation earlier that day with the conspiracy enthusiast. Dorian Dabrowski had been seeing a lost girl in reflections. Might she be real? Mr. Dabrowski was wrong more often than he was right, but might he be actually detecting something supernatural?

The little girl might even be connected to whatever was bothering my aunt.

I wondered what Zinnia Riddle was doing at that exact moment.

That morning, when we'd said goodbye before heading to our respective workplaces, I'd made her promise to contact me at the first sign of anything spooky.

But would she? The woman could be so stubborn about handling everything herself.

It might be nice to shoot her a text message to let her know I was ready to help, just in case she was on the edge.

I lifted my hand to catch my phone as I called it to me by magic.

Just then, the light on the television shifted tone, drawing my eye.

A self-help guru was sitting cross-legged, being interviewed. As he looked at the camera, he seemed to be looking at me.

"We are all the architects of our own problems," he said.

I snorted.

"Not all of them," the interviewer, a young woman of mixed ethnicity said. "You can't blame people for their circumstances. That's called victim blaming."

Calmly, he repeated the statement. "We are all the architects of our own problems."

Her dusky cheeks flushed. "What about genetics? What about all the things we don't have a choice in? What about other people? What about fate, or bad luck?"

The guru reached out and pinched the air, as though physically grabbing the one question he was interested in responding to. "Bad luck," he said, as though announcing an essay title.

"Exactly. What about bad luck? Or good luck?"

He gently rocked from side to side. "Good luck, bad luck, who can say? It depends on where you stop the story. The road itself is always turning."

"Always turning." She chewed her lower lip. "Do you mean people should always look on the bright side? Trick themselves with positive thinking?"

"There is no trickery," he explained. "A man's dog is sick. He takes the dog to the vet, but the appointment lasts too long, and the man misses the flight for his vacation. He goes home, he turns on the news, and he hears that the plane has crashed. There are no survivors. Was it good luck that he missed his vacation? Was it good luck that the dog was sick?"

"It's... *good* luck," she said. "I get it. What you're saying is that everything is actually good luck when you step back far enough. That's a nice way of putting things, Mr. Thackery Toaster. I can see why your books and international tours are so popular!"

"Tollster," the man said, enunciating his last name carefully.

She giggled. "Did I say Toaster again? My bad. I'm so sorry I was wrong, Mr. Tollster."

The guru smiled with his mouth only. "Who can say that my way of saying my name is right and your way is wrong?"

The interviewer's face twitched. She was not very experienced, and didn't have a good poker face to keep her emotions from showing. I felt sorry for her. She was likely having trouble assimilating the words the man was saying with his passive aggression.

"Right," she said. "Thank you for explaining about the good luck, Mr. Tollster."

"I haven't finished," he said. "What about the person who took the man's seat on the airplane? Go back two hours, and now we see her. She has no dog to get sick. She's at the airport, but the flight is overbooked. She is trying to get to her sister's wedding, and she doesn't think she'll make it, so she's fighting back tears. Then they announce her name. There is one seat available. She is so happy, she cries with relief. She grabs her luggage, and she is the last one on the flight." He closed his eyes briefly. "She is carrying her luggage, running, and the heavy bag is bruising the side of her leg."

The interviewer shifted uncomfortably. "Is this real?"

"Her name is Susannah. She's getting on the plane," he held up one finger and looked at his watch, "right now."

"What?" The interviewer looked around, searching for a producer or a cue card to rescue her. "Are you joking?"

The guru pressed his hands together and leaned back, smiling. He looked satisfied by the woman's apparent confusion. What a guy.

I spoke sternly to the television: "Stop it, you little troll. Your name should be Trollster."

The guru stared directly into the camera lens and said, "Good luck, bad luck, who can say?"

"Oh, shut up." I changed the channel.

Or at least I tried to, but what I had in my hand was my phone, not the remote control.

I remembered I'd been about to message my aunt.

On the TV, the guru was still going on, irritating me with his riddles while the interviewer tried to establish whether or not he was making a terrorist threat.

I tossed the phone in the air and sent it back to the charger.

I'd had enough of that day, and enough of other people and their good luck, their bad luck, and who knows.

If Zinnia needed my help, she could put on her big girl pants and ask.

CHAPTER 9

Zinnia Riddle

While Zara Riddle thought about texting her aunt, across town, Zinnia Riddle felt the tingle of a premonition.

Zinnia summoned her phone and waited for the text that would be coming from her niece.

It didn't come.

After a full fifteen minutes, she concluded that her niece wasn't going to message her after all. Sometimes the psychic power could be buggy. She returned the phone to the charging station on her way to the kitchen for something to drink.

There was a buzzing in the kitchen that didn't belong to any appliances. She listened to the hum a moment, then chalked it up to a nonmagical cause: tinnitus. Her ears always buzzed more when she was sad. Did a blue mood down-regulate her liver's production of glutathione, or was it the other way around? Who could say. Once the downward spiral started, it was difficult to pull out of. Those old neural circuits, once lit up, were like clean steel tracks for train cars of bad thoughts.

She boiled water and brewed a cup of tea with the most astringent of powders: three bitter fruits from India, plus koodzuberry enzyme for its multiplier effect. The tea would work wonders on her tinnitus, which some witches —not Zinnia—believed was caused by magical bees.

After getting down the bitter tea, she opened her refrigerator in search of something to cut the taste.

She was out of pickles and olives. Also limes, lemons, and all sorts of things. Had she missed a shopping trip? Or several?

Since late September, when Halloween decorations had started appearing around town, she'd been off her usual schedule.

At work that day, she'd forgotten about the staff meeting in the third floor boardroom.

Margaret Mills had returned to the office to get her, tutting and stomping around as usual. Then Margaret had started a fight over nothing, and they'd bickered all the way up in the elevator, throughout the meeting, and until the end of the day, when Zinnia had challenged Margaret to a duel in the supply room and Margaret had wisely declined.

After a thorough ransacking of the refrigerator, Zinnia returned to the living room with a box of stale crackers, a jar of raspberry jam, and a tiny spoon.

She took a seat on the sofa, and was about to dig into the jam when the room began to vibrate. The temperature dropped rapidly. The mirror above the fireplace showed movement in the room, though nothing in the room was moving.

The lamp next to the sofa suddenly flared and burned out.

Zinnia remained seated, waiting.

The other lamp flared and burned out.

She was in the dark.

The formless shapes in the mirror were still moving.

Was it him?

She couldn't trust herself. She'd thought once before that he'd come to see her, but it had been someone else.

This time, though, the haunting felt different.

Zinnia called out softly into the darkness, "Aiden?"

Three Years Ago

March

The lamp fell to the floor with a clatter. The bulb flared as it broke, as though the light inside had been a trapped swarm of luminous insects, suddenly set free by the smashing of the glass.

Mitchell Harrington bolted upright on the couch, spilling his wine.

"Aiden!" His voice was hard and stern.

When it came to his son, Mitchell had no patience. Any sign of disobedience sent the professor straight to yelling. It was a point of contention between the couple—Mitchell and Zinnia—or at least it would have been if Zinnia hadn't learned long ago to leave it alone.

Aiden was Mitchell's son, not Zinnia's. She had never called herself the boy's stepmother. Not even now that she was living in the New York brownstone with the family. She always referred to the boy as "Mitchell's son."

Mitchell practically howled, "Now you've done it!"

"I didn't do it," Aiden said, grinning impishly, denying it even as he stood over the evidence of the broken lamp. "It must have been a ghost."

Mitchell handed the remainder of his wine to Zinnia and got to his feet.

Please don't, she thought but didn't say.

Mitchell boomed, "You're not supposed to fly that thing in the house!"

"But Dad! It's raining outside, and you said you'd take me to the park today, but you didn't, because you never do what you say you're going to do!" Aiden did have a point. Zinnia bit her tongue.

Mitchell lunged for his son's toy. It was a remote-control, battery-powered drone. As Mitchell lumbered around grasping for the drone, the swinging of his long limbs reminding Zinnia of King Kong, clinging to that pointy building and swatting at airplanes.

Like the mythical ape batting airplanes, Mitchell caught the drone, threw it down, and crushed it under his foot.

Aiden screamed in anger, hurled obscenities at his father, then ran upstairs to his bedroom.

Mitchell wasn't far behind.

Zinnia stayed where she was on the sofa with both glasses of wine. She yawned. Family life could be tiresome.

She knew what would come next. For the next thirty minutes, there would be yelling and crying, threats and ultimatums, plus a few door slams. There would be no physical abuse—she would not have tolerated that—but the evening would still be ruined.

She set the glasses on the coffee table, checked that she was alone, and cast a spell to remove a red wine spill from the sofa cushion.

Then she cast another spell to gather the broken light bulb glass, which had sprayed out in a dangerous radius. She righted the lamp, used a weaving spell to mend the cloth shade, and got a fresh bulb from the hall closet.

Once everything had been set right, Zinnia turned up the volume on the television and waited for the latest power struggle between father and son to settle. The yelling and crying had hit a fever pitch faster than usual, which meant it might sputter out in time to salvage some of the evening.

Mitchell finally came down from his son's room. He was still tall, but looked about two inches shorter than he had earlier. The bags under his eyes were puffy. Sometimes both parties in the power struggle cried, which

Zinnia found curious but didn't comment on. She wasn't the boy's mother.

Mitchell stopped at the lamp and peered over the shade at the bulb. "I thought this broke," he said.

"It did, but just the bulb," she said. "I swept up everything."

"You didn't need to do that. You should have rang for Fiona. It's her job."

"It's late, and she goes to sleep early." Also, the maid's name wasn't Fiona. Zinnia kept herself from correcting Mitchell on that point. Like weighing in on parenting techniques, her keen insight was only appreciated by Mitchell when she was pointing out other people's mistakes.

He sat down heavily. "I don't know how much more I can take. He's barely eleven. What am I going to do when he's a teenager?" He rubbed his bald temples. "Zinnia, what am I going to do?"

She nodded thoughtfully. It was a rhetorical question, which was a shame.

Zinnia had plenty of ideas about what might be done differently to elicit better behavior from the boy. She had read a few child psychology books. She had observed certain patterns. However, unlike truly incompetent people, she lacked the confidence that a tiny bit of knowledge gave the fools of this world. The more she learned, the more she realized how little she knew.

And besides, she wasn't the boy's mother.

Mitchell was still waiting for some kind of response.

"You'll handle it," Zinnia said. "Even when he's a teenager. You'll handle it, one day at a time."

Mitchell used one long hand to rub both eyebrows at once. "It's just..." He strained against the idea, then let it out. "It's just that he can be so hard to love."

So hard to love.

Zinnia had heard many complaints about the boy, but never anything this harsh, this searing, this permanent.

So hard to love.

Zinnia's eyes stung, and her throat ached.

The words could not be taken back, or unheard.

She felt shame rolling in her stomach—shame on behalf of Mitchell, who had so *much* shame, but for all of the wrong things. The man would apologize for overly good behavior, proudly calling attention to himself. "Sorry I'm spoiling you with these lavish gifts, Zinnia!"

But apologize for actual rudeness? For hurting someone's feelings? Never.

Zinnia listened for sounds that Aiden might be within earshot. The house was quiet. He probably had his bedroom door closed, but what if he heard his father talk about him that way?

"I don't mean that," Mitchell said, sounding genuinely regretful. "I don't mean what I said."

"I know," she said soothingly.

She didn't need a spell to know he was telling the truth. At that exact moment, he really didn't mean what he'd said, but at the moment he'd said it, he had meant it. He wouldn't have said it if he hadn't. There were so many other words in the English language, so many other things to say. The truth came out. Only the most duplicitous of people could easily say things they didn't mean.

Mitchell rubbed at his eyebrows until they were flecked with dandruff. "I do love him," he said.

"Of course you do. He's your son."

"He *is* my son. My only child. The day Aiden was born was the most spectacular day of my life. Being a father means everything to me. But why does he have to make it so hard?"

He was looking at her, expecting an answer to another rhetorical question. Mitchell did this a lot.

And why wouldn't he? Zinnia Riddle had never claimed to have all the answers, and yet, over the past couple of years, she certainly had come up with a lot of them.

The man seated next to her, Mitchell Harrington, must have noticed that ever since the mysterious redhead had come into his life, things had been falling into place. He'd come across a vein of life's gold, a streak of good luck. Whenever Zinnia was around, all of his lost items, from cuff links to entire boxes of papers, would be found. The top restaurants would take their reservations, even at the last minute. And he'd even secured tenure at the university, years ahead of schedule. Even his parents, who expected the best, had been surprised with the apparent ease at which he'd been appointed.

Zinnia had celebrated each victory at his side, buoyed by his gratitude.

When they'd first met, she was surprised to find herself drawn to him, the Mitchell who was trudging through life as though it were an obligation, an unwanted gift card that had to be spent.

When she had awakened the joy inside him with the sheer power of her love, she had felt his transformation as though it were her own. She had been trudging through life, too. Now she had purpose. She had a family. She was not a mother, or a wife, but she did have lunch dates with ladies who were mothers and wives, and treated her as one of them.

After a whirlwind romance, she'd agreed to move in with Mitchell. His life continued to be on the upswing, except for one aspect: his relationship with his son. That aspect seemed to be in decline. Or was it? The other mothers in Zinnia's social circles assured her this was perfectly normal. Like the moon, relationships with kids waxed and waned as the children went through developmental phases.

Mitchell was still looking at her, waiting for a response. He asked, "What else can I do?"

"Nothing," Zinnia said. "You're already doing the best you can." She wished it were not true. She wished he could try harder and do better, but the man had his limitations. He didn't even have any supernatural powers.

"Thanks for saying that." He let out a big breath and relaxed into the sofa. "I know I'm doing everything I can, but it's good to hear it from another person." He reached for the wine and drank it down. "He's probably acting out because the doctor made him uncomfortable."

"The doctor?"

Mitchell grabbed the remote control and started changing channels. "I took him in for a checkup this afternoon because he was complaining about stomach pain to the school nurse, and you know how they are. Every little sniffle has to get medicated away."

"How long has he had stomach pain?" This was the first she'd heard of it, but a pattern was already forming from her recent memories: Aiden picking at his food. Aiden turning down his favorite dessert.

"Everyone has stomach pain," Mitchell said, ignoring the question.

"No. They don't."

He shrugged. "Everyone in my family."

Zinnia said nothing. The news came of no surprise. Out of the whole Harrington clan, Mitchell was the easygoing, happy one.

She asked, "What happened at the doctor?"

"The usual," Mitchell said. "The doctor poked and prodded him. Aiden started screaming bloody blue murder about the man's cold hands." Mitchell chuckled. "It was nice to have all that hostility directed at someone else for a change."

Zinnia said nothing. The boy hadn't mentioned anything to her about stomach pain. Had he been hiding an illness, or was today's visit to the doctor simply an excuse to get out of school? Aiden could be creative about getting out of classes.

"That old doctor didn't back down," Mitchell said, chuckling. "He finished the exam, cold hands and all, and ordered a bunch of blood tests and scans."

"That doesn't sound good. I can understand why Aiden would be upset. Did the doctor say it could be serious?"

"You know doctors. They always say the same thing. *It's probably nothing, but it's good to be careful, just in case.*"

"They do say that," she agreed, extra-knowingly to cover for the fact she'd rarely been to see a doctor.

"I'm sure it's nothing," Mitchell said. He rubbed his stomach. "I'm going to get some antacid." He got up from the couch, then hesitated, looking at her expectantly.

"I'm sure everything will be okay," she said.

It would not be.

CHAPTER 10

Zara Riddle

Friday

24 Days to Halloween

After I finished with my library work on Friday, I went to meet up with my aunt at her workplace.

I walked into City Hall's bottom-floor office for the Wisteria Permit Department. It was a hive of activity, with six people so fixated on their respective tasks, they didn't notice me coming in.

"Look at all these busy workers," I said. "Forget the police department. Clearly this is the hardest working WPD in town."

Karl Kormac, who'd been hunched over some office equipment, straightened up proudly. "You got that right," he said, thrusting out his ample front, which made his rumpled suit jacket strain at the buttons. "My staff work hard, and we play harder. Are you bowling with us tonight, Zara?"

"If you'll have me," I said. "My own team bailed, but I'm available as a swinger. Wait. That didn't sound right. I mean I'm available as a spare. A substitute."

"You're hired," Karl said, then he looked down again and muttered something ugly at a printer.

Margaret Mills stomped over to join her boss. The poor machine was bleeping a sad tune. A piece of paper was audibly crumpling as it shot partway out, then got sucked in again.

Karl cursed the printer some more, this time shaking his fists in addition to verbally berating it.

The printer's bleeping amplified to a cacophonous, almost musical sound.

Margaret gasped. "Now you've done it," she said. "You jinxed the printer for real. You have to be more careful in an office full of people with our talents." She pounded the wailing machine's buttons. "It's all hexed up."

"It's just crying wolf," Karl said. He reached for the buttons, but the frizzy-haired witch smacked his hand away.

Two people giggled—the WPD's youngest employees, Xavier Batista and Liza Gilbert. They shared a work space, and were also dating.

Over at another shared work space, Dawna Jones sighed at her desk. "Not again, boss."

The office gnome, Gavin Gorman, grinned and said, "Good one, boss. Let's order a new printer. That one's ancient. The new ones are much better."

"It's only two years old," Margaret said.

She cast something with her hands, and a puff of purple smoke rose from the printer.

"You can't casually curse at electronics," she said, shaking her head. "This hex is bad."

Karl waved his hands. "Well? Unhex it. Do your thing."

Margaret coughed and waved the purple smoke around. "I don't know if I can remove it by myself." The clouds parted, and she looked across the open-plan work space at me. "Zara, help a witch out, will you?" She beckoned for me to come over. "Let's witch-pool for a tandem spell."

Liza asked, "Witch-pool?"

Xavier chimed in. "Is that like car-pooling, but for witches?"

Neither witch answered.

Gavin said, "Witchcraft is so needlessly complicated."

Dawna said, "Anything worth doing is either hard, or complicated, or both."

"Not necessarily," Gavin said.

Xavier asked, "Can witches pool their powers with people who aren't witches? Like, say, a really strong and handsome young man?" He flexed one arm to show off his bicep, which did appear to be larger than the last time I'd seen him.

Liza chided him. "You don't have to try so hard all the time."

While the group bickered with each other, I glanced at the door leading to my aunt's private office. It was closed, but it didn't appear to be soundproof. Did she know I was there? Was she sitting inside, cackling to herself over the prospect of me being drawn into her office politics?

Over by the printer, Margaret stomped one foot, like a rhino delivering an aggressive warning. "Zara! Did you hear me?"

"Sure," I said. "No problem."

Between my fight with Bentley on Monday, then breaking the news to my daughter about her genie father dying, I'd had a long week. I'd come to City Hall to meet up with the gang because I was looking forward to unwinding over a few drinks at the bowling alley with them.

I certainly didn't *want to* merge my power with Margaret's to unhex a printer that her sprite boss had cursed. But Margaret was a member of my coven, and chipping in to witch-pool powers was exactly the sort of thing we were supposed to do without quibbling.

I walked over, took her clammy little hand in mine, and opened my gates to boost her spellwork with my power.

Energy zinged around, enfolding us. A pool of mist surrounded both of our bodies. Our heartbeats synchronized. I sensed everyone gaping at us. I shut them out of my mind and focused on the energy, and on Margaret's will.

"Your will is my will," I murmured, further opening the gates.

"Other way around," she said. "My will is your will."

"That's what I said."

"Wrong again." She squeezed my hand. "You transposed it. Curse you and your sloppy syntax. You're sucking the power out of me, you novice witch." She yanked her hand away and glared at me. "Are you trying to melt me into a puddle?"

"I wasn't. But, for the sake of clarity, how would one witch melt another witch into a puddle?"

"You're worse than your aunt," she said, fuming. "Does anyone around here take me seriously?"

The others in the office murmured a chorus of no's.

Margaret reacted to the insult by raising both hands high overhead, her palms crackling with fireballs in her signature color of green.

I stepped in front of her and joined my palms to hers, as though giving a double high five. A high ten.

As we slowly lowered our arms together, I gently said, "Let's try again with the printer, Margaret. If it doesn't work this time due to me messing it up with sloppy syntax, I'll help you beat up every supernatural in this building, including the big boss on the top level."

Margaret shuddered at the mention of Mayor Paula Paladini, exactly as I knew she would.

"Okay," she said. "We can try one more time."

I pulsed power her way through our existing connection. "I give to thee my will." I repeated the phrase in Witch Tongue.

"Nicely done," she said with an eyebrow raise. "A bit old-fashioned, but no room for misinterpretation."

The printer let out a meek chirp.

The other office workers went quiet as they watched.

Margaret cast a diagnostics spell. Another mist formed, enclosing both of us as well as the printer. As the mist settled, the hex revealed itself.

Together, Margaret and I whispered, "Secrets revealed, trouble unsealed."

The spell had worked. I could actually *see* the curse. It resembled tin foil, crinkled and wrapped around the printer.

The next part would be as easy as peeling actual tin foil off a frozen lasagna.

Margaret and I were able to let go of each other's hands while remaining linked. We non-verbally communicated as we worked together to peel off the curse.

As we finished, there was a round of applause.

The piece of paper finally emerged, unwrinkled and perfect.

Margaret and I released our energetic embrace and took a step back from each other. The frizzy-haired, middle-aged woman's cheeks were flushed pink. She was breathing heavily, like a schoolgirl who'd just been cast in the school musical, or who had spent several minutes in a dark closet with the boy she fancied.

People were cheering. I had been lost in the flow state of magic—lost inside Margaret Mills—for an unknown amount of time. Now, hearing the reactions of the other office workers, I suddenly felt self-conscious. I'd never realized how intimate it was to share magic with another witch. It wasn't romantic, or sexual, but it was... *something*.

Gavin took an accurate reading of my discomfort and, being the gnome he was, made it worse.

"Now kiss," he jeered.

His deskmate and on-again-off-again girlfriend, Dawna, tossed a pink eraser at his head. "Don't be such a gnome," she said.

Karl cleared his throat and said gruffly, "Good work, team. Commendations all around. I'll make a note for your next performance review, Margaret." He adjusted the straining button on his suit jacket and blustered, "Back to work, everyone. There are at least ten minutes left on the clock. Maybe not on your clocks, but definitely on the new, tamper-proof one in my office."

The workers went back to what they'd been doing when I'd arrived: tapping on their keyboards and sorting through file drawers.

Margaret didn't go back to her desk. She pulled a gray handkerchief from her pocket, wiped the sweat from her brow, and nodded for me to follow her. She led me to the far corner, by the exterior wall.

It was cool by the wall, which I appreciated.

Margaret looked past me with worried eyes and asked in a hushed tone, "Are you here about your aunt?"

I followed her gaze to my aunt's office. Zinnia was in charge of special buildings, which allowed her to have a private work space. The door was still closed.

"I'm not here *about* her," I said. "I came for the bowling."

Margaret frowned and wrung the damp handkerchief in her hands. "But there *is* something wrong with Zinnia," she said.

"Is there?" I didn't know what information Margaret was privy to, so I had no choice but to play dumb.

She raised her eyebrows. "Zara, are we really doing this? She's my best friend. Something is wrong with her, and we both know it. If you haven't noticed, you aren't much of a niece."

"Fine," I said. "There *is* something wrong with Zinnia. She's been avoiding me since Monday, but I picked up on it anyway. The woman is not nearly as subtle as she thinks she is. The loud sighing is kind of a dead give away."

"I thought she was over the hump," Margaret said. "She seemed like her old self when she got back from vacation with your mother. Like she'd completely gotten her groove back. But something must have happened. All week, she's been moping around, doing everything at half speed, and she's missing things."

"Missing things with her job?"

"How should I know? I'm not in Special Buildings. I mean *other* things."

"Such as?"

Margaret swished her lips from side to side, then reluctantly said, "I changed my hair, and she didn't even notice."

I took a closer look at Margaret's hair. It was long, curly, gray, and frizzy. One shorter curl hung in the center of her forehead, like a rhino horn. Hadn't her hair always looked that way? I squinted. It might have been a bit less gray, but more frizzy. Or the other way around. More gray, less frizzy?

"It looks nice," I said. "I like what you've done."

"I changed it back."

"Well, if it works, it works."

"Never mind my hair. We have to do something about Zinnia."

"Do we? She's not a damsel who needs rescuing. Riddle women are tougher than they look."

"We have to do something," Margaret insisted. "The coven is only as strong as its weakest witch."

"Really? If you're that worried about the strength of the coven, I've got a few ideas for restructuring."

Margaret stamped her foot in warning. "Zinnia needs to get herself together."

I sensed my heart rate increasing and my anger rising. The anger wasn't mine. Margaret and I were still linked from our tandem spell.

"Take it easy," I said. "Don't you dare give us a pair of witch strokes." I shook my head. "Not over a jinxed printer, Margaret Mills. I'm not going down like that."

Her nostrils flared as she deliberately took in a deep breath.

I spoke gently, for her sake, but mostly for mine. "We need to be patient, and cut her some slack. Everyone slows down a bit this time of year. The days get shorter, and people start talking about sunny vacations. It's probably seasonal."

"It's not seasonal. Or maybe it is," Margaret said, thankfully calmer now. "Do you think it's seasonal? She was bad last year, too, about this time."

"We could try some sunshine spells."

"She doesn't want the light. She wants the dark. I feel her cravings." Margaret lowered her tone even more. "She's been taking that poison again. The one that puts a shield around her feelings."

"Poison?"

Margaret nodded.

I asked, "Actual poison at poison dosage, or at a vitamin dose for hormesis?"

"Poison dosage." Margaret shivered. "She feels dark inside, Zara. So dark." The two friends had a special psychic link, and Margaret had a habit of unintentionally reading Zinnia's mind.

I nodded. "Does she put the poison in her tea?"

Margaret rubbed her arms and nodded.

"I knew it."

"You knew?"

"Not exactly. I saw her slip something into her tea cup on Monday morning at my house."

"We can't let her do this to herself again," Margaret said. "We can't ignore this and hope it goes away. We need to face it head on and confront her. Together. Me and you. Or me and you and the whole coven."

"Not so fast," I said. Zinnia would hate that. Head on confrontation worked on some people, but not my aunt. Her boundaries would clamp down like high security roll shutters on a jewelry store in a bad part of town.

"We have to do something," Margaret repeated.

"I'll talk to her about the tea, and whatever else is going on. She stayed over at my house on Sunday after dinner because she thought she had a ghost tailing her, but I didn't see one. Do you think she's being haunted?"

"You tell me. You're the ghost whisperer."

"I'm Spirit Charmed."

"Exactly." She leaned over and frowned at my aunt's closed door. "Whatever you have planned, don't wait too long. We have to fix her. I can't stand by again while she fades away." Margaret held very still, and I felt the hot tears she was holding back as though they were my own. "I need my best friend."

"And I need my aunt. I'll talk to her."

"Do it now." Margaret, not one for patience, immediately stepped into my personal space and herded me toward Zinnia's office.

I tapped gently on the door, then opened it.

Zinnia was seated at her desk, using her computer. The desk was set up so that her back was to a wallpapered wall and she was facing the door. She looked up at me, showing no surprise on her expression. No emotion at all.

She wasn't alone. A little girl, about ten years of age, stood behind her.

"Oops," I said. "I didn't realize you were in a meeting."

"Don't be silly," Zinnia said, waving me in. "What a nice surprise, having you visit me here at work. Is it lunch time already?"

"Aunt Zinnia, it's five o'clock. I'm here for bowling. We talked about it this morning."

She checked the time. "It is five o'clock." Her expression didn't change.

"Are you okay?" I sensed Margaret lurking nearby, listening in and urging me to grill my aunt. I sent a psychic shush her way.

"Just busy," Zinnia said breezily. "Busy, busy, busy. You know what they say: If you want something done, ask a busy person."

Meanwhile, the little girl behind my aunt stood very still, as though her job was to witness our interaction without taking part in it.

I nodded at the girl and asked, "Is it take-a-kid-to-work day? Are you going to introduce me to your friend?"

Zinnia twirled in her chair, looked through the girl and around the area behind her, then twirled back to face me. Her expression hadn't changed, but her light skin was more pale.

She spoke slowly and calmly. "Zara, please don't joke about such things. It's tiresome." She took a sip of tea from a mug next to her keyboard, grimaced, and asked, "Answer me honestly. None of your jokes. Is there a ghost in this office with us?"

"Possibly," I said. "There appear to be three people in this office. Me, you, and another party. At first glance, I didn't think it was a ghost, because ghosts are usually see-through."

The little girl stared at me, as expressionless as my aunt. Despite appearing to be solid, she was hard to look at. When I tried studying her directly, she blended with the floral wallpaper behind her, partly disappearing, but not by changing opacity. It was more like camouflage.

Zinnia's eyes widened. "The ghost is behind me? Doing what?"

"Just standing there."

"Did you say it was... a child?"

"Yes," I said. "It's a little—"

Before I could finish, my aunt's eyes rolled up, and she fainted.

CHAPTER 11

After making sure Zinnia was still breathing, and as comfortable lying on the floor as an unconscious person could be, I called in the nearest witch.

"Close the door behind you," I said as she entered.

"Are we doing the intervention? Where's Zinnia?" Margaret was too short to see over the desk to the floor where my aunt was convalescing.

"She's... resting her eyes."

"Resting her eyes?"

"Margaret, do you see anything strange inside this office?"

She looked around, squinting. "Is this about the wallpaper? Honestly, none of us understand your aunt's obsession with florals." Margaret tugged at the curl on the center of her forehead, making it spring. "Don't we all have more important things to discuss?"

"This *is* the important thing," I said with an eyebrow raise. "Zinnia is being haunted. There's something in the room with us right now, and it's not responding to my ghost spells."

"How do you know something's in the room?"

"I can see it." I tapped my temple next to my eye. "One of the perks of being Spirit Charmed."

Margaret rolled her eyes. "No need to lord it over everyone else how powerful your specialty is. If you really can see this ghost, then who is it?"

"I don't have a name, but it's a little girl, age ten or so."

Margaret walked over to a corner of the office that was nowhere near the entity we were discussing. She blindly started waving her hands through the air and casting reveal spells.

After a moment, Margaret said, "I don't see anything. It's not fair. I hardly ever get to see ghosts." She gave up and sat in the visitor's chair, arms crossed.

We stared at each other a moment.

Margaret's eyes twitched, as though she'd just thought of something. "You said it was a little girl. Are you absolutely sure it's not a boy?"

"I can't be entirely sure. I assumed it was a girl. She's got long, blonde hair." As I turned to study the mysterious entity, her blonde hair shimmered and changed color. "Make that black hair. Medium-length, black hair. No. Red."

Margaret huffed impatiently. "Which is it? We need to get a positive visual ID."

I tilted my head to the side, squinted, and tried to get a better look. The girl kept shifting, hiding her features within the wallpaper pattern behind her.

"It's the strangest thing," I said, blinking repeatedly. "Her face keeps changing, blending in with the surroundings. Like a squid."

Margaret's face lit up with recognition. "Like glowfish," she said. "Zinnia had a bunch of glowfish in a globe, in this office. Then they got out. I thought they were gone, but maybe a few stayed behind." She rubbed her chin. "Which reminds me. I was going to research a camouflage spell so I could blend in with the inside of my house and finally get some peace and quiet. But that was back before Mike moved out. Funny. I get plenty of peace and quiet now. People never talk about the up side of divorce and shared custody."

I snapped my fingers. "That's it! There's that object camouflage spell. The one you can use on piles of unfolded laundry and other messes when guests drop in unexpected."

Margaret snorted. "I never use that. My whole house would disappear."

The spell didn't make anything invisible, but it did put a sort of perceptual veil over select objects.

I cast the camouflage reversal on the little girl while talking through what I was doing so that Margaret could follow along.

The girl's appearance seemed to become a little less vague—to my eyes, anyway—but Margaret reported that she still couldn't see anything.

"Are you sure?" I asked. "When was the last time you had your eyes checked?"

Margaret scoffed. "My eyesight is perfect. Enough fooling around." She waved her hand impatiently. "Do your big, spectacular ghost spell. The one I'm always hearing about. Where you latch onto the spirit like it's a new library book."

I had already tried that technique before calling in Margaret, but I did so again. It didn't hurt to be thorough. The acquisition still didn't happen, but something did change.

The girl's face showed an emotion for the first time. She raised one eyebrow in curiosity.

Feeling encouraged, I tried the spell once more, this time inhaling deeply, with my nostrils facing the stranger.

Again, failure to acquire.

"Is it working?" Margaret asked.

"You don't think I'd tell you if it was?" I winced inwardly at my tone. Margaret's attitude was rubbing off on me. Plus I was frustrated that nothing was working.

"No need to get sassy. Where is Zinnia, anyway?"

"Zinnia's unconscious on the floor over here. She fainted after I told her about the ghost, or whatever it is."

Margaret sprung from the chair and raced around to kneel beside her friend. "Zinnia, stop faking," she said, then, to me, "She's faking. Zinnia never faints." Margaret slapped Zinnia's cheeks. "Open your eyes. We're having an intervention."

My aunt didn't move.

Margaret summoned her purse. She yanked out its contents, then started testing various powders and bottles by waving them under my aunt's nose.

Without looking up, Margaret asked, "What's the ghost doing now?"

"Just watching us."

"What does it want?"

"I haven't asked."

"Well?"

My cheeks burned. Margaret Mills did have a way of making me feel every bit the novice I was. Bossy though she was, the woman could be clever and insightful. It was part of what made her so annoying.

I turned to the camouflaged girl and smiled. "Hello, dear. My name is Zara Riddle. What's your name?"

She gave me an amused smile. She reminded me of my daughter at that age, even though her features kept changing.

"Do you know your name?" I asked.

She smiled serenely.

"Do you know someone named Dorian Dabrowski? He's a man I know from my job at the library. Mr. Dabrowski told me he saw a little girl who's lost. He says she can't find her way home. Is that you?"

There was a glimmer of recognition in her ever-changing eyes.

"Are you the lost girl?"

Her head moved slightly up and down. Was she nodding, or was it a trick of her camouflage glamour?

I kept trying to communicate. "Is your last name Dabrowski? Or are you connected to the Dabrowski family?"

Again her head moved, this time from side to side. It was a no.

"What about the Riddles? Are you connected to that family?"

She nodded, then pointed at Zinnia.

Down on the floor, Zinnia's limp body began to twitch, then seize.

The girl took a step closer, and Zinnia's jerking movements increased.

Margaret shrieked. "What's happening?" She whipped off her suit jacket and used it to cushion Zinnia's head from the floor.

I quickly explained, "The ghost, or whatever it is, is trying to communicate."

Through gritted teeth, Margaret snarled, "Where is it standing right this minute?"

I indicated the space halfway between me and Zinnia. The girl was no longer advancing. She had stopped, and was trembling, holding both hands over her mouth. She seemed concerned about what was happening to my aunt.

Margaret flung up one arm, grabbed magic as it pooled in the air, and whipped it at the little girl. Her aim was true. The energy lit the girl green.

"I see her," Margaret gasped.

Green sparks splashed around the room.

The girl was gone. All that remained were some dark patches in my vision from the bright blast.

Margaret's missive hadn't been the usual defensive fireballs. It was powerful banishing magic—the type that sent supernatural entities back to their home base. The spell was a variation on the magic that gnomes used to teleport their way free of danger.

On the floor, Zinnia's body relaxed. Her breathing returned to normal.

I held my own breath, waiting.

Her eyes fluttered open.

Margaret said to me proudly, "That did the trick."

"It sure did," I said to Margaret. "The little girl is gone."

"You're welcome," Margaret said. "Why didn't you banish it in the first place? That horrible entity has been sucking out Zinnia's life force. It was here to finish the job, and you just stood there, making small talk with it."

"That's not exactly—"

"Don't tell me you're one of those soft-hearted witches that tries to make friends with everything and everyone." She helped my aunt sit upright. "It's a good thing I was here."

Groggily, Zinnia said, "Thank you, Margaret."

Margaret said, "Any time. Why didn't you tell me you were being tailed by some sort of psychic leech?"

Zinnia smiled wanly. "Oh, Margaret. I don't think of you that way."

Margaret shot me a look and said dryly, "As you can see, she's fine now. Rude as ever."

I asked, "Did you know you were you being tailed by a psychic leech?" There was no single psychic leech. It was more of a category for a variety of ills that few people actually understood.

"I didn't know I was," Zinnia said to both of us. She looked at me. "Did you see him? A little boy?"

"Not a boy," I said. "It looked to me like a girl, about ten years old, but her appearance kept changing."

Margaret said, "Boy, girl, who can say? All I saw was a big, green flash of light when it turned its tail to run back to the hellfires from which it spawned." She did a replay of her physical gestures. "Pow! Take that, foul beast!"

Zinnia ignored Margaret and stared ahead blankly. "Not a boy," she said. What little color had returned to her face drained away.

"It was probably a Wallflower Ghoul," Margaret said. "They creep around feeling sorry for themselves because nobody notices them, but they never actually do anything about it until things have gotten way out of hand."

Zinnia's expression remained blank.

"Sure," I said noncommittally, the way people registered that their true answer was a no without saying no. "If it were a psychic leech, that might have been what kind of psychic leech it was." The camouflage aspect certainly matched up. I had never seen one before, but I had read about Wallflower Ghouls in the DWM Monster Manual. "But aren't they supposed to be seven or eight feet tall? This one was small, like a child."

Margaret shrugged. "Might have been a new one." She helped Zinnia to her feet. "Want me to put some banishment in a bottle in case that thing comes back?"

"Yes," Zinnia said.

"No," I said. "We should do tests to make sure that's what it was, and then find the root cause. Ghouls don't come around for no reason."

Margaret rolled her eyes. "If we witches tried to find the root cause for every little thing, we'd never get anything done."

"Some things simply *are how they are*, and there is no explanation," Zinnia agreed.

That didn't sound like the Zinnia Riddle I knew and loved.

Margaret rubbed her hands. "It feels weird to use magic in here. I never use magic at the office."

My aunt rolled her eyes so hard they practically squeaked.

There was a tapping on the closed door, and Gavin yelled through it, "Are you witches busy stirring up a cauldron of eyeballs in there, or are you coming to bowling?"

My aunt answered, "Bowling. We'll be out in a minute." She shooed us toward the door.

I didn't move. "Are you sure you're up to it?" I asked. "You were passed out cold for several minutes."

Margaret answered for her. "Of course she's up for it. Everything's fine, now that we've banished that nasty old thing that was bothering her." Her chest inflated as she said to Zinnia, "You should have seen us. We were quite the team, your niece and I."

"Quite the team," I agreed.

The other two left the office to join the others.

I held back a moment, staring at the spot where the entity had been. There were a handful of pale ashes on the floor, from the smiting.

Wallflower Ghouls were at least seven feet tall, and anything but silent. Whatever Margaret had banished, it hadn't been a Wallflower Ghoul.

Whatever it was, it would be back.

CHAPTER 12

Saturday

16 Days to Halloween

My gorgon best friend, Charlize Wakeful, kept one hand on the steering wheel while she rooted around in the back seat of her car with the other.

"What's the plan?" I asked.

"It's a surprise," the pretty but deadly blonde said.

We both had the day off work and free of other responsibilities—my boyfriend was working and my daughter was out of town—so she'd suggested a full day of girlfriend time. Whatever she had in mind, it would almost certainly involve tequila. My witch powers usually protected me from hangovers, but Charlize loved to test me.

"Good surprise or bad surprise?"

Instead of answering, she handed me what she'd been rooting around for in her messy backseat: a slip of shiny material similar to the foil blankets that paramedics hand out after emergencies.

"It's stretchy," I said. "And tiny. Is this a headband?"

"Guess again."

"A thong? Gym shorts?"

"More of a gym jumpsuit. The top is attached, so you don't have to worry about the shirt riding up when you do handstands."

"Oh, good. That is the main reason I don't do handstands more often."

"I had it custom made by the seamstress who does all my clothes."

I should have guessed that. Charlize dressed like an advanced-technology alien from a sci-fi movie. I'd never seen her in blue jeans. White jeans, sometimes, but she preferred shiny silver jumpsuits.

Some supernaturals kept a low profile, but not Charlize. The gorgon didn't mind if she drew stares. Her own stare—should she choose to use it—was far more deadly than anyone's. She could turn any living thing into a statue. Her powers also worked on the recently deceased, or *parts of* the recently deceased. One time she turned a ribeye steak into a cute door stopper. Taking Charlize along for sushi was a great way to test if the fish was as fresh as the restaurant claimed.

Charlize reached back again and retrieved a granola bar from the back seat—wrapper open already—and took a bite. As she chewed, she offered the bar to me.

I declined. "I'm trying to cut back on raisins."

"Raisins? Yuck. Do you take me for some sort of sicko? I would never buy raisins." She looked down at the granola bar, which was dotted with something black. "Those must be chocolate chips." She took another bite. "Or not." She rolled down the window and spat out the mouthful, then tossed the half-eaten granola bar behind her, back into the back seat.

She kept her eyes on the road as she spat out the window a couple more times, then asked, "Aren't you wondering what the jumpsuit is for?"

"I already know. We are both running away to join the circus."

"We're going to a hot yoga class." She flashed me a grin. "That jumpsuit is all yours, for keeps. It's different from mine. Notice the V-cut on the neck, and the keyhole detail."

"It's very pretty. I should save it for something special. I wouldn't want to get sweat all over something so pretty."

"Don't be a wimp. You'll love hot yoga."

"I've been to yoga before. I tried to be a yoga person, but it didn't take."

"When have you been? Not recently, I bet."

I thought back. "It hasn't been that long. When one of the Four Eves tried to bring on the apocalypse, she made me kneel in supplication. And then, just last month, at a funeral, Helen Highbury invited me to her new Yoga for Seniors class at the community center. I didn't go, for obvious reasons, but that night I had some very vivid nightmares about doing yoga, which I think counts."

"It doesn't count."

I folded the silver garment and set it on my knee. "Can't we go window shopping and eat cheeseburgers and onion rings like usual?"

"Everybody knows you have to earn your lunch with hot yoga."

"I've never heard of such a thing. You're making that up." I looked out the passenger side window at the changing scenery. We'd left town limits and were turning onto a dirt road. "Where are you taking me? You'd better not be kidnapping me. My boyfriend's a detective. He'll find me, and you'll be in big trouble when he bites you on the neck."

"Oh?" She gave me a playful eyebrow waggle. "Bentley's allowed to bite other women? I thought you two were exclusive."

I gave her a dirty look.

She smirked and nodded at the road ahead, which wove up the mountainside through a thick forest. "The yoga studio is at an A-frame cabin up this way. It's wood heated."

"Like a flatbread pizza oven?"

"You'll love it. When the class finishes, we all run outside and jump in the cold creek."

My skin tightened all over. "Just when I thought it couldn't get more horrifying."

"You'll love it," she said, not convincingly.

I examined my new silver jumpsuit and tried to warm up to the idea. It was a cute outfit. I did enjoy events that required special clothes.

I asked, "Have you picked out a costume for the Monster Mash?" I wasn't going, but I was still interested in hearing about it.

She groaned. "Zara, you have no idea." She shook her head, her loose blonde curls tousling. The snakes that lived within her hair hissed softly. "I should stay in town and hand out candy with you. If any kids try to egg your house, I'll be happy to put them on timeout."

She meant she'd turn them to stone with her gorgon powers. Temporarily, of course, and without killing them. Even so, it would not be ideal for my reputation in the neighborhood. The locals already referred to my beloved home as the Red Witch House—a tradition that started long before I moved in.

"If you promise not to zap anyone, you're welcome to hang out," I said. "You could even bring Chloe and Jordan Junior." They were her gorgon sister and nephew.

"Maybe I will," she said, then muttered, "Stupid NHR Department."

"Are you having a problem getting your costume approved?"

"I submitted three different proposals, each tamer than the last. NHR shot down all of them. They said my Little Bo Peep costume was offensive to shepherds. To shepherds! Can you believe it?"

"Do you even have any shepherds working there?"

"Not that I know of, but there is a sheep shifter in payroll. It has to be her. She's the quiet type, so you just know she's plotting something. What kind of sick person chooses a career working in payroll?"

"I guess someone who can't handle the high octane thrill of programming code all day."

Charlize snorted.

"A sheep shifter," I said. "Is she the one who always has salad in her teeth? Are you sure it's her?"

"Who else would object to someone dressing up as a shepherd girl?"

I shrugged. "Who knew your coworkers were so uptight." I crossed my arms and looked out the window as we passed rocky terrain with small waterfalls. The landscape changed quickly as soon as a person left Wisteria.

"I'm glad I'm not going to the ball," I said. "I'm glad I get to dress up however I want on the most fun night of the year, but I do hate the idea of missing out."

"You won't be missing out," Charlize said. "At this rate, nobody will be going, or if they do, it won't be in costume. It's not just me who's having a problem. Everyone's getting the corporate run-around from NHR."

"So much fuss over nothing. Don't get me wrong. I totally understand the issue with cultural misappropriation, and trampling all over other people's identities. I think we, as a society, have a long way to go, and, yes, there is a line people shouldn't cross. I'm glad it's a talking point. But objecting to fairy tale costumes?" I took a big breath. "I mean, come on. Some people have *real*problems."

"No kidding," she said softly. "How is Zoey taking the news about Archer?"

I paused to let the lump in my throat settle. "You know Zoey. She's so stoic, especially when it comes to the big stuff."

"It's like I always say. People are stronger than they think they are. The granite is already inside them. I just bring it out."

"Zoey's always been tough. She did go through that moody patch when her boyfriend left for college, but she snapped out of it quickly. Honestly, I haven't heard much from her about Archer getting reincarnated."

"She's probably pouring her heart out to that demonic teenager."

Charlize was referring to Ambrosia, who was not in my good graces. Technically, she never had been, but things had gotten worse recently.

I'd talked to Zoey about the drinking allegations, and it turned out Ambrosia had been casting inebriation spells on both of them. I'd been angry and disappointed, yet not surprised. It was the sort of thing normal teenagers did to test boundaries, and I knew how important it was to Zoey to do some of the things "normal" people did.

So, I'd let her off with a warning. Bentley hadn't approved. But Bentley wasn't her parent. I was. And she was already being punished enough, having to deal with the coming loss of her father.

I explained all of this to Charlize, along with my concerns about Ambrosia being a bad influence.

When I was done, the gorgon said, "Admit it. The real reason you don't like Ambrosia is because you're jealous."

"No way. It's because she's a little freak with no self control, and she's been getting my daughter drunk."

"So? I'm a little freak with no self control, and I'm always getting you drunk." She batted her eyelashes my way. "But you loooove me."

She did have a point. I was quiet for a minute, then asked, "Is it bad that I'm jealous of their friendship?"

"Does it feel bad?"

"I know that I hate feeling this way. I never wanted to be one of those moms whose whole identity revolves around being best friends with her daughter." I pretended to gag.

"It's not your whole identity."

"It's not?"

"If it *were* your whole identity, and you had nothing else going for you, I'd have to put you out of your misery by turning you into a nice granite statue."

"Remind me not to cross you."

She turned and winked at me, her blue eyes sparkling. "I just did."

Then she took a hard left, testing the limitations of her Beetle.

After a dozen roller coaster bumps, as she nailed every pothole dead on, we pulled up in front of an A-frame log cabin.

We stepped out of the car as the dust settled. Birds chirped. The air smelled of tree oils and loam soil.

The cabin's porch was deep and inviting, with sturdy pine furniture. The overhang was decorated with tinkling wind chimes, glittering sun catchers, and colorful streamers that twirled hypnotically in the light breeze.

Charlize led the way, pulling open the heavy wood door. A wave of heat escaped and washed over me like the hot exhalation of a very large monster.

I paused before entering.

Over the tinkling of the wind chimes and the rustling of the streamers, I could hear the nearby creek babbling. It was the one we were going to jump into. It sounded very cold.

CHAPTER 13

Wednesday

12 Days to Halloween

The coven didn't meet every Wednesday, but many of our non-emergency meetings seemed to fall on that day of the week. We met between one and three times a month. None of us picked the dates. Maisy Nix, the tall and intimidating owner of Dreamland Coffee, was the keeper of a magic calendar that set our schedule for us.

The coven had six members: Maisy Nix; her niece, Fatima Nix; my aunt, Zinnia; Zinnia's best friend and coworker, Margaret Mills; myself; and our newest witch, Ambrosia Abernathy. She was my least favorite, and, to make matters worse, the others had taken to calling her New Zara to annoy me.

What the coven needed was one more member to serve as a tie breaker during our many debates. We had discussed the possibility of allowing non-witch members to attend meetings. Back before my time, the former owner of my house, who'd been some kind of healer mage, had been part of the group.

Margaret, was a fan-girl when it came to the local gorgons, had been vying to include the baker gorgon, Chloe. I didn't have the heart to tell Margaret that the gorgons found the idea of a coven laughable, and would never want to be part of it.

My aunt had suggested inviting her coworker, Dawna Jones, whose skills as a card mage gave her some ability to predict the future.

It seemed reasonable enough to invite mages, since there was some overlap in skills between witches and mages, but the group couldn't agree on where to draw the line. Dawna might want to bring her boyfriend, Gavin Gorman, and nobody wanted that.

Gavin was a gnome, and gnomes couldn't be trusted. We all felt it in our witch guts. It was probably an unfair prejudice, but Gavin's uncle Griebel had ruined the reputation of gnomekind. Some coven members still dealt with the repugnant little man, but always with great caution. Except for Zinnia. She claimed her old pal was "basically harmless."

Harmless, my butt! She hadn't caught one of Griebel's spiky death traps with her bare hands like I had. And she hadn't channeled the tortured spirit of a girl who'd been killed by a poisonous potion delivered by the gnome himself.

The meeting tonight would be, like all the others I'd attended, witches only. We only brought up the idea of expanding our membership when we ran out of things to bicker over.

After a quick dinner, I drove toward the downtown Dreamland Coffee.

I hit a streak of good luck. Every traffic light—not that there were many on my route—was green.

I arrived at the coffee shop several minutes ahead of schedule. I entered through the back door, and immediately realized my green-light luck had been bad. Only a single witch was there. The proprietor of the coffee shop was seated at the round table, doing something with coffee grounds, test tubes, and a komodo dragon.

Maisy Nix was mid-forties, six foot two, with tan skin and shoulder-length shiny black hair. She was thin but not skinny, and did everything with a confidence bordering on brute force. She pushed me like few did. She'd trapped me in a room to boast about her romantic conquests, and she'd siphoned off my magic to power a broomstick flight without asking. Like my mother, she wore plain, tailored clothes, such as gray trousers and white blouses. She was a stunning woman, with large, sensual lips and eyes the color of black coffee.

The komodo dragon was... big and gray. Like a typical komodo dragon.

Both looked up at me as I entered.

"Whoops," I said, stopping in my tracks. "I must be early."

"You're not early," Maisy said. "Everyone else is late."

"But clearly you're busy with something. I'll just step out into the alley to give you a few minutes to finish doing whatever it is you're doing. I'll do what people do in alleys. I've been thinking about starting a new bad habit. Maybe I'll try smoking."

"Don't," Maisy said. "If you start smoking, I will assume you're on fire and extinguish you."

"I'm sure you will." Maisy helped fight wildfires, so her threat was far from empty.

"Try this one," Maisy said to her lizard friend.

The komodo dragon grabbed one of the liquid-filled test tubes with his scaly, clawed forefoot, and slurped it back.

Maisy used magic to whip out one of the chairs. "Come. Join us."

I stayed near the door. "I, uh, think I hear someone coming. I should stay by the door in case anyone has trouble with the lock."

"Sit." She pointed at the chair. "You can help taste test some new beans."

"Beans? I'm assuming you mean coffee beans. I do have an adventurous palate, but I've found that all other beans pale in comparison to coffee beans, except peanuts, which are technically legumes, unlike coffee beans, which are technically seeds."

Maisy raised an eyebrow. "Do I make you nervous, Zara?"

"No." I forced myself forward and took a seat. I wasn't *nervous*. It wasn't *nervous* to keep a respectful distance from a dangerous creature and her komodo dragon.

As I settled in my chair, the dragon began to move. It swayed from side to side, slapping and scratching the table as it turned its thick body around, rotating on the round table like a big, burly hand on a clock. It stopped, facing me.

"Hello there," I said to the big lizard.

It did nothing.

I felt Maisy's eyes narrowing at me.

I remembered what Margaret Mills had said about me being too friendly toward unknown entities. She'd mocked me for trying to make friends with all of them.

I tilted my face up to the ceiling, pretending to lose interest while I continued to study it out of the corner of my eye.

It had scales, like Ribbons, but it was much beefier. And it had a smell. A zoo smell.

I couldn't ignore it any longer. And why should I? I was a naturally friendly person. Nothing wrong with that. Plus Margaret wasn't there to mock me.

I smiled at the creature and said, "My name's Zara."

Maisy snorted. "Don't flirt with Humphrey," she said.

"All I did was say hello and introduce myself."

"With Humphrey, it doesn't take much. Stop making bedroom eyes at him."

"I wasn't." The nerve of her. She was the one with the bedroom eyes.

Maisy tapped the creature's beefy tail. It didn't budge. Maisy got up and walked around to my side of the table. She leaned over my shoulder and looked it—*him*—in the eyes.

"Great," she said. "Now Humphrey is fixating on you."

Fixating? How could she tell? The komodo gazed in my general direction with expressionless reptile eyes. I couldn't even tell if we were making eye contact.

Humphrey's mouth opened, and when it did, warm breath came at me. I had not been wondering which orifice had been emitting the zoo smell, but now I knew it was the mouth.

I leaned back, but the smell followed me. My eyes started to water.

"He likes you," Maisy said. "Look at him. He's practically shooting love beams at you."

As I stared into the komodo's eyes, I started to see something that might have been romantic interest. Or I was giddy from the breath fumes. The stink was worse than the paste that came from the glands of Banded Tree Hoppers.

As the komodo shot his breath and love beams at me, I self-consciously pulled my blouse closed at the neck. "Thanks, but I'm seeing someone," I said.

Maisy grabbed the beast by the tail and forcibly turned the whole thing—approximately one hundred and fifty pounds of it—around. Humphrey protested by snapping at her, but the witch rebuffed the attack with casual magic shielding. She was so quick with her defenses, she made it look effortless, which I knew it wasn't.

As Humphrey completed his rotation, the table underneath him wobbled noisily. The table had been hexed one too many times and wobbled a lot even under better circumstances.

Maisy took her seat again, crossed her very long legs, and said, "Back to testing the new roast samples." She looked at me pointedly. "It's just regular coffee. Not any sort of magic beans. Not tonight."

"I'm in," I said. Why not?

Maisy explained the differences between the roasts, and we began the taste test, drinking samples out of test tubes.

Humphrey rated the new roast blends on a scale of one to three, holding up claws as fingers.

Maisy said to me, "You and Humphrey have something in common."

"We both prefer the golden roast," I said.

Her large lips spread in a mean smile. "And both of you can eat up to eighty percent of your body weight in one sitting."

"Ha ha. Have you been sitting on that comment a while? Have you been planning it all day? Is the whole point of having a komodo dragon here all part of a setup so you could make that crack about me and my appetite?" I rested my chin on my hand and leaned in like an interrogator. "Did you make all my traffic lights green?"

"Oh, Zara. Lighten up."

"You're not denying it."

She rolled her eyes. "Don't be such an OCW."

She meant Overly Cautious Witch. It was an insult that didn't necessarily mean a witch was being too cautious. The shorthand term could be used in all circumstances where one witch disapproved of another witch's attitude. Calling another witch an OCW was a good smokescreen whenever one was about to get busted for her own bad behavior.

The back door opened. Maisy's niece, who was as short as Maisy was tall, and as sweet as Maisy was mean, came in with her usual cheery smile.

Fatima pushed her oversized, white-framed glasses up her stubby nose and asked me, "How's Boa? Has she said any new words?" I had consulted Fatima shortly after the whole Clockbird incident.

"Not yet," I said. "Just ham."

"That must be all she has on her mind. I'm glad she has such a good life in her *furever* home."

"Me, too, but can we get her to stop talking about it?"

Fatima, who worked at a veterinary clinic, and whose specialty was communicating with pets, looked horrified. "Why would you ever want your furkid to stop talking?"

"It might be hard to explain a talking cat to certain people who might visit the house," I said.

Fatima waved one small hand. "People only hear what they want to hear. They will assume she's saying *meow*."

"*Ham* sounds nothing like *meow*."

"Actually, cat meows sound nothing like M-E-O-W. If you actually listen, you'll find that very few cats say meow. They say oww, or rurrh, or groww, or meeew, or ehh, or any number of things."

"Maybe to you."

Fatima shrugged. "People hear what they expect to hear."

I scratched my neck. "I'd still like to return Boa to her factory default settings, and I'll admit it's for a selfish reason: my sanity. I've been dreaming about ham every night for the last two weeks. I have a suspicion Boa has been sitting on my pillow, whispering in my ear while I'm sleeping."

"That does sound like something a cat would do," Fatima said, nodding seriously. "Has anyone witnessed her doing this? Have you asked the Shadow Man who watches you sleep?"

Maisy cut in to say, sharply, "The Shadow Man isn't real, Fatima."

Fatima's tan cheeks flushed a dusky pink. "Of course not, Aunt Maisy. It was just a joke." Fatima gave me a secret wink. *Not a joke.*

The door creaked open, and Margaret Mills came stomping in.

"Men!" Margaret didn't wait for a response before launching into a tirade about how divorce was liberating, but she should have learned her lesson and stayed single, because dating two men who shared one body was not a picnic in the park.

Ambrosia Abernathy arrived next. The teen witch entered, waved hello and took a seat, all without taking her eyes off her phone screen.

Once seated, Ambrosia gave the others brief eye contact, skipping me. She knew she was in the doghouse with me for casting inebriation spells on my daughter, but it would go unmentioned at the meeting. It was best to not involve the whole coven unless absolutely necessary.

When Ambrosia finally set her phone down, and saw that a full-grown komodo dragon was sitting on the table and gazing at her amorously, the teen witch shrieked.

The dragon, startled by the scream, reflexively whipped its beefy tail and snapped its jaws in warning.

Ambrosia pulled back in alarm, causing her chair, which was nearly as jinxed and unreliable as the table, to topple over backwards.

As Ambrosia spilled on the ground, her untrained powers zapped out in all directions, shocking all of us on the tips of our noses.

"Ow!" Margaret rubbed her nose. "Ambrosia, pull yourself together!" Margaret's hair curled itself into tight ringlets, no frizz at all.

Fatima, who'd apparently noticed the change in Margaret's hair, gave me a knowing look. Some of us shared a secret theory that Margaret might have some gorgon blood in her family tree.

Ambrosia groaned on the floor. Nobody went to help her. I almost felt sorry for her.

"Do better," Maisy said sharply to her mentee. "*Be* better."

"Sorry, Maisy," Ambrosia said. She got to her feet, dusted off, and righted the chair, which now wobbled worse than ever.

"Stop flirting with Humphrey and pull yourself together, New Zara," Maisy said to Ambrosia. "You're as bad as Old Zara."

The others snickered. The only one who agreed with me that Ambrosia shouldn't be called New Zara was my aunt, and she wasn't there. She was late, which wasn't like her.

Maisy removed the komodo dragon from the table "to protect him from unrequited love," and tucked him into a cage in the corner. When she locked the door on his cage, that was when I realized Humphrey was an actual komodo dragon, and not a shifter. I'd assumed he was Maisy's latest supernatural love interest, but I was wrong. Then again, maybe I wasn't. With Maisy, you never knew.

The other four witches ducked out to the front counter to get their favorite beverages. I stayed behind and furtively checked through messages on my phone. I didn't dare use my phone in front of the others and get compared to our teenaged, phone-obsessed coven member.

There was nothing from Zinnia, so I started to compose a text asking where she was.

Before I hit send, she'd already replied, thanks to her psychic powers: *There's a meeting tonight? Why didn't anyone tell me?*

I started to compose a message that she would have known if she kept up on the group chain, but her next psychic reply came in immediately: *I'll be there in ten minutes. Bone-dry cappuccino, please.*

* * *

When Zinnia finally arrived, even later than she'd promised, her coffee was cold.

I took her with me to make a fresh cappuccino. The others stayed in the back room, engrossed in a chaotic cross-talk conversation about Halloween costumes, scarecrows versus zombies, dating two men in one body, and the existence or non-existence of something called the Shadow Man.

"Thank you for not forgetting about me," Zinnia said.

"I'd never forget about you. Don't be silly. How have you been?"

She rubbed her forearms. The heat was off in the main coffee shop area, and it was as chilly as a meat locker.

"Fine." She nodded toward the back room. "Did I miss anything important?"

"What do you think?"

There were squeals and cackles from the back room.

She pursed her lips in a tight smile. "I suppose we ought to be grateful that things are slow enough lately for us to indulge in gossip and girl talk."

"Why is it slow? Halloween is in twelve days. Shouldn't there be zombies and goblins rising from every crypt in town?"

"That's just a myth. One of those urban legends people like to believe in."

"Are you sure about that? Even legends are usually based on some truth."

"Statistically speaking, the month of October tends to get no more uprisings of evil entities than any other month."

"So it's just an average month."

"More or less. The locals do get awfully excited. I suppose all the jack-o-lanterns, corn mazes, and scarecrows do add a certain festive spirit to the air."

"I love Halloween. I always have."

"Yes. Well..." Her eyes glistened. She blinked quickly and looked away. "I don't," she said.

"Why is that?"

She stuck her nose in the air. "All the popular depictions of witches are unflattering."

The brittleness to her tone told me she was lying.

"I asked how you were doing, and you didn't answer," I said. "I'm going to hazard a guess and say that you know that whatever's been haunting you is back. It wasn't a Wallflower Ghoul after all, was it?"

"Of course it was," she snapped. "I'm fine now. I haven't even thought about the matter in days. I don't know what you think you saw, but it must have simply been," she waved her hands, "a Wallflower Ghoul traveling through the area."

I didn't let my eye contact waver.

I didn't look behind my aunt, or directly at the little girl sitting on the edge of the counter behind my aunt.

As usual, she was watching us silently. I was almost getting used to her presence.

In the days since I'd first seen the entity at City Hall, I had seen Zinnia three times, and I'd observed the entity nearby each time. I had tried some different spells each time, but I hadn't cast a banishment spell. Other than making my aunt forget the coven meeting, it didn't seem that harmful.

By not attacking it as Margaret had, was I going about things the wrong way? I usually had my aunt to mentor me, but she was so locked in denial about this, she wasn't much help.

The coffee machine gurgled and beeped.

"You need to flip the switch," Zinnia said. She shooed me away from the espresso machine and took over. Having been to many more coven meetings than I had, she was more experienced with the machine.

As my aunt worked, the little girl hopped off the counter then stood at my aunt's elbow, watching the coffee brewing with interest.

Zinnia shivered.

I asked, "Did it just get even more cold in here?"

"I don't believe so, but it will be good to warm up with an extra-hot cappuccino."

"Aunt Zinnia, there's a reason you shivered just now. That thing that you claim isn't bothering you is standing at your left elbow."

"Oh." She kept her gaze steady on her ceramic mug as the espresso dribbled down.

"I can see her."

"I suppose you would."

"Margaret is worried about you."

"*Margaret* has more than enough to worry about with her boyfriends."

"I'm worried about you."

She glanced up, a wounded expression in her hazel eyes. "I can take care of myself. I was doing just fine before you moved here. Riddle women are tougher than we look." She rubbed her thumb.

"Is that why you're dosing yourself with poisonous potions that lock up your emotions and numb your heart?"

Here comes the intervention Margaret has been planning since day one.

"I know about the poison," I said. "Margaret and I are both concerned you've been abusing it."

My aunt's lips all but disappeared. "That's my business, not yours."

The little girl with the shifting features remained at my aunt's elbow. She flicked her ever-changing eyes back and forth as we talked. She offered no emotional reaction, but I had the impression she understood what we were saying, as well as everything we weren't saying.

"It's not just your business," I said. "I have no choice but to notify the coven about," I waved at the entity, "the situation."

My aunt reached for the milk and began steaming it. "Please don't."

"You know the rules. Whether you meant to or not, you brought that thing here, into our meeting."

"But I didn't mean to."

"Now it's watching and listening, and unless we blast it with a banishment spell, which I feel is unwarranted, it's going to follow us into the back room. If I don't inform the coven, we'll be in violation of the rules, and if Margaret finds out we're in violation of the rules, we'll never hear the end of it."

"So be it." She took a breath and straightened up. "Perhaps it's for the best. The group can do a spell and banish it for good."

"Or make everything ten times worse, like when we tried to cure Ambrosia's pimples and turned her green."

Zinnia frothed her milk without comment.

"Then it's settled," I said. "We will make it a coven-wide issue."

"If you insist. I won't stop you."

She wouldn't stop me, and I would soon find out that, like Ambrosia's skin problem, some things had to get worse before they got better.

CHAPTER 14

Zinnia sat quietly while I told the coven about her unwanted companion.

Margaret squawked at me for not informing her sooner that the problem was back, and that it was apparently not a Wallflower Ghoul after all.

Zinnia leaned over and took Margaret's hand in hers. To my surprise, the gentle touch worked wonders, and Margaret became the most cooperative member of the coven during our discussion of the problem.

We quickly reached consensus and performed our first spell as a group.

Spell number one did not go as we'd hoped. The result was the overhead formation of a fluffy, white cloud that dropped a localized rainstorm on our table. It was better than no result at all, but not by much.

Time for stronger measures.

The cloud continued raining while we talked. I cast a fountain circulation spell to keep our laps from being splashed until the cloud decided to go away on its own.

Our second attempt, which was a completely different category of spell, made the cloud larger and turned the rain into icy hail. Large, square chunks the size of dice came crashing down, bouncing noisily on the table before passing through the surface and disappearing.

The shadow girl stood behind Zinnia, watching impassively.

"It's not working," Fatima said.

Margaret shot me a look. The younger Nix witch's specialty was being Whisper Graced, but she certainly had a minor in Stating the Obvious.

"There's no change with Zinnia's shadow," I said.

Fatima asked, "Is that what we're calling it? Zinnia's shadow? Isn't that a bit... You know..." She puffed out her cheeks and made wide eyes as she nodded in Zinnia's direction. "Victim blame-y?"

"I'm sitting right here," Zinnia said icily. "Don't talk about me as though I'm not even here."

Everyone glanced around uncomfortably. Zinnia could be so easy to offend, but nothing offended her quite like people trying hard to not offend her.

"It *is* my shadow," Zinnia said. "But we all know how dangerous it is to name that which ought not be named. Shall we call it *the* Shadow?"

Maisy led us in a quick vote, and we agreed unanimously to call her, or *it*, the Shadow.

One thing that didn't resolve was the storm cloud. It continue to spew down hail stones.

"This needs to stop," Margaret said, fanning both hands at the nuisance rain cloud ineffectively, the way campers fanned the smoke of a campfire.

Fatima held both hands over her ears. "The sound is making my poor ears ring." The young woman was sensitive to loud noises. Rumor had it she needed to be fitted with a modified straightjacket—a thunder shirt—during the town's fireworks celebrations.

"You're the rain and cloud expert," Margaret said to Maisy. "Is this one of those clouds you and the fire crew use to contain forest fires?"

"Not exactly," Maisy said. She leaned over, looked below the table, then gazed up at the cloud in wonder. "I've fought fires all over the world, and I've flown through every kind of weather, and I have never seen anything like this before."

Ambrosia, who'd been quiet until now, stood and stroked the cloud, as though petting a woolly creature. "It's soft," she said with surprise. "Like a sheep."

Margaret and Maisy got to their feet to pet the cloud. They agreed that it was soft, like a newborn lamb. Fatima didn't get up, and kept covering her ears.

Zinnia remained seated, her expression neutral.

The Shadow continued to stand behind Zinnia, closer than I'd ever seen it. As I watched, the Shadow lifted one small hand and rested it on Zinnia's shoulder. Contact? That was new.

Zinnia twitched her shoulder, dimly aware of the entity's touch, even if she couldn't see the hand. The only other witch who could see the Shadow was Ambrosia.

For the moment, I was glad to have Ambrosia be part of the coven. We hadn't figured out the teen witch's exact specialty—my aunt's magic codex couldn't make up its mind—but we suspected the teen witch was, like me, Spirit Charmed.

Ambrosia met my gaze through the hailstorm and raised her eyebrows. She flicked her gaze to Zinnia's shoulder, then back to me as she raised her eyebrows even higher. Her question was clear. Should we inform Zinnia that the entity had progressed from standing nearby to actually making contact? I shook my head. No. What good would it do?

"Well," Maisy said, in the tone she used when she was tired of our company and wanted us out of her coffee shop. "It is getting late."

The cloud took the hint and stopped hailing. It remained overhead, though.

"Are you kicking us out, Aunt Maisy?" Fatima dropped her hands from her ears. "After only two spells?"

"Two spells that should have worked," Maisy said. "There's no rule that you always have to try three spells, and no evidence that the third one is the charm."

"Then why does it always seem that way?" Fatima asked. "You try and try, then the third one works."

Margaret looked at Zinnia and asked, "What do you think? Should we try a third spell?" She waved her hand in front of Zinnia's face. "You look half dead, Zinnia. How much of that poison have you been taking? Are you trying to kill yourself?"

"Margaret," I said sharply. "And you wonder why she doesn't open up to people. Take it down a notch."

Heads turned my way. Eyes widened. Everyone present stared at me with horror, as though *I* was the person who'd overstepped boundaries, and not Margaret. In the absence of the hailstorm, the room was way too quiet.

"It is getting late," Margaret said. "And I don't like the look of that rain cloud. If we try another group spell, it might start spewing out tarantulas and scorpions. Speaking of which, I really should be getting home. My children are making the most of their parents getting divorced. The number of ill-advised pets they've been acquiring might be some sort of record."

The tension broke as several of us chuckled. The last thing Margaret's kids needed was more pets.

Maisy said, "You can borrow Humphrey any time."

"A komodo dragon?" Margaret snorted. "That's the last thing they need. They don't even take care of the pets they have."

"That's not what I meant." Maisy smiled a carnivorous grin. "Humphrey has an excellent appetite. He'll make short work of any household creatures you deem extraneous."

Across the table, Fatima squeaked in outrage.

Maisy tilted her head, bringing one finger to her cheek. "Margaret, how many pounds is your youngest offspring?" She tilted her head the other way and waved her hand. "Never mind. I'm sure it'll be fine. "But just to be safe, don't remove Humphrey's collar while your smaller children are in the room."

Margaret asked, "Why would I remove his collar?"

Maisy stroked her own neck vertically. "So he can swallow the bigger pets."

Margaret nodded thoughtfully.

Fatima, the pet lover, sat in stunned silence, her mouth open in horror.

The cloud started dropping a light mist. I felt the moisture on my face.

"I have an idea," Ambrosia said.

The group gave her their full attention, and she squirmed as though surprised.

Shyly, in her upspeak that made everything sound like a question, she said, "We've been going at this like it's not a ghost? But what if it is a ghost?" She looked at me through the cloud's mist and winced in what I guessed was a pre-apology for what she was about to say. "What if Zara's conclusions aren't correct?"

Everyone looked at me.

I shrugged. I'd been wrong before. The Shadow didn't act like my other ghosts, so I'd concluded it wasn't a ghost, but I wasn't more invested in being right than I was in helping my aunt. It stung a little to have Ambrosia questioning my judgment, but I could take it. *Zara tries to be a good witch. Zara keeps growing as a person.*

"Go on," Maisy said to the teen witch. "We all appreciate your input, and your unique perspective as a novice witch. We can try a third spell if you have one in mind."

The others murmured in agreement. Maisy wasn't in charge of the meetings, but she did provide the location and free coffee, so nobody objected when she ran things.

Ambrosia swallowed, then continued. "Just because Zara's acquisition attempts didn't work, that doesn't mean it's not, you know, a ghost? The ghost communication spell might work?" Her voice kept pitching up, which did make it difficult to take her seriously.

"That one's easy," Margaret said. "We can do that spell. All we need is a minimum of two witches and a mirror."

Maisy, pushed her chair back, jumped up, and loped off on her long legs. She called back over her shoulder, "I'll grab one of the big mirrors from the bathroom. If I can remember the screwdriver spell."

"Don't bother," Margaret said. "We'll move this party into the bathroom. It's hard to focus on anything with this mist pouring down." She tagged Fatima on the shoulder, then grabbed Zinnia by the arm. "Come on. Let's get you fixed, for once and for all, so we can all go home, and you can stop pickling yourself silly."

Ambrosia and I were the last to get up. She intercepted me before we'd even left the mist radius.

In a hushed tone, she asked me, "Are we actually doing the communication spell? In the bathroom?"

"It was your idea, kid. Don't suggest the crime if you can't do the time."

She wrapped her arms around herself. "But big bathroom mirrors are freaky enough as it is."

I shrugged. She wasn't wrong.

She whispered, "What if something comes through from the other side?"

"Then we'll put on our big girl pants and deal with it."

"Okay, but..."

"But what?" The young witch and I were alone in the back room. Well, if you didn't count Humphrey the komodo dragon, whose pet-gobbling breath I could now smell.

Ambrosia tucked her bleached hair behind her ears nervously. "Doesn't the Shadow look familiar to you?

How can she look so familiar, if we can't even see what she looks like?"

"She's probably one of those *abstract* ghosts. They're only vague and unfinished because they're lazy."

Ambrosia's expression relaxed. "That makes sense." She turned and walked out to join the others.

I snorted to myself. *Abstract ghosts.* It was so easy to fool novices. I could have told her the moon was made of Parmesan cheese.

I grabbed some of our used dishes from the table so I could drop them in the kitchen along the way. The coffee cups had been washed clean by rain, hail, and mist, but I couldn't be sure the magical precipitation met food safety regulations, so I left the dishes by the sink.

By the time I got to the washroom, I realized I'd been too slow. The coven hadn't waited for me.

I stepped in just as the lights were flickering and all the witches were cackling with excitement. Cackling! You really noticed how witchy they sounded when you walked into it.

When the fog cleared and the lights went back to normal, there was a single word written in the condensation on the mirror.

Ambrosia said, "It's a name?"

It *was* a name.

None of us dared speak it.

The name was Aiden.

We all turned to Zinnia for a reaction.

"Oh, no," my aunt said, backing away until she bumped against a wall. She covered her eyes with her palms. "No," she said weakly. "No."

The Shadow stood beside her, also covering her eyes with her palms and mouthing the same word. *No.*

CHAPTER 15

Zinnia Riddle

Three Years Ago

June

"He's such a D to the B," Aiden said.

Zinnia shot the boy a warning look. "Language."

"I didn't say it. I didn't say the actual word."

"That doesn't matter. You meant it." Zinnia gathered the empty dishes from the side of Aiden's bed. The food had barely been touched. An uneaten grilled cheese sandwich was wedged between two plates, making the whole stack wobble.

"But I didn't say it," Aiden argued. His tone was cheeky but playful. He enjoyed these discussions.

Zinnia continued her lecture. "Words matter, including the ones we imply. We ought to be mindful of all of our words."

"Why do you talk like that? Are you a teacher?"

"All of us are teachers, in a way." She set the tray aside and sat on the edge of his bed. "Why? Do you think I'd be a good teacher?" She grabbed her long, red hair and twisted it up onto the top of her head. "Like this? With a bun? I could stick a pencil through my bun, just like a real teacher."

Aiden smiled. "The teachers at my school don't wear their hair like that." He licked his chapped lips. "But I like it. You know, you're kinda pretty."

She fanned her face. "Such flattery. You're making me blush."

He laughed, which was good, until it turned into a hoarse cough.

Mitchell came running in.

He asked Zinnia, "Is he coughing again?"

She held out both hands. The child was still coughing.

Mitchell looked at Aiden. "Has this been happening all night? When did it start?"

Aiden finally stopped coughing. He didn't answer his father. He pulled away the pillows that had been propping him up and pushed himself down in the bed. He rolled over so that he faced away from his father.

Mitchell put his hands on his hips and walked around the bed to the tray of dishes. "Why is this mess here? Where's Fiona?"

"She's sleeping," Zinnia said. "It's three o'clock in the morning."

He waved at the silent boy. "Then why are you in here? What are you doing in here, besides keeping him awake and making him cough? He needs his sleep."

More sweetly than he deserved, she replied, "I got up to use the washroom, and I noticed the light was on, so I came in to check on him." She cast a spell to make her voice more calm and convincing. "Everything's fine, Mitchell. You ought to go back to bed and not worry about this."

The lights sparkled in front of his face. Zinnia could see the visual confirmation her spell was working, but others could not. It was working, and she saw the change in Mitchell's eyes—the hypnagogic response—as he accepted her suggestion.

"I'm going back to bed," Mitchell said, turning. "I'm not going to worry about this."

"I'm coming with you," she said.

Mitchell left the room.

Zinnia followed him to the door, but didn't leave. She closed the bedroom door softly, then came back to the side of the bed.

Aiden immediately rolled over and sat up.

"Show me how to do that," he said.

"How to speak to someone with respect and kindness?" She leaned forward and touched him lightly on the nose. "You don't need me to show you. The secret is already inside you."

"Not that." He rolled his eyes. "I'm talking about," he lowered his voice to a whisper, even though they were alone, "the M-A-G-I-C."

A tingle of alarm ran up her arms and over her body. Did he know? He couldn't possibly know. She'd been so careful.

She smiled warmly and said, "What a wonderful imagination you have, Aiden. When you grow up, you're going to be a famous author."

He grabbed her hand and squeezed it. "I'm not joking around," he said. "I know you're a wizard."

She blinked rapidly. "A wizard? Little ol' me?"

"Don't lie. I heard those weird sounds when you were telling that D to the B to get lost. I've heard them before. Lots of times. It's like a whistle, but upside-down, like you're doing something with your tongue."

Frowning, she reached over to the dresser and grabbed his anti-nausea medicine to read the label.

"This must be messing with your ears," she said, shaking the bottle, then opening it to sniff. "Ew. It smells exactly like something that messes with your ears."

"But I've only been taking that stuff for a few days, and I've been hearing the whistles for at least a year. You're doing it. It's magic. I know because it always happens right before you calm *him* down." He sat up on his knees and looked her straight in the eyes. "Zinnia," he said solemnly.

"Aiden," she said with equal seriousness.

"I'm dying," he said. "If you can't tell your big wizard secret to a little kid who's dying of cancer, who can you tell?"

"Aiden, are you faking this illness of yours to get secrets out of people?" She was only half joking.

"No. You don't have to tell me *how* to do the magic, but at least admit you've been doing it. Tell me. Right now."

She sighed. "Fine. You got me. I'm a secret wizard. My best friends are Harry, Ron, and Hermione, and I got sorted into the Hufflepuff House."

Aiden frowned. "You're going to feel so bad when I die. You're going to wish you told me when I was alive." He turned away and wriggled himself back under the blankets.

He muttered something else she didn't catch.

"Aiden, if you can't sleep, I can read you a story. Is that what you want? Something about magic to take your mind off everything?"

He pretended to snore.

Within minutes, his fake snore became real. He had been tired.

Zinnia sat on the edge of the bed until morning.

She barely noticed the time passing, and didn't move until the morning shift nurse came in to check on the boy.

In a whisper, the nurse asked, "Was it a difficult night?"

"Not as bad as some," Zinnia replied.

"It might be time to add a night nurse to the schedule."

"Not yet," Zinnia said. *Please, not yet.*

The night nurse wasn't supposed to come until it was nearly over.

Everything was happening too quickly.

It had only been two months since the diagnosis. It was too soon to give up on the treatments, even though they weren't making him better.

She stayed seated on the edge of her bed, and she decided something. She would be there herself, every night. They did not need to call a night nurse. Not yet.

CHAPTER 16

Zara Riddle

Saturday

9 Days to Halloween

"Booties up," said the perky yoga instructor, clapping her hands for emphasis. "Hey, you two. I want to see those shiny silver booties in the air."

She meant us. Charlize and I were the only ones present with shiny silver booties.

I shot a look over at the blonde gorgon computer programmer. She was struggling to maintain her pose next to me. Sweat streamed down her face and dripped on the mat. Her face twisted with exertion as she pushed her booty higher.

I had no choice but to also push mine higher, risking a nosedive on my mat.

The instructor rewarded us with praise. "Good work, silver booties! Now, make them wag!"

Wag? Did she mean literally?

Charlize wagged her bottom, so I had no choice but to do the same.

"Now that's how you do a Downward Dog," cheered the instructor.

We moved on to the next pose. Charlize caught my eye and whispered, "Don't act like this wasn't *your* idea."

I spat a sweaty lock of hair out of my mouth.

She was right. I had only myself to blame for being back at the A-frame cabin just one week after I swore I'd never return.

It turned out the hot yoga's restorative effects were slow to activate. It wasn't until Friday night that I realized that some twisted, sweat-loving part of me was actually looking forward to doing it again. I was eager to wear the custom-made jumpsuit, even though it put a big silver target on my booty.

"Keep your faces serene," the instructor said. "When adversity comes at us, we do not show weakness by letting our beauty fade."

I relaxed my face out of the grimace I'd been holding.

The instructor was a rubbery woman named Riverflow, and she was the perfect hot yoga teacher, the ideal mix of kooky and earthy, bossy and encouraging. She had a good point about maintaining grace under fire. We were there to get healthier and find inner peace, not to acquire frown lines.

Satisfied with the angles on our silver booties, Riverflow turned her attention to our other sweaty friend, Carrot Greyson.

"Skyward," Riverflow urged. "The sun's not behind you or below you, Lemon Yellow." She might have known Carrot's name, but she referred to people by their booty colors. "It's up, Lemon Yellow! The sun is up, up, up!"

Carrot Greyson gave the pose one more try, her eyes practically popping out from effort as her lemon yellow yoga shorts shakily rose skyward. Her tattoos were vibrantly glowing under a sheen of sweat.

Once in position, Carrot tilted her face and shot me a dirty look.

Me? It had been Charlize's idea to invite Carrot along, not mine. I was only getting the flack because Carrot knew better than to give a gorgon a dirty look. Carrot had the power to magically paint on all surfaces, from walls to humans, but she was just a mage. Mages weren't as resilient as witches.

Riverflow cooed musically, "I wish you all could see what I see! What a beautiful rainbow of booties!"

Then she hopped up on the platform and did a one-handed handstand with an ease and grace most people couldn't achieve on two feet.

* * *

The hot yoga session consisted of thirty-three poses and lots of heavy breathing.

After the hot part, all twelve of us—eleven students plus the instructor—ran outside for the cold part.

Giggling and shrieking like children at play, we all jumped into the freezing cold, mountain-glacier-fed creek that babbled behind the studio.

Most of us wore our yoga clothes into the water, since we were drenched anyway. A few older ladies stripped naked. Nobody found that odd. It was that sort of crowd.

Carrot waded over to where Charlize and I were standing, her skinny, tattooed shoulders pulled up to her ears.

"It's so cold," she whimpered. "I haven't been this cold since I went camping with my cousins Jeremiah and Jebediah. They refused to have a campfire because they didn't want to participate in the senseless murder of a tree."

Charlize gave her a sidelong look. "Couldn't you have made a fire out of the fallen branches? They were already dead anyway."

Carrot sighed. "You don't know my cousins."

"They wouldn't last a minute in my family," Charlize said.

"That's funny," Carrot said.

"Funny?"

"Because the Wakeful clan and the Greysons have hated each other for generations." Carrot quickly added, "Not me, of course. I don't care about the past, or whatever your grandfather did to my grandfather."

Charlize raised a blonde eyebrow along with a single hair snake. "I'm sure whatever happened, your grandfather was the one who started it. Greysons are always collecting weapons and bragging about killing monsters. If you ask me, the so-called monster hunters are the real monsters."

"Ladies," I interrupted. "I'm sure both your grandfathers are equally horrible."

They both turned to me, looking confused. Then, when they realized I was joking, the tension broke and both laughed.

"Angelo Wakeful was no saint," Charlize said.

"But he wasn't as horrible as your grandmother, Diablo," Carrot said. "Or so I've heard."

The gorgon smiled. "Thank you."

The two of them, who hadn't spent much time together until now, chatted away about town history and their family trees. I didn't have much to add. The Riddles' involvement in town history dated back to the 1950s, but only on a technicality based on time travel. My aunt was the first of our clan to live there—that we knew of. We suspected there might have been others, who had gone by different last names.

Carrot smiled and laughed as she talked to the gorgon.

I was glad to see we had successfully taken Carrot's mind off her genie boyfriend's imminent demise. Unfortunately, upon noting that, I remembered it was happening, and sadness gripped my heart.

Hot yoga and other distractions could make you forget about the past and the future and simply exist "in the moment," in the present, but you couldn't be there all the time.

I looked back at the cabin. The windows were opaque with steam.

The conversation lulled, and Carrot said, "I'm so cold."

"Adversity is good for you," Charlize said. "Hot and cold exposure are essential for a good life."

That sounded familiar. "Charlize, that's what you always say tequila is for," I said.

"Tequila is also essential, but there are downsides," she said. "The dose makes the difference between poison and cure, and tequila is a lying devil who only says more, more, more."

I bit my tongue.

Carrot made a brrr sound. "This cold exposure sure is w-w-working," she said. "I'm not thinking about anything except this w-w-water."

I turned to Charlize and gave her a chin lift. "Do the thing," I said. "Do your little trick."

Carrot asked, "What trick?"

"Wimps," the gorgon said, then, with a sigh, "All right. I'll do it."

Carrot gave me a worried but excited look. Her mind was still off Archer. My mind went back to him. Why did he have to get an unstable body that wouldn't last longer than a potted fern?

Now I was worrying about him. And worrying about my aunt, too. I couldn't even remember a time I wasn't worrying about someone.

Meanwhile, Charlize looked happier than a clam escaping a clam bake.

Speaking loudly, addressing the whole group, Charlize said, "Everyone gather around and watch the freak perform her circus sideshow trick."

Carrot whispered to me, "She's not going to turn us into stone, is she? I was on the fence about the hot yoga, but I'm really not comfortable with becoming a statue." She looked down with alarm. "Is it already happening? I can't feel my feet."

"Relax," I said. "She's just going to make the water warm."

Carrot frowned and narrowed her eyes. "Like how boy cousins offer to make the water warm?"

"Not like that. Look."

We both watched the gorgon. I'd witnessed the feat the previous Saturday, but I saw it again for the first time through Carrot's eyes, and it was magnificent.

Charlize raised her shapely arms in the air. She turned both to granite, then to bubbling, red-hot lava, which she plunged into the creek. The water hissed, and steam plumed up in great billows.

"It's working," Carrot said, her skinny shoulders relaxing and her tattoos returning to their usual shape. "The water's getting warmer." She looked around. "How much heat is she generating to warm up this whole creek?"

"It's not the whole creek," said one of the naked older ladies as she joined us. "We're in an eddy, dear," she said to Carrot. "The water's swirling around in between these rocks here, like a hot tub."

Carrot sighed and leaned back to soak her bright orange hair. "It's so nice."

The naked lady beamed at the gorgon. "Thank you, honey!" Her chest bobbed happily, unfettered by clothing.

"My pleasure, Adelaide," Charlize said with a wink.

The other yoga class attendees happily waded over to join us, careful not to touch the gorgon's lava arms directly. Nobody screamed, because they were all supernaturals, and they'd seen Charlize do her trick after previous classes.

Riverflow saw what was happening and barked, "Wimps," but then reluctantly joined us in the hot tub party.

All twelve of us basked in the late autumn sunshine, warm and snuggly as a pot of chili beans. We listened to the creek babble and the birds chirp. The leaves overhead rapidly turned yellow and red, then drifted down on a light breeze. One of the others in our hot tub must have been responsible for speeding up the leaves, but I didn't know who. Some of the women had shared their powers with the group in formal introductions, but others were too shy, or too smart.

Eventually, people drifted away to their towels and dry clothes one by one.

Only the three of us who'd arrived together in Charlize's car, Bugsy, remained.

Carrot, looking right at home in the steaming water, said to me, "Margaret told me about Zinnia's Shadow."

I didn't volunteer more information.

Carrot glanced at Charlize, then at me. "Is it okay to talk about the Shadow?"

I waved at Charlize, accidentally flicking water in her face. "She knows everything, and it sounds like you do, too." I cast a sound bubble to limit our conversation, though the others didn't strike me as the snoopy type.

Carrot said, "It's so sad about that little ghost boy being stuck between worlds."

"That's just a theory of Margaret's," I said. "And it wasn't even the first conclusion she jumped to."

"You don't think he's a stuck ghost?"

"I don't know if there even is a ghost. If there were one, my powers should have worked. Why would a ghost hold back when they've got a Spirit Charmed witch around to do their bidding?"

"But if it is a ghost, what I don't understand is why nobody noticed him until now. He died two years ago, didn't he?"

"If it's the Aiden that Zinnia knew, yes. Margaret said he passed away around Halloween."

Charlize turned to me. "What's this about a little boy? I thought your aunt was being followed around by a chameleon *girl*."

"She is. But at our last coven meeting, we did a communication spell, and something wrote the name Aiden on a mirror. I told you all of this."

"That almost sounds familiar," Charlize said. "Was I listening when you told me?"

I splashed more water in her face, on purpose this time.

There was a flash of movement in the nearby woods, and a wolf strolled out. The wolf was on the small side, almost dog sized, and trotted toward us in a friendly manner.

"Of course," I muttered under my breath. "Riverflow has a pet wolf. How did I not expect this?"

"It's not hers," Charlize said.

Carrot threw her hands above the water and exclaimed, "Alfie!"

Alfie?

The orange-haired woman quickly explained to us, "This is the doggie, I mean the wolf, that got hurt in Towhee Swamp. I helped him get better. Excuse me while I go see how he's doing."

She stepped out of the hot tub eddy, her colorfully-illustrated body steaming in the cool air.

Charlize elbowed me. "And then there were two," she said.

I looked at her. "You know, I don't think I told you about the coven meeting, did I?"

"Was it the one where all the witches acted witchy and self important about everything, and nobody let anyone else's ideas stand whole without putting their own stamp on it?"

"Ha ha," I said. "I'll have you know, we can cooperate sometimes."

Charlize pressed her lips together smugly.

"We did three group spells to try to figure out what's haunting Zinnia," I said. "And we tasted some new coffee blends."

"I don't know how you get anything done with all those other people involved. Whenever I'm facing a problem, I don't want anything or anyone between me and the problem. Just a keyboard, thanks."

"Can you program an algorithm to figure out what the Shadow is, or how it relates to a boy who died two years ago?" I glanced over at Carrot, who was play-wrestling with the tame wolf. "Or how it connects to Archer dying?"

"I could come up with something that can use AI to detect patterns within a system as complex as real life, but it would probably try to take over the world again. And I promised I wouldn't touch AI ever again."

I tucked my chin and gave her a look that said oh really? She knew that I knew that she was working on a dozen secret projects. She had to. If Charlize had too much free time on her hands, the chaos around her amplified. Every space she inhabited started to resemble the back seat of her car, which was bad enough. Earlier that Saturday, before picking up Carrot, I'd help clean up the seat, shoveling the contents directly into a biowaste dumpster at the DWM.

Charlize said, "Maybe I could feed some parameters into a program. What do you know about this boy, Aiden?"

"Zinnia didn't want to talk about it."

"Big surprise."

"But Margaret knew about it, so she told us. A few years back, Zinnia was living with a man. He was a professor at a university. No magic. He worked in the economics department."

"That's an interesting match."

"He didn't even know she was a witch."

Charlize wrinkled her nose. "And she didn't tell him? That never works out."

"And it didn't. But he had a son from his previous marriage, Aiden, and the kid bonded with Zinnia. According to Margaret, Zinnia was planning to leave the guy, but the boy got sick, and she stuck around." I swallowed hard. "Until he died, two years ago."

Charlize made a sympathetic sound. "That's awful. Watching someone die is the worst."

We both glanced over to Carrot, who was now sitting next to the wolf and stroking its ears.

"I can only imagine," I said. "It was hard for me when my mother was ill, but at least she pretended to die quickly. It didn't drag on..."

I couldn't finish. I felt awful talking so offhandedly about another person's intimate tragedy. In a hot tub. It wasn't right.

I'd been exposed to many gruesome deaths through my calling as a witch, but this one was different. The boy had died of natural causes, from a natural disease. Zinnia hadn't been married to his father, but she must have felt some responsibility for the boy. Had he called her mother?

I shivered, despite the warmth of the water.

Aunt Zinnia, someone's mother.

I'd never thought of her that way. Suddenly I felt retroactively terrible for all the times I must have sassed her about parenting advice when it came to Zoey. She must have felt it. She must have felt motherly love. And now he was gone.

No wonder she was haunted. I would be, too.

Charlize asked, "How long was the boy sick?"

"A few months," I said.

"Did Zinnia...?"

"Did she use her potions to treat the child?" I shook my head. "That would have been crazy. Every witch knows you can't use magic to treat something like that. It can't be done."

"But she must have tried."

"Margaret got angry and defensive when we asked, so who knows."

"Angry and defensive is a good cover for guilty."

She made a good point. "I talked to Maisy for a few minutes in the alley, and she said, just between us, that if Margaret and Zinnia did something that violated the laws of nature, that might be why the Shadow is here."

"To rebalance," Charlize said.

My teeth chattered. The water had turned chilly. Charlize had been focused on our conversation and not on heating our eddy.

Charlize looked up at the bare branches overhead, unworried by the temperature change. "This reminds me of something my grandmother used to talk about," she said. "The nature of disease and decay versus the life force of magic."

"Were there magical cures for cancer in the land she came from?"

Charlize kept staring skyward. "No, but only because they didn't have cancer in the first place. What I mean is..." She squinted. Her hair snakes woke from their slumber and started hissing around, eyeballing me suspiciously. "I wish I could remember what she said. Don't you hate that? When something's on the tip of your tongue, so to speak?"

"If it's in your head, I could try searching through your memories like a book," I said. "There are spells."

"You are not going to hypnotize me, witch." She snorted.

"It's not hypnosis," I said, except it sort of was.

Charlize took in a sharp breath. "I know!" She tapped her head. "Zinnia went to my grandmother's world recently. They have a lot of shadowy things over there. I bet this Shadow tagged on and followed her over here, like a hitchhiker."

"That is... spooky."

"It was a major breach. Between the red wyverns and unclassified creatures three-hundred-and-ten through seventeen, it kept everyone very busy. Your aunt's Shadow would have easily been overlooked."

"How do we get rid of it?"

She winced. "I'm not sure. I'll have to start an official case file at the Department. Sorry."

"You do what you gotta do. If the DWM can help, I would welcome them with open arms." I looked down. "Speaking of open arms, you need to either turn up the heat or carry me out of here. I can't feel my legs."

Sweetly, she said, "You need to warm up? This is perfect timing. Riverflow is starting the next session in a few minutes. Come on. It'll be fun. You're already dressed for it."

She put her arm—still warm but not lava—around my waist and helped steer me toward shore.

Despite my chattering teeth, I managed to say one word: "Monster."

She smiled proudly.

CHAPTER 17

After our second hot yoga class and creek dip, Charlize and I dropped Carrot off at her tattoo studio, then rolled up to Wisteria's new all-you-can-eat Indian buffet restaurant.

We opened the door to the warm fragrance of spicy curry. Pleasant music streamed over hidden speakers. Colorful scarves decorated the high ceiling.

A petite woman in a sarong greeted us and directed us to serve ourselves from the buffet and take any seat we'd like. After two back-to-back yoga sessions in one day, I couldn't think of anywhere I'd rather be. Even the vegetables looked good. I rubbed my rumbling tummy as Charlize and I picked up our plates to begin.

I asked my friend, "What kind of restaurant was this place before? I don't think I've been inside this building."

"That's because it used to be an autobody repair shop." The blonde gorgon pointed at the large wall of windows. "Those are roll-up garage doors."

So they were. "I like what they've done with the space."

"Me, too. If the food's as good as it smells, this could be our new hangout."

"You're assuming I'm not going to get us banned for life," I said with bravado. "Brace yourself, for tonight you shall witness your best friend consuming eighty percent of her body weight in one sitting."

Charlize, who knew better, rolled her eyes. "Big talk from a puny human." She jumped in front of me, grabbed the spoon from my hand, and started heaping rice with cranberries onto her plate.

"How wise of you to cut in line in front of me," I said. "You'd better stay two steps ahead if you want any food for yourself."

A deep, male voice behind me said, "She needs to stay ahead of *you*, Zara? What about me?"

I turned to find the burly DWM agent Knox, and behind him, his friend and fellow agent, Rob. They must have just arrived, minutes after us.

Rob grinned at us and said, "You three had better leave some food for me." He wagged a finger. "And behave yourselves. This town hasn't had an all-you-can-eat buffet in years. Don't put them out of business their first week."

We all laughed.

"What's this I hear?" A black-haired, tan-skinned man in his thirties approached us with friendly outstretched arms. His black hair was buzz cut, and he wore wire-rimmed glasses with tiny round lenses. His face was skinny and his body was not. He was dressed in a gold tunic and matching pants.

We all said hello.

The man spread his arms even wider. "Friends, I invite you to eat all you can." He spoke in an Indian English dialect. "Rest assured, we have no intention of going out of business. I am not my cousin, after all." He paused, and his smile broadened with the barely-restrained excitement of someone delivering a corny punchline. "My cousin who sells rugs."

The four of us murmured noncommittally and exchanged looks.

"It is a joke," the man said. "Because rug stores are always going out of business. Please, you must laugh at my joke."

Did we have to? I'd lost so much perspective lately, I wasn't entirely sure what was funny anymore.

He went on. "My family and I have worked very hard for this grand opening, and all that is left is to fill this place with the sound of laughter."

Rob spoke up for the group. "You'll have to forgive us for not laughing at certain types of humor. We're all a little gun-shy lately. Halloween's coming up, and there's been a lot of talk about who can say what or wear what." Rob shoved his hands in his pockets. "The fact that my own ancestors came from China has ruled out a lot of my costume options."

Knox said to his friend, "What about me? I wanted to be Elvis, but they said I couldn't be Black Elvis. I told them I didn't want to be Black Elvis. Just regular Elvis."

"You'd make a great Elvis, big guy," Rob said.

"But I am not allowed," Knox said.

The restaurant owner looked aghast. "Who told you that? You, my large friend, should be able to dress as anything you want. The whole lot of you could go as Black Elvis, Chinese Elvis, Gorgon Elvis, and Redheaded Witch Elvis." His brown eyes twinkled. "Unless you have something better in mind that you believe your underground bosses will approve of."

Charlize froze, except for her hair snakes, which twitched up in alarm.

Knox leaned down and asked me in a low tone, "Do we know this guy?"

"I sure don't," I replied. "Get out one of your Men in Black weapons. Shoot him into a cocoon or something."

Knox's brow furrowed. "Who told you about the cocoon gun?"

Rob, who'd also leaned in, said, "Good idea." He pulled a silver weapon from his pocket, and aimed at the overly familiar restaurant owner. Rob pulled the trigger, and something string-like emerged from the device.

Seconds later, the man who'd casually revealed half of our group's powers was fully wrapped from head to toe in something white and silky.

The white shape fell to the floor and wriggled frantically.

"You forgot the air holes," Charlize said, stepping over the cocoon casually to get at the ginger beef. She loaded her plate and said over her shoulder, "I recommend three holes. Nostrils and mouth." She glanced down at the wriggling cocoon. "You'd better do it before he passes out."

Rob pulled out a small knife and quickly put air holes in the cocoon. Then he and Knox hauled the wriggling parcel away for something they called "processing."

I sidled up next to Charlize at the buffet. "I was only joking about the cocoon gun. I had no idea." I glanced over at the dining room, which was empty. I could hear the sounds of food prep emanating from the kitchen, but we were alone for now. "What are they going to do to him?"

"Why are you so concerned?" She moved along the buffet. "Is that naan bread?" It was. She took a stack. "I wouldn't normally have both rice and bread in one meal, but that does smell good."

By the time we reached the end of the buffet, the guys returned. All three of them. The stranger walked in front of Knox and Rob, hands clasped and head nodded forward.

"My apologies," the man said to Charlize with a nod, then repeated it to me. "I was without my manners. I did not mean to imply anything." He winked several times. "You are, of course, normal human women."

His mind hadn't been wiped, but now he understood that he'd violated the local supernatural customs, at least when it came to DWM agents.

If I'd been there alone, I probably would have talked it out with the guy. Margaret wasn't wrong about my friendly approach. But the DWM had their own ways.

Charlize said, "Apology accepted." Her hair snakes relaxed and disappeared in her golden curls. She extended her hand and introduced herself.

We made official introductions all around.

The man's name was Vijay Kulkarni, no relation to the Bollywood star, wink wink.

Not wanting to offend, the four of us pretended to know which Bollywood star Vijay meant.

The restaurant owner explained that he had been living in London until recently, running a restaurant that catered to hungry supernaturals. He learned about our little town of Wisteria from some new customers, the Moore family. "Lovely people," Vijay said of them. "And what a cute little boy. Such big eyes."

Hearing about our town had inspired Vijay. He realized it was time for a big life change, so he packed up his wife and children, and moved stateside to start a second restaurant.

"Vijay's is now an international franchise," he said. "We started with one, now we have two, and soon we will have many more." He took a step back and waved his arms. "Now eat! Look at all this food! I have taken enough of your time, and you have given me the warmest of greetings."

Rob snorted.

Knox, confused, said, "We did?"

Vijay smiled blissfully. "I have not been shot with a capture device in far too long, let alone interrogated."

"You're welcome," Rob said. "Any time."

Vijay urged us again to eat. We did as he instructed, loading up our plates.

We seated ourselves at a round table twice as big as what we needed, and began eating.

For the next half hour, I enjoyed catching up with Rob and Knox. I hadn't seen them face-to-face since my fake birthday party at the DWM cafeteria. That event had resulted in far too much bloodshed and death, and not nearly enough presents.

Contrary to my threats about eating the restaurant out of business, I only had three helpings of dinner. I would have stopped at two, except Vijay came by and urged us to sample the new dishes the staff had just set out.

Just when we thought we couldn't eat another bite, we discovered the dessert buffet.

We had to grab petite square plates and start all over. There were impossibly sweet round donuts—Gulab Jamun—and other items I'd never tried before.

Rob leaned back in his chair, rubbing the sides of his stomach. "Good thing I hit the gym today," he said.

Knox furrowed his brow in confusion. "You came to the gym for five minutes, to borrow some of my clean socks."

Rob shrugged. "It still counts."

Changing the subject, Charlize pointed her thumb at me and said, "Zara refuses to attend the Monster Mash. She's protesting NHR's heavy handedness with the costumes."

Rob and Knox exchanged a knowing look.

I waved my hand. "Don't you guys go blabbing about it and getting me in trouble with the powers that be. I'm simply not going. It's apolitical." I licked the spoon for my cardamom rice pudding. "Besides, someone's got to hand out candy at the Red Witch House. The local hooligans will be so disappointed if nobody's home when they egg it."

"I'm with Zara," Charlize said. "I'm handing out candy with her this year. Forget about the Monster Mash. We'll have our own party."

"A party?" Rob leaned in. "Can we come, too?"

"Sure," Charlize said. "The more the merrier."

"Yes," I said, making it official. "I'd love to have you guys over."

Knox gave me a serious look. "Will there be costumes?"

"I can't see why not," I said. "Wear the most outrageous costume you can think of. No limits."

Rob asked, "Can I bring someone? A date?"

"Of course," I said. "Bring two."

Charlize guffawed.

Rob grinned. "That's generous of you to think I could round up not just one date but two."

Charlize turned to me. "We have to invite Carrot and Archer."

"Do we? Carrot seemed excited about going to the ball at the castle."

"She might have changed her mind if they turned down her costume ideas."

"I'll talk to her about it," I said.

For the next hour, we lingered over our desserts and chai tea, chatting about catering and music choices for the party.

When Vijay came by with a hot pitcher of chai tea refills, we invited him and his family.

"I will do the catering," he said.

"You don't have to work," I said. "Come as a guest."

"I insist," he said. "At a party, everyone loves samosas. My wife uses magic to make them. She is a pastry mage." His chest broadened. "And I am a spice mage."

We all made ahh sounds. Two food-related mages in one kitchen? That did explain why the food was so incredible.

"My sister Chloe should meet your wife," Charlize said. "Chloe and her husband run the Gingerbread House."

"They can meet at the party," I said.

"Perfect," Charlize said, and we all agreed that the relaxed, non-corporate costume party at my house was going to be the highlight of the year.

And it would happen in nine days.

CHAPTER 18

Sunday

8 Days to Halloween

Since my move to Wisteria, my whole social life had really leveled up. I had a bunch of new friends, I regularly hosted dinner parties, and soon I would be throwing a great Halloween party. I had so many ideas for decorations, party food, and the music play list.

But first, that Sunday night, I had to prepare for a regular family dinner in my dining room. The prep work wasn't heavy, since it would be potluck. The others didn't trust my cooking abilities. You serve people macaroni sandwiches with ketchup dipping sauce *one time,* and they never let you forget it.

I had been put in charge of appetizers. Typically, that would have meant sorting through the five open boxes of crackers I usually had on the go at any time, and picking out the unbroken ones. But everyone was in for a surprise that night, and not the bad kind, like that time I used a spell on my oven to make extra-fluffy soufflés and nearly summoned a cacodemon.

My contribution would be a platter of mouth-watering samosas. Vijay had brought them over in the afternoon as a preview of what he'd be serving at my Halloween party. He'd actually brought over three platters and more of those round donuts, but who was counting?

At quarter to six, Zoey and I were setting the table.

Correction: I was setting the table, and Zoey was moping, looking tortured, and adjusting the angles of everything I set out. My sixteen-year-old daughter was a shifter, not a witch, but she would have fit right in with the coven. She couldn't leave another witch's handiwork alone.

"Aunt Zinnia's invisible spider traps seem to be working," I said. The spiders were invisible, but the traps were not. "I don't see nearly as many cobwebs on the chandelier."

It wasn't true. The cobwebs were worse than ever. I was feeling optimistic, possibly a side effect of eating two platters of charmed samosas.

Vacantly, she said, "That's nice."

That's nice.

She'd been saying that a lot lately, and not much else. I'd had to get reports about her and Ambrosia's work on the fake haunting at the Inn from Ambrosia.

"I also bought you new deodorant and put it in your drawer," I said.

"That's nice."

"I'm thinking of letting Carrot give me a tattoo."

"That's nice."

"On my face."

"That's nice."

"It will be a tattoo of lizard scales, to make me into a lizard woman. Green scales with purple highlights, like Ribbons'. I'll have to get a new photo taken for my driver's license, of course. And my passport."

Without looking up, she said—you guessed it, "That's nice."

This was not good.

If Zoey was still moping when the others arrived, and if Zinnia was still moping from her ongoing haunting—and why wouldn't she be—that would be way too much moping. All that bad energy would force me to bend over backward making jokes, trying to change the mood of the room, to no avail. Then my new half-sister, Persephone, would give me that mortified look that told me she was experiencing second-hand embarrassment on my behalf. I would double down. It would become the kind of bad dinner party you couldn't blame on the food alone. A total misfire.

Something had to be done to snap my daughter out of her funk.

I cast a spell, turning one of the table's cloth napkins into a white bird. I sent the napkin bird flapping around the room. The bird's linen wings stirred the cobwebs, dusting the table.

She scarcely noticed.

"Is that Marzipants?" I asked theatrically. "How did that darn bird get in here? Mrs. Pinkman must have sent him all the way to Wisteria using magic, or FedEx."

No reaction from Zoey. I'd been hoping for a squeal, at minimum. Mrs. Pinkman's bird, a budgie, used to terrorize her.

"Watch that lower lip," I said. "You'd better pull in that pouty drawbridge before Marzipants does you-know-what on it."

Zoey didn't pull in her pout, let alone laugh at my attempt at levity.

She flashed into her fox form, jumped in the air, and nabbed the flapping bird.

The spell expired upon contact, and the linen budgie went limp. Zoey-Fox gave it a death shake anyway. She landed lightly on all fours. I was reminded of Boa murdering Clockbird. Had Boa's death pounce been instinctive, or had she learned it from my daughter? Was my regular kid educating my furkid? What an interesting new thread in the tapestry of our family life.

I looked down at my daughter's fox eyes, which looked even sadder in animal form. The limp napkin bird was still in her mouth.

"It's perfectly understandable that you're feeling sad about your father going away," I said. "Do you want to talk about it?"

She dropped the soggy white napkin at my feet, then rested her chin on her paws. She couldn't speak in her shifter form, and she wasn't changing back.

"I can take a hint," I said. "You don't want to talk to me about it. I hope you're talking to someone, though. Maybe Ambrosia?"

Her ears twitched up straighter, which I took to mean yes.

"I guess it's true," I said with a sigh. "Ambrosia really is the New Zara, and not just at coven meetings."

Zoey-Fox stood and turned, then slowly walked out of the dining room. She dragged each paw across the wood floor noisily. Nobody could mope quite like a teenager, except a shifter fox teenager, due to having twice as many feet to drag.

I wasn't alone with my thoughts for very long before someone else came along. Charlize, who must have let herself in without ringing the doorbell, appeared in the dining room doorway.

"Hey, good lookin'" she said.

"Hey, yourself," I replied.

She sniffed the air and asked, "Is Rhys back in town, or is that your daughter I smell?"

"Zoey shifted into fox form right before you got here," I said. "All the better to not talk about things with her mother."

Charlize remained in the doorway, leaning on the frame. She had both hands behind her back. "My sisters and I used to hate it when our mother pried into our lives."

"I wasn't prying," I said.

"Of course you were. Isn't it your job? Checking on your child's emotional state in between disasters?"

"Fine. I was prying. Guilty as charged."

"You're not guilty of anything. My sisters and I hated it back then, but we'd give anything to have my mother back to do it one more time." Her head tilted forward and her smile went away. "Life can be a real stomp on the tail," she said hollowly.

"It sure can," I agreed.

"That's why I brought these." She straightened up and proudly brought out two bottles she'd been holding behind her back. One was white wine and the other was tequila. She waved the wine. "We can start slow and work our way up."

"Booze?" I shook my head. "Charlize! You were in charge of the main course."

"Which is why I brought tequila." She waved the second bottle. Her hair snakes hissed with amusement.

"So much for the whole potluck idea," I said. "They'll never let me host Sunday dinner again."

The gorgon laughed. "Lighten up, Zara. I also brought a big pot of beef brisket." She nodded in the direction of the kitchen. "I stuck it in your oven to keep it warm." She tilted her head to one side. "Speaking of which, why is your oven so clean inside? Is it new?"

"I had to do a deep clean after the soufflé incident."

"I bet you did." She reached into the breast pocket of her silver jumpsuit. "Speaking of summoning the dark forces to befoul all that you hold sacred and dear, I brought over that thing we talked about."

"You found it?"

She pulled from her pocket a gold chain holding a pendant, then tossed it at me. The chain snagged a few low cobwebs on its way to my hands, sending dust fluttering all around us.

The gorgon sneezed. "Don't clean up on my account." She rubbed her nose. "Why the cobwebs? Do you have invisible spiders?"

"Yes, but I put out traps."

"Those don't work," she said.

"What does work?"

She shrugged. "Ignore the problem and hope it goes away?" She looked pointedly at the pendant in my hand. "Don't you have bigger fish to fry?"

Yes, I did. The pendant was for a spell I was planning to use on my aunt's Shadow.

When Charlize and I had talked about my aunt's problem the previous day in the creek, she had theorized the entity was a hitch hiker from another world, an entity that had crossed into our world with my aunt.

Margaret's banishment spell had worked on the entity, but not permanently. To get rid of it for good, we needed something more powerful. The key was using an object from its home world as an anchor.

I examined the pendant Charlize had brought. I'd expected something flashier. The stone wasn't any sort of gemstone I recognized. It wasn't even shiny. It looked like a plain ol' pebble.

I asked, "This belonged to your grandmother, Diablo Wakeful? It's so..." I couldn't lie and say it was pretty.

"It's a rock," Charlize said.

"Did you or one of your sisters change the gemstone into a rock?"

She laughed. "Sometimes a rock is just a rock." She came over to the table, popped open the white wine, and poured two glasses. "When my grandmother immigrated to this world, it was on short notice. They didn't have time to pack. What you're holding is a pebble that was stuck in the treads of her boot. My grandfather had it set in gold as a gift."

"Aww." I curled my fingers around the pendant and held it to my chest. "That's so sweet. This is a family heirloom." I tried to hand it back to the gorgon. "I can't use this for my spell. It might get ruined. You saw what happened with the soufflés."

She pushed it back to me. "Our family's fates are intertwined," she said. "Maybe the whole reason my grandfather had a pebble mounted in gold was so that nobody chucked it out. That way it would still be here for right now, when we need it to help Zinnia."

I gave her a sidelong look. "Intertwined fates? Have you been analyzing ancient scrolls again?"

"A girl's gotta do something to keep her mind busy when all available computers are compiling data."

"Thank you," I said, holding the pebble to my chest once more. "It means a lot that you trust me with a family heirloom."

She rolled her eyes. "You're so corny." She handed me a glass of wine, then sipped some of hers.

I took a drink. As always, the first sip did eighty percent of the job the full glass would do. Wine magic.

Charlize asked if I had the other objects and supplies ready for the banishment spell.

I showed her the pewter-framed hand mirror I'd selected for the ritual. The spell didn't require much else beyond the anchor object, the mirror to serve as a portal, a couple of basic combustibles, and the participation of a minimum of two witches. Zinnia was the subject of the spell—or the *object*—it wasn't clear—so she couldn't cast, but Ambrosia could.

To permanently banish an entity back to its origin, we had to float the anchor object on a pewter-framed mirror, then chant the spell in Witch Tongue in tandem, in perfect harmony. I wasn't sure Ambrosia even knew how to harmonize, but I had a plan, and that was something.

"That could work," Charlize said, finishing her glass of wine. "And if it doesn't, you're still one step closer to the solution, because at least you'll know what doesn't work."

"Thanks for the vote of confidence."

"Forget what I said." She poured another glass and hiccuped. "It's going to work. You're a brilliant and powerful witch, Zara Riddle. Why wouldn't it work? Of course it's going to work. You've got a plan and everything."

"I do. So why do I have the feeling I'm forgetting something?"

She looked around. "Where are the crackers?"

The crackers! It wasn't a Riddle family dinner without the crackers.

I got the crackers, and we decided it was better to dispose of the entire bottle of white wine than admit we'd started before the others.

As we toasted our brilliance, my confidence in the plan grew.

By the time Zinnia and the other guests arrived, I was absolutely, positively, one hundred percent sure the spell was going to work.

CHAPTER 19

Well, folks, you heard the setup: I had a detailed plan. I had magical supplies. I had confidence. I had crackers and cheese. Everything should have worked.

However, I'm sure someone as clever as you can imagine exactly how things went down, based on the aforementioned factors, as well as the fact it was still eight days until Halloween.

My latest attempt to deal with Zinnia's tag-along went so poorly, it made everyone's memory of the whole souffle incident seem, by comparison, as wholesome and pleasant as a small town charity bake sale.

Not only did my dining room ceiling get covered in ectoplasm—again—but the terrifying abomination that came through the mirror smashed up my favorite teapot.

The worst part was that I hadn't even realized I had a favorite teapot—it was the rose-patterned one—until it was being unceremoniously crushed under an enormous cloven hoof.

Actually, that's not true.

The worst part—the *actual* worst part—happened when the dust settled. Ambrosia and I saw that not only had we failed to banish Zinnia's Shadow, but we had made the problem worse.

The Shadow was now more of a medium sized girl than a little girl. It had grown in size and was at least a foot taller. And Zinnia—poor little Zinnia—was smaller.

On the plus side, we did finish the evening with the same number of living people with which we'd started. There were six of us: Me, Charlize, Zinnia, Ambrosia, Zoey, and Persephone Rose.

I'll spare you the gore of the failed tandem spell, and cut to the aftermath.

The screaming had stopped, though our ears were still ringing from the gunshots.

Zinnia was staring at me in disbelief. We had just measured her height in the doorway. The news wasn't good.

Zinnia's eyes were as round as the rose-patterned saucers that had been smashed. "I'm two inches shorter?"

Ambrosia was also staring at me. "I harmonized with you perfectly, Zara. I don't understand what went wrong."

Charlize, who was holding the tape measure, said to my aunt, "If you started out the same height as Zara, then it's not two inches. You've shrunk three and a half inches." Charlize waved the tip of the tape measure at Ambrosia. "Don't sweat it, kid. I called it. This hare-brained scheme of Zara's was never going to work."

Zinnia looked down and patted her clothes. "Everything's loose." She looked around dazedly. "My clothes are loose."

"The shrinking seems to be proportional," Charlize said. "You got shorter, and narrower. Look how loose your belt is."

Zinnia asked, "Why would my body shrink but not my clothes?" Before we could answer or apologize again, she waved away any possible explanation and repeated a phrase I'd heard many times. "Because magic has a mind of its own."

It sure did. I looked around surveying the damage.

The Shadow was still stubbornly there. The medium-sized girl stood behind Zinnia, partly blending with the destroyed room.

Gooey ectoplasm dripped from the ceiling above her, and shards of broken mirror were embedded in the wall behind her.

The pebble, which had started out the size of a gemstone, was now the size of a boulder, and still smoking.

Zoey, who had shifted into red fox form at the first sign of trouble, was warily circling the enormous boulder, sniffing it.

Persephone Rose, in black fox form, was also sniffing the boulder. My sister had shifted while everyone was screaming in terror, but not until after unloading her service revolver into the summoned beast. Shooting it with regular bullets hadn't damaged the beast, but it had distracted it long enough for Charlize to push it back through the portal.

And that was how we'd managed to survive the encounter. Barely.

The black fox stepped away from the boulder and shifted back to human form. Persephone plucked some fried calamari from her long, dark hair. "Ew," she said. "Was this from our potluck dinner or from the other side? Don't tell me. I don't want to know." She picked out three more pieces, then said to the red fox, "Zoey, do you want to join me outside for a run? It does a shifter good to move rapidly through natural terrain after a traumatic event." She glanced over at me sheepishly. "If it's all right with your mom."

They both looked at me with hopeful eyes.

"Go ahead," I said, then, formally, "You may be excused from the dinner table." I coughed. "Or what's left of it." The beast had stomped it cleanly in half.

Persephone shifted back into a black fox, then jumped outside through the spot that had been a window. The dining room's window was neither open nor smashed, but simply *no longer there*. It was just a rectangular hole.

Then there were four of us: Me, Charlize, Ambrosia, and tiny Zinnia. Or five, if you included the Shadow, who was getting too big to miss.

Charlize looked out through the ripped-open wall and watched the two foxes. They tumbled over each other playfully, then disappeared over the fence. I worried for them, but I knew they would be safe under the cover of dark, as long as they stayed quiet.

The house creaked.

Charlize, Ambrosia, and a reduced-in-size Zinnia looked at me.

The house groaned.

Charlize, Ambrosia, and Zinnia started moving toward the only human-sized exit that wasn't blocked with a smoking boulder.

I saw what was causing the creaking and groaning.

"Don't leave yet," I told them, and pointed to the former window. The loud noises were from the house itself, and its magic. The wall had begun repairing itself. Unlike previous renovations, the house wasn't being shy or doing it in secret. The hole was filling in with a new window material right before our eyes.

The new window was wider than the previous version, and prettier, with a stained glass detail. The construction finished in less than two minutes, and then there was silence.

Something went CRACKLE.

"The floorboards," I said. "Everyone get away from the boulder!"

"Relax," said Charlize. She was breaking the seal on the lid of the tequila. By some miracle, the bottle had survived the incident. "I think we've earned this," she said.

"None for me," Zinnia said. "I should be heading home now." She took two steps and stopped. "My boots are too big," she said. "Everything is too big now."

"You'll probably be back to normal by morning," I said, with zero confidence.

"Or dead."

I said nothing.

Ambrosia piped up. "I don't know what went wrong. I was harmonizing perfectly with Zara. You heard it, didn't you?"

"The spell was performed adequately," Zinnia said. "Something else must have gone wrong, or..."

Charlize took a swig of tequila from the bottle, then offered it to Zinnia. "Or what?"

Zinnia waved off the bottle. "Or the entity isn't from another world." She pulled up her loose clothes, gathering the extra fabric in one hand, and lifted her chin as she looked up at me. "Zara, I appreciate everything you've done for me, but clearly this is something I ought to handle on my own."

"I'm sorry things didn't go perfectly—"

The damaged chandelier came loose from the ceiling and crashed onto the remains of the table.

The room was pitch dark.

I cast an illumination spell, and restarted. "I'm sorry things didn't go perfectly, but we are getting somewhere. Now we know what doesn't work."

Zinnia stepped over a pile of charred calamari and left the room. The Shadow followed, pausing briefly to give me a look that broke my heart, though I couldn't put my finger on why.

A moment later, I heard my aunt sigh loudly as she opened the front door. Her sigh was drowned out by the sound of approaching sirens. A neighbor must have heard the ruckus and called the police.

And then there were three of us. Me, the gorgon, and New Zara, whose harmony hadn't been as flawless as claimed.

We waited for the police to bang on the door, but the sirens kept going, then receded. It didn't cheer me up much, because it only meant that someone else was having a worse night than we were.

Charlize handed the bottle of tequila to Ambrosia. "Here you go. Bottoms up."

Ambrosia looked at me hesitantly.

"Go ahead," I said. "You've been messing around plenty with your intoxication spells. You might as well graduate to the real stuff."

"Drink up, hatchling." Charlize waggled her eyebrows. "What's the worst that can happen? If you drink too much and throw up, it won't be the worst thing to get spewed in here tonight."

All three of us looked up at the goo on the ceiling, the spatter on the walls, and then the pile of calamari.

Without another word, we moved the party to the living room.

CHAPTER 20

Zinnia Riddle

Three Years Ago

August

"You can't use magic to do that," said Margaret Mills. "You can't cure a non-magical disease with spellwork, no matter how careful you are. It breaks all the rules."

Zinnia replied testily, "Breaking the rules isn't the same as not being able to do something."

Margaret scowled.

"I can, and I will," Zinnia said. "Whether you help me or not."

Margaret crossed her arms and leaned back in her chair. They were sitting at a table for two in a luxurious restaurant on the Upper East Side of New York. Neither witch had needed to cast a sound bubble for privacy. Not because the restaurant wasn't busy at lunch time—it was busy—but because the tall-backed booths that surrounded every table in the place provided plenty of privacy.

Best of all, the booths were upholstered in rich velvet, in the loveliest shade of fuchsia. Being surrounded by so much color, after living for the past year in the dreary beige and gray brownstone, made Zinnia feel alive. The fuchsia velvet made her feel hopeful.

The waiter arrived with the starters.

Margaret sniffed at hers, a stack of delicacies perched on a slice of cucumber.

"This is it?" Margaret asked. "I've sneezed bigger appetizers."

The waiter politely said, "I shall bring Madam the soup course right away."

"Do that," Margaret said. "But forget about using the eyedropper to put it into the itty bitty tea cup, or the shot glass, or a thimble from a dollhouse. If you've got soup, just bring me the whole pot."

The waiter shot Zinnia an amused look. "Perhaps a *bowl* would be more to Madam's liking," he said to Margaret. He cupped his hands together, overlaying his fingers to create a bowl. A small bowl.

Margaret took the man's wrists and shifted his hands apart to form a larger bowl.

The waiter nodded to show that he understood, and left them to their conversation.

"I can't take you anywhere," Zinnia said.

"You used to be more fun," Margaret said. "You've been spending too much time around the other rich ladies. The ones named Mimi, and Fifi, and Kiki. With the Botox faces and the butt implants."

"I don't know anyone named..." Zinnia trailed off. She did know a Mimi, a Fifi, and a Kiki. Plus there was Mitzi, and Dottie, and Bootsie. And that was just the women. Their pedigreed dogs had even more outlandish names.

Margaret picked up the cucumber slice and ate her *amuse-bouche* in one not-very-amused bite.

The soup came quickly, and Margaret happily gave the waiter two thumbs up for the bowl size.

The two old friends made small talk through three more courses before Zinnia brought up the taboo topic once more. Zinnia didn't need to hear that the magic she wanted to perform was against the coven's rules. She was going to do it anyway. What she needed was a friend. A friend who was a witch, and who was willing to help so that the spell didn't kill Zinnia.

Margaret listened as she ate her soup.

After Zinnia had made her case, Margaret seemed to consider it as she lifted the soup bowl to her lips and finished the last drops.

Margaret set down the bowl. "I knew it. I knew you didn't pay to fly me all the way here to New York just because you missed me."

Zinnia said nothing.

Margaret shook her head. "Zinnia Riddle, I can read you like a book. Like a book I've already read three times."

"Margaret, I've been completely transparent with you. I asked Maisy first, but she can't get away during forest fire season. After Maisy, you are the coven member I trust the most."

"Thanks," Margaret said flatly. "That means a lot that you'd pick me over the only other witch in the coven. The one who's always begging us to join her crusade to eradicate fleas world-wide."

Zinnia smiled. "Is Fatima still going on about that?"

"Yes. And you wouldn't believe who Maisy is dating."

"Oh, I probably would."

They both nodded. There were few people or beings Maisy wouldn't date.

Zinnia asked, "Is the hotel room to your liking?"

Margaret leaned in. "Don't you think a suite at the Ritz-Carlton is a bit much? I'm a simple woman. I don't need a view of Central Park, but... it sure beats staring at piles of dirty laundry and crayon art."

"I'm glad you're enjoying the room."

"You don't need to bribe me with fancy hotels. I'm your friend, Zinnia. All you have to do is ask."

"And that's what I'm doing. I'm asking."

Margaret leaned back and slumped in her seat.

Zinnia said, "I'm asking you to help me save a young man's life. I wouldn't ask if I didn't need your help. I haven't found any other way, and I've been through all the literature I could get my hands on."

"And you still haven't found the cure for cancer?" Margaret sniffed. "Zinnia Riddle, do you honestly think you're the first witch who's tried?"

"Of course not. I just..." The lump that was always present lately rose in her throat. Her eyes stung. She fought to regain her composure and said, "I was hoping you might know of something."

Margaret was quiet for a long time, then she said, "I thought you hated the little brat."

Zinnia winced. *Hated* was such a strong word, but yes, she had used that word to describe her feelings toward her boyfriend's son. She had certainly disliked the way he ruined all their family outings. She had also disliked the fact that, since the boy's mother was dead, he would not be going anywhere any time soon.

In the beginning, the child had seemed like the one big flaw attached to an otherwise excellent boyfriend. Mitchell Harrington was far from perfect, but he had many good qualities, and those had drawn Zinnia to him. He was worldly, and inquisitive, and bright.

Mitchell had also recognized those same qualities in Zinnia, and he was generous with his praise. No matter what she wore for a date, he would do a double-take and pretend to be stunned.

"I can't believe I'm going out with the most beautiful woman in the world," he would say. And she would blush every time, because she knew he meant it. She'd cast a spell to be sure. To him, she truly was the ideal woman.

For a while, that was enough for her. All the wealth, the staff, the chauffeur-driven towncars were just a bonus. Zinnia was not, as some suspected, a gold digger. She had magic at her fingertips, and, like most witches, could have easily acquired any material thing she wished for.

She was with Mitchell because she genuinely enjoyed his company, and spending time in his world. He wasn't perfect, but who was? There was a fine line between *settling* and being smart enough to want what you already had. She sat astride that fine line. Things might have stayed that way forever, if not for Aiden's diagnosis.

Since March, and the invasion of the Big C, things had changed.

Aiden was still Aiden, and household items were smashed regularly by the boy, but he wasn't the only destructive force in the family. Zinnia began to see that the root cause of much of the familial strife was the father.

Mitchell Harrington had a demon inside him.

Not an actual demon—Zinnia checked—but a metaphorical one.

He'd been born into old money. A lot of old money. And, like too many children who came into the world that way, he'd been raised by members of staff. They cared for him well, and some of his nannies may have even loved him, but it was never enough. He carried a deep resentment that manifested even at the best of times, as anger, or self-pity, or both.

The resentment levels had been high for months now, because having a sick child wasn't even close to the best of times. And the worst was yet to come.

Zinnia might have left him by now, if it wasn't for Aiden.

Aiden.

Was there anything she wouldn't do for him?

Margaret was still there, sitting on the tall-backed fuchsia booth, waiting for an explanation. Why would Zinnia want to save the boy who was the cause of so many problems?

Rather than opening her mouth and trying to say the words, Zinnia opened her mind to her old friend.

Margaret really could read her like a book, thanks to a one-way psychic connection the two had.

Zinnia let Margaret feel the truth. The boy had been a source of irritation, but then, gradually, he had wiggled his way through her defenses and into her heart.

As her affection for Mitchell had faded, her love for Aiden had grown, and now it was stronger than any love she'd felt before.

"I understand," Margaret said softly. "Kids. They drive you up the wall, but they steal your heart. They take a piece of your soul, and they won't let go. They always know how to..." Her frizzy gray hair suddenly curled up into ringlets the way it did when she got excited. "That's it!"

"What?"

Margaret slapped the table with one hand. "I'm a genius!"

"Of course you are," Zinnia said, laughing lightly. "That's why I asked for your help. I only asked Maisy first because..." She had nothing.

"Because you knew Maisy would say no, and you were scared I would say yes."

Zinnia exhaled in relief. When Margaret read her mind, Zinnia felt understood. Margaret understood Zinnia in ways she didn't even understand herself.

"Well, here I am, my dear friend," Margaret said. Her cheeks were rosy and her gray ringlets curled tighter. "And we're going to save that boy. I know a way that might work."

"What about the rules?"

Margaret blinked. "We're in New York now. A different jurisdiction. The rules here must be different."

"Oh," Zinnia said. "I hadn't considered that."

"That's why you need me," Margaret said, tapping her forehead. "Now, where do you suppose New York witches get their combustibles?"

CHAPTER 21

Zara Riddle

Wednesday

5 Days to Halloween

It took us three days to clean up the mess from Sunday's dinner and accidental demon summoning. And by *us*, I mean the professional cleaning service that the house itself called in.

The head housekeeper, a pointy-faced, small-eyed woman named Ruth, had started her career at City Hall, and still worked there. After a few incidents during the summer, she'd learned about magic, and then had been promoted to a special task force directly under the mayor.

When October rolled around, things slowed down, so she was currently working on her side hustle with her domestic cleaning business. She had the mayor's blessing, and assured me there was nothing her team couldn't handle. Discretion was guaranteed. Ruth gave her word as her bond, and swore that anything she or her crew saw, smelled, or scraped out of a crevice would not be reported to anyone but me.

Ruth and her uniformed crew were still cleaning when I returned home from work on Wednesday.

"I thought you'd be done by now," I said.

"We found another problem," Ruth said gravely. "You have invisible spiders."

"Still? I guess those traps really don't work."

"Traps are for amateurs," she said, dead serious. Ruth didn't joke about matters of cleaning. "Traps do nothing."

"I take it you have a better solution?"

She grinned, exposing two large, sharp-looking front teeth. "We have our ways."

"Do whatever it takes," I said. "They keep eating anything waxy I bring home, and I can't live a life without candles. First world problem, I know, but it is what it is."

"We will take care of the spiders," Ruth said. "No extra charge. It will be my pleasure." She pushed up her sleeves, revealing some fresh tattoo ink swirling on her forearms. Carrot Greyson's handiwork, I surmised.

"Ruth, you and your crew are the best. Are you available for a party?"

"Yes. We clean up after parties."

"I meant... would you like to come to one? Right here? I'm having it on Halloween."

She blinked repeatedly, and her pointed features softened. "That is so kind of you to offer, but I may have other plans." She bitterly added, "If I can get approval for my costume."

I bit my tongue and didn't say what I thought about costume censorship. Ruth seemed like a hard-working and reasonable person, but you couldn't be too careful and it was a touchy subject.

Ruth asked, "Can I get back to you?"

"Of course. You're welcome to come to my party. You and your whole crew, and their dates. And you can wear anything you want."

"I'll think about it," she said. "Thank you."

I popped my head into the dining room to say hello to the crew and extend the invitation to them. They had similar stories about having other plans that weren't quite ironed out.

One of the men—his name tag read Wesley—plugged in an industrial-looking machine that might have been a vacuum cleaner, or a space ship.

Gruffly, Wesley said, "Sorry in advance for the noise. The Sucko Three Thousand is going to make a racket."

I waved a hand casually. "Make as much racket as you want." I noted that I enjoyed telling a big, burly man to make a lot of racket in my house. Having hired help was fun. I could see why rich people did it.

"It's really loud," he warned.

"No worries. I only popped in to check on the cat, and change clothes before heading out again." Boa had been sequestered to the basement for her own safety, and Zoey would be working late at her school library because she was not comfortable sitting around while the crew cleaned our house.

The man with his finger on the power switch for the Sucko Three Thousand asked, "Fancy date?"

"Just book club," I said.

"Librarians are in book clubs? Don't you get enough books all day long?" Wesley laughed at his joke.

"You'd think so," I said. "You certainly would think so."

* * *

Book club was actually—you guessed it—witch club, also known as coven. Calling it book club wasn't much of a lie, technically, since many of our discussions were about books of the magical variety.

That Wednesday evening, I walked in through the back door of Dreamland Coffee to find the usual gang there. They all had their usual hot beverages. There was a flowering plant on the table. Humphrey the komodo dragon was nowhere in sight, and his cage was gone. His scent lingered.

Zinnia had made it on time, or at least ahead of me. She was seated at the jinxed table with Fatima, Maisy, Margaret, and Ambrosia. Looming behind Zinnia, quiet as ever, was the Shadow.

I hung up my jacket and walked over to the table to get a closer look at what the coven was doing.

There was a potted cactus on the middle of the table, actively sprouting yellow blossoms at a rapid rate.

"Nice of you to finally join us," Maisy Nix said icily. The cactus pushed out three more blossoms.

"Sorry I'm late," I said. "I had to stop at home and check on the cleaners, and the cat."

Fatima asked, "How is Boa?"

"She's still asking for ham, but she won't be asking the cleaning crew. She's locked in the basement so she doesn't fall victim to the Sucko Three Thousand."

I pulled out a chair but didn't sit down. I'd skipped dinner, and was dying for a coffee, but I wasn't sure if I should push my luck and make myself even more late for the meeting.

"Can I get anyone anything?" I asked sweetly, looking for an excuse. "Refills?"

Nobody spoke up.

Ambrosia was staring down at her phone, twirling her bleached hair absentmindedly.

Margaret had apparently nodded off, and was lightly snoring.

Zinnia was staring straight ahead. She was still smaller than usual.

Maisy and Fatima were quietly casting a tandem spell on the cactus.

"Refill, anyone?" I asked again. "Aunt Zinnia?"

"Maybe later," Zinnia said weakly. "I'm a little busy right now."

She reached forward and pushed her fingers onto the spiky needles of the cactus.

I yelped and jumped backwards. "What are you doing?"

She winced, but kept her fingers where they were, with cactus needles sticking into the tips. The plant's yellow blossoms reversed their growth, shrinking in on themselves and withering.

Fatima looked up at me and answered, "We're making her full-size again. The cactus should help speed up the natural restoration. We believe—"

Maisy cut off her niece. "We are restoring Zinnia after what *you* did to her, Zara. The poor woman has been tripping her way around town in oversized shoes for three days now. What were you thinking? Did you expect her to simply sleep it off?"

I gripped the back of the chair and kept it between myself and the bossy witch.

"Yes, actually, that's exactly what I thought would happen," I said, calmly and carefully. "The Foucalt-Frost-Fassbender Manual clearly states that, except in the case of an emergency, we should let the Witch Nature mend our injuries."

There was a chorus of judgmental sounds from the other witches.

Like most covens, we had disagreement within our ranks about whether the teachings of the Benedict-Baxter-Brosnan Compendium superseded the Foucalt-Frost-Fassbender Manual. They had been published within minutes of each other. It was unclear which one was the newer publication and thus the preferred one, so both had been republished the very next day.

Again, both books were released within minutes of each other, and so each prepared to re-release the next day.

This battle for recency continued for four hundred days, until, finally, the six authors called a truce.

Unfortunately, the damage had already been done. Each of the hundreds of times the books had been revised, a small alteration had been made to the contents to justify a new edition.

The witch community feared that, while there was some good information to be found in both magical reference tomes, the constant changes might have adulterated the contents to the point where the books were useless, or even dangerous.

That didn't stop witches from choosing an alignment in the whole FFF-BBB debate, or from digging in their heels on one side or the other at any opportunity.

My mere mention of The Foucalt-Frost-Fassbender Manual started an argument.

While Zinnia sat there with cactus needles jabbing into her fingers, the others quibbled over syntax and typefaces.

I quietly slipped out to get the coffee I needed.

Tonight felt like a rose petal latte sort of evening.

I was taking my first sip, lingering by the espresso machine, when Maisy Nix came out and joined me.

"Just tidying up," I said. "And I do realize The Benedict-Baxter-Brosnan Compendium has the exact same advice regarding witch healing as the Foucalt-Frost-Fassbender Manual, so there's no need to correct me."

She crossed her long, toned arms and looked me up and down. "That's not what I came to talk to you about."

"If you came out to make me feel bad about what happened to Zinnia, don't bother. I already feel terrible."

"Actually, I came out here to thank you," she said.

"Oh?"

"For helping me with Ambrosia," she said. "Novices rarely learn from verbal warnings alone. By including her in your little disaster, you have done more to impress upon her the importance of preparation and research than I could have taught her in months."

"You're welcome."

She uncrossed her arms, and they fell limply at her sides. "Oh, Zara. Aren't you as exhausted as I am from this constant power struggle?"

I was confused. Her posture had become nonthreatening. Her voice was practically warm.

I gave her a sidelong look. "What power struggle?"

Maisy pointed at my chest then hers. "Between us. The struggle for Alpha Witch."

I almost laughed. "What are you talking about?"

"How you're constantly undermining me. You never listen to anything I say, and you'd rather take anyone's advice but mine."

"I do?"

She gave me a pointed look.

I replayed some of our interactions, trying to see things from her perspective. I was not the most impartial judge of my own behavior, but if I really tried, I could see what she meant.

But there was no way I was going to admit it.

Apologize and let her lord it over me forever? Let her win? No way. I hadn't been perfect, but she'd started it.

I grinned and said through bared teeth, "I'll do better." *Zara tries to be a good witch. Zara does not battle for Alpha Witch dominance.*

"Good," she said, also baring teeth. "And be more careful from now on with my novice. Better yet, keep your distance."

"She's my daughter's best friend. She's at my house all the time. The wards do nothing to keep her out."

Maisy's eyes narrowed. "So, this is how it's going to be? More of your arrogance?"

I shrugged and took a slow, relaxed sip of my latte.

Maisy turned on her heel and walked away, calling over her shoulder, "Wipe the milk foam off the steamer, please and thank you."

I bobbed my head from side to side and mimicked her. "Wipe the milk foam off the steamer." I used a cloth to clean the machine.

By the time I returned to the back room, the whole enterprise with the cactus had been wrapped up. Zinnia wasn't quite back to her full size, but she was close. The Shadow was still there, and still a medium-sized girl who blended with the background.

"Good work, everyone," Maisy said. There was a smattering of applause. "What's next on the agenda?"

Fatima pulled some papers from her book bag. "I'd like to revisit my proposed campaign to eradicate the common flea."

Everyone groaned.

CHAPTER 22

Thursday

4 Days to Halloween

At the library on Thursday, I updated my coworkers on the status of my aunt's Shadow.

"That's too bad," Kathy said. "Your aunt is such a lovely woman. It's a shame she's being haunted by whatever it is."

Frank said, "If I see that nasty thing at your Halloween party, I'll tell it to take a hike."

"You're coming to my party? But you were so excited about the Monster Mash."

He fluffed his pink hair. "Frank Wonder has a fabulous time wherever he goes."

"Me, too," Kathy said. "I have a fabulous time wherever Frank Wonder goes."

The two linked arms, exchanged a look, and giggled. They'd been doing that a lot lately.

Kathy's husband was out of town most of the time, traveling with their sons, who played professional sports. In Mr. Carmichael's absence, Frank had been spending a lot of time at the Carmichael house. He'd even been crafting with Kathy. He tried to hide it from me, but I saw the sequins, and the embroidery, and the handmade pottery mugs that had been proliferating in the staff lounge.

"I'm glad you two are coming," I said. "But I should warn you: It might be standing room only. Charlize has invited half the supernaturals in town."

"Oooh," Kathy said. "Your house party is going to be the social event of the year. Whooo could pass that up?"

"My sister, for one," I said. "She's going to the DWM costume ball. She says it's political, because of her job, and she has no choice. Whatever. She's young. She's still impressed by things like ballrooms."

Kathy said, "I'm sure your sister would choose you over work if she could."

Frank asked, "How are you two getting along? Siblings can be difficult. They're always trying to change the established pecking order." He raised his eyebrows at Kathy. "Get it? Pecking order?"

The two, who still had their arms linked, giggled some more.

* * *

Toward the end of my shift, I phoned my sister. I invited Persephone Rose for dinner in my freshly-cleaned house. She didn't believe me that Ruth's cleaning service and the Sucko Three Thousand had fully erased the evidence of Sunday's disaster.

"Let's go jogging together instead," she had suggested.

"Jog-ging," I said, sounding out the word carefully. "I've heard of *jogging*. It's that adjective people use for the comfy shoes with the laces."

"If you can go to hot yoga with Charlize, you can go jogging with me."

I groaned. "This is exactly why I should be more secretive about my activities. Curse me for being an open book."

My spine tingled. I may have actually cursed myself.
Just a little.

* * *

Persephone Rose and I met in Pacific Spirit Park.

The lamps were flickering on as the sun set for the day. The sky was darkening, and there was a chill in the air. My sister's pink shirt looked white in the blue light.

"You look sporty," she said.

"I am wearing the sport-mandated attire," I said. "These are my couch pants and my laundry day shirt. My comfy shoes are confused about why they are being worn out of the house."

Persephone smiled, looking cuter than ever, like a doll, with her big, brown eyes and her thick, dark bangs. She didn't look as much like our father as I did, but I definitely saw the resemblance when she flashed her foxy grin.

I lifted my loose T-shirt to show her my new acquisition, a sports bra. "These chest flatteners come in many pleasing colors," I said.

"You do look the part." She walked us over to a park bench and used it for balance while she stretched her calves.

I did the same, and we chatted while stretching.

She was particularly interested in my interaction with Maisy Nix.

I told her about our recent coven meeting.

Persephone's big, brown eyes went wide with interest. "Maisy Nix did what?"

"She basically challenged me to take her down and bite her on the scruff of neck."

"Literally?"

I shrugged one shoulder, then turned it into a side bend stretch. "Not literally. I may be exaggerating a smidge. But she's so mean, Persephone, and people don't believe me. Everyone sees her as this glamorous businesswoman who's always so gracious to customers at Dreamland

Coffee. Whenever I tell anyone she's mean to me, people say I must be imagining things."

Persephone nodded. "That sounds familiar."

"It's not fair," I said. "She's got no reason to pick on me. Being a witch is no excuse to be, well, a witch."

"Mm hmm." Persephone smirked down at her running shoes, as though I'd said something hilarious and didn't know it.

"So," I said, "I need your advice about how to deal with her."

"You need my advice about how to stop another woman from picking on you for no good reason?"

"Yes." I thought I'd made it perfectly clear.

Persephone kept smirking. "Why don't you tell her she's your sister?"

"What? I'm not related to the Nixes. Not that I know of."

More smirking.

"You are so wacky sometimes," I said. "It must be from your mother's side of the family. Our father is weird, but not like that."

"Must be." She finished stretching, then started jogging at a leisurely pace, or at least at a pace that would be leisurely for someone who jogged regularly.

"Hey! Wait up!"

I zapped myself with the buoyancy spell we witches used for flying on broomsticks. I put on the speed to catch up to Persephone and her swinging ponytail.

The spell worked too well, and I flew past her.

"Cheater," she yelled at my back.

"It's not cheating if you have no other choice." I turned and jogged on the spot while she caught up. "You sure are fast. What are you? Part fox and part jackrabbit?"

She caught up, and we jogged together along the path.

The forest was dark, but Persephone had a waist-mounted light that would help us avoid large, loose stones. Plus we both had great night vision. The light was mostly for cover.

I glanced up, checking the trees and sky for giant flesh-ripping birds, as I always did, ever since the first time I had been attacked in that forest.

"So, the local Alpha Witch is causing you grief," Persephone said. "How am I supposed to help?"

Our footfalls fell in rhythm, and two became one, sound-wise.

"Teach me how to be a better Alpha and achieve dominance," I said.

She said nothing.

"Pretty please?" I begged.

"You do know that my shifter form is a black fox."

"I know."

"Black foxes don't run in packs," she said. "Most small canids prefer pairs or family groups. And, even if we did run in packs, I'm not a fox. I'm a person. The fact that you think I'm some sort of authority on pack behavior is, to use the jargon of the day, triggering."

"I didn't mean to offend you. It's a compliment. I figured you'd be the person to ask because you work with a lot of tough guys at the police department. You must be around a lot of Alpha and Beta behavior."

"That's true," she said. We jogged for a moment, then she said, "Zara, if you promise not to tell anyone else, I can let you in on a trick we use around the station."

"Ooh."

"You can't tell anyone I told you. Not even Bentley."

"I promise not to tell. My word is my bond."

Slowly, she said, "Our secret trick is... we all keep open cups of our own urine in our desk drawers. The scent establishes distinct territories."

"Open cups of what?" I lost my jogging rhythm and stumbled awkwardly.

She laughed and ran ahead at top speed. Her dark ponytail swung merrily.

She had been pulling my leg. What a joker! Just like our father.

Even with my buoyancy spell, I had to run hard to catch up.

"You got me," I said. "Brat."

"It's about time I got you," she said. "I can't wait to tell everyone at the station. Your reaction was priceless."

"I said you got me. No need to rub it in."

"Wow," she teased. "You can dish it out, but you can't take it."

"Dish *what* out?"

We jogged for a while, me getting back in rhythm, before she explained, "Zara, you're always giving people a hard time. Sure, it's funny sometimes, but not always. What you think is a joke can hurt someone's feelings, for real. That's why you're having this problem with another witch."

"You're saying it's my fault whenever someone is mean to me? That it's my fault when I'm the one getting bullied? Talk about blaming the victim."

She shook her ponytail and jogged faster. "What I'm saying is that people are like funhouse mirrors. They reflect back to you some version of how you treat them in the first place."

My buoyancy spell was wearing off already. It wasn't designed for jogging. I breathed harder, my lungs straining.

I asked, "You think I should suck up to Maisy? Kiss her skinny butt?"

"That's not what I said."

"It's not?"

"A little flattery can't hurt, but you don't have to overdo it. Basic civility and respect can go a long way. I didn't get this far in my career by being abrasive to my coworkers."

No, she hadn't. Persephone had gotten promoted to the rank of detective by being in the right place at the right time. She had provided intel on criminal behavior. She was a snitch. But she'd probably been a nice snitch. Say what you would about Persephone Rose. She was always polite, even when people didn't deserve it.

My first impression of Persephone had been inaccurate. I'd seen her as a kid playing dress-up in borrowed high heels: young, naive, and weak.

But it wasn't true at all. That was just what she'd wanted me to think.

Ten points to Ms. Rose.

An underestimated woman was a powerful force, witch or otherwise.

CHAPTER 23

Friday

3 Days to Halloween

All day Friday, in between helping patrons at the library, I puzzled over something that didn't make sense. How was it that other people had such completely different opinions about me and my personality?

Margaret Mills said I was too friendly, always trying to cozy up to threats when I should have been chasing them off with balls of lightning.

Persephone Rose said I was too aggressive, always offending people with my casual jokes.

Maisy Nix thought I was arrogant, and that I flirted with giant, smelly lizards.

Thinking about it too much made my brain short circuit. I fantasized about canceling my party. Who needed a bunch of judgmental people around, judging me in the house where I lived?

Didn't they know I was trying to be a good witch?

Even Bentley, who believed that everyone was always striving to do their best, seemed to have lost his faith in me. We had hung out a few times that month, but our relationship hadn't been the same since the night we'd argued about whether or not Archer Caine's death was a tragedy.

I hated myself for thinking it, but I was actually looking forward to the whole thing being over, so we could start grieving him and move on.

You can imagine how bad *that* made me feel about myself.

On top of being foolishly friendly, aggressively Alpha, and flirtatiously arrogant, I was also kind of a heartless witch.

That's why, when I bumped into Archer Caine on Friday night, I felt extra guilty about mistaking him for a homeless person.

I was walking along the sidewalk, heading toward Mia's Kit and Kaboodle, when I noticed what I thought was an elderly man sitting on the sidewalk. He was huddled in layers of torn and tattered clothing, looking forlorn and hopeless.

We didn't have many homeless people in our town, so I was more than surprised to see this downtrodden gentleman.

I stopped, fished out some money, and held it out for the fellow.

"Here you go," I said. "I hope things turn around for you soon. My name is Zara, and I work at the library. We have some programs, where we help people with their resumes and—"

"Zara?" The old man's head lifted, and a pair of familiar green eyes met mine.

It was Archer Caine. His gaze went to the money in my hand, and his whole body jerked back, as though it was a lit stick of dynamite.

"Sorry," I said. "I didn't recognize you, Archer."

The formerly energetic genie grabbed the hem of my jacket, and used me to get to his feet. As he rose, I saw that the layers of clothing he wore were all clean and fashionable, in that shabby, faux-hobo way of some designer clothes.

He spat out a question. "What are you doing here?" Then, "Are you spying on me?"

I put one hand on my hip, lifted my chin, and stared the genie in the eyes. "Archer, if I truly wanted to spy on you, I would do it, and you'd never know."

He lifted his chin and stared down his nose. "Is that so?"

I was puffing out my chest, preparing to put him in his place, when I remembered people's criticisms of my personality.

What could I do that wasn't wrong by someone else's assessment?

The weather, I thought. People talk about it all the time.

I took a step back and tucked my chin down.

"The weather's chilly tonight," I said.

His body language immediately relaxed. "It is," he said. "People tell me it can snow as early as the first week of November."

"I've heard the same, and also that the first snowfall doesn't stick."

He looked up at the dark sky. His eyelashes had turned gray. "I'd like to be around to see it," he said.

The cold got through my layers of clothing and I shivered.

"Archer, can I buy you a hot cup of coffee? Or soup? Or both? Not together, but separate. In a cup and a bowl. Or in two cups. Who's judging? Some people like a cup of hot soup. On the other hand, I hear the French enjoy bowls of coffee."

As I rambled about cups and bowls, his expression went slack, and it was not a pretty sight. The body he'd stolen came with a conventionally handsome face—Chet Moore's—but it was now as tattered as a hundred-year-old leather recliner. Deep lines ran in the usual spots, as well as in spots where faces weren't supposed to get wrinkles, ever.

I stopped talking and swallowed hard. I'd heard about the genie's worsening condition from a number of people, but all the warnings hadn't prepared me for the reality. He was decaying. He didn't look like he would make it through the night, let alone until the first snowfall.

He looked into my eyes, and time stood still.

My hand went up, and before I knew it, I was touching his cheek. "Oh, Archer," I said. His skin was so dry.

He brushed my hand away. "Don't," he growled. "Your powers cannot fix what must not be stopped."

"I wasn't trying to heal you. I was..." Just showing human kindness.

He turned his dilapidated features, looked through the window into Mia's Kit and Kaboodle, then turned back to me.

"My companion is inside of this place, examining the wares," he said, sounding ancient. Like he'd sounded the first time we'd met. Or, actually, the second time we'd met.

"Your companion is inside Mia's? You mean Carrot?"

"She will be occupied for some time."

"Do you want me to go in and get her for you?"

"Let her have her fun," he said. "She has been buying dress after dress for that ball." His green eyes twinkled within their deep lines. "In time, a person might discover that girl to be a princess."

"Carrot?"

"She may be of royal lineage. I would know. I have met many princesses over my many lives. I suppose you could say I *have a type*." He gave me an eyebrow waggle.

I smiled. However sick he was, the guy wasn't too ill to leer at me.

"I'm glad you're making the best of it, all things considered," I said.

He leaned to the side and looked behind me, across the street. Then he licked his lips, which looked as dry as his cheek had felt. "Your offer of hot liquid would be acceptable."

"Soup or coffee?" I offered him my elbow.

"Both." He limped past my elbow and moved toward the crosswalk with surprising speed.

* * *

We entered Lucky's Diner. The restaurant's claim to fame was having been in business for over seventy years at the same location.

We had come for soup and coffee, but our plans were dashed when the busty waitress informed us that the day's soup special was sold out, and the coffee maker was busted.

"Would you like pie?" she asked.

"I like pie," I said, stating the obvious. Who didn't like pie?

When asked which flavor of pie and milkshake he wanted, Archer said, "Bring us one of each, and two forks."

I jerked my head back in surprise. One of each, and two forks? I'd heard him utter that exact phrase once before. Seventeen years and three months ago. It was the night we'd made our daughter. We'd gone for pie with some other kids before we'd started drinking.

Archer guffawed.

He was watching me, and I knew that he knew exactly what I was thinking about.

"Some things never change," I said. "You're exactly the same as you always were."

Those stolen green eyes of his twinkled under the opaque layer of cataracts.

The waitress, who was still standing at our table, gave me a sympathetic look. "Aren't you sweet, honey. Taking this handsome fella of yours out for pie. I sure do miss my own grandpappy." She winked at me before leaving.

Archer pushed one wrinkled hand back through his white hair. He stared after the waitress and her round bottom, his upper lip curling. "When I come back in my next life, I'm going to make her sorry she was blessed with the gift of speech." He gave me a look of disbelief. "That woman used to flirt with me. I had her wrapped around my finger. And now she doesn't even recognize my face. She believes I am someone's grandfather?" The wrinkles around his nose deepened. "She believes I am*your* grandfather?"

"She was just being friendly, Archer. It's what waitresses have been doing since day one. Since someone hung a carved wooden sign over the door of the very first tavern." I leaned forward, chin on hand. "Speaking of which, were you there? When the first tavern opened?"

He leaned back, stretching out his arms along the back of the booth. "I was *somewhere*," he said cryptically.

"Please, Grandpappy, tell me about the good ol' days."

His eyes sunk deeper into darkness. "You mock me," he growled.

"I do," I said. "People seem to think it's a flaw to have a sense of humor."

"I've always liked your sense of humor." He pointed a finger at me. "Stay away from people who have none. They are narrow in vision. We have a saying, in a language you wouldn't know, that has been long forgotten. People without humor cannot see very far until you throw them in the air and set them on fire."

"That sounds familiar," I said. "But I do live with a wyvern."

"Their kind has respect for history."

"Speaking of which, I am curious about your history. Is it true you were King Arthur?"

He scoffed. "Were? I *am* King Arthur."

"Really? Tell me about it."

He yawned. "You can hear those stories anywhere. Watch one of the movies. Honestly, I've told the tales so many times, I'm not sure which details happened and which were embellishments to impress serving wenches."

Right on cue, our serving wench arrived with a tray full of slices of pies.

With surprising force, Archer raged at the waitress, "These are mere wedges! You promised us pies! Bring us pies!" He banged one wrinkled fist on the table.

The waitress jumped in alarm, then giggled apprehensively as she looked to me for guidance.

"Bring my grandfather the whole pies." I apologetically added, "He doesn't get out much." I used my finger to twirl a circle above my ear in the universal symbol *for my companion is a few hazelnuts short of a jar of Nutella.*

A few minutes later, she returned with the whole pies, the milkshakes, and a quivering bus boy who wanted to personally apologize to us for breaking the coffee maker.

"That's more like it," Archer said. Then, brandishing a crooked finger at the waitress, he said, "Do not return to this table. Do not come when I have a bite of food in my mouth and ask me *how it is tasting so far*. If the pie is not good, you will know." He thundered, "Be gone!"

The two left, and did not return.

In fact, they disappeared completely. Everyone did.

* * *

Hours later, after Carrot had tracked us down and joined us at our table inside Lucky's Diner to help finish the many pies, we would discover the Lucky's Diner staff had disappeared.

I would need to manually add up the bill myself, leave some cash by the register, turn off the lights and kitchen equipment, and use my magic to lock the door after we left.

As I drove home, alone in my car, the voices of Archer and Carrot echoed in my head. They were a cute couple. They were complete opposites, and yet they were a perfect match. Her quirkiness complemented his oddness. Both were slightly out of sync with the modern world.

The man didn't want to talk about his days as King of Camelot, but he sure could go on about aqueducts and medieval plumbing. I learned more about ancient irrigation and sanitation than any person should—while consuming pie.

The sound of those two chattering happily and laughing was stuck on repeat in my brain, like a catchy pop song that's so bad it's good.

I thought about what Archer had told us about the long-ago debut of his new design for an indoor toilet, and I started laughing.

I laughed so hard that I forgot he was dying.

For a moment.

And then I remembered.

The car was very quiet for the rest of the drive home.

CHAPTER 24

Saturday

2 Days to Halloween

My party was coming up fast, and I still needed a costume. Bumping into Archer Caine on Friday night had diverted me from my planned trip to Mia's Kit and Kaboodle. That meant I had to go shopping for my costume at practically the last minute, on Saturday.

Folks, take it from me, you do *not* want to be inside a thrift store on the Saturday before Halloween. I barely escaped with my life.

By some divine miracle, by which I mean a sneaky spell or two—it's not cheating if you have no other choice —I managed to snag the perfect costume. It had to be perfect. There was no time for second guessing. Halloween was in only two days.

Costume taken care of, I visited the bulk warehouse store to pick up mixers and plastic cups.

Folks, I may sound like a broken record, but you do *not* want to be inside a bulk warehouse store on the Saturday before Halloween.

After barely escaping with my life for a second time, I popped into the drugstore for some cheap accessories to finish off my look. While there, I picked up a restock on lipstick and deodorant, since my house was now free of invisible spiders, thanks to Ruth's cleaning crew.

What was my costume?

Not telling. It would be a surprise for everyone at my party.

I'll give you a hint: It was the most upsetting thing I could think of.*

*That still had a vaguely human form.

I had to stop shopping when my car couldn't hold any more stuff. I might have gotten more in by using a Bag of Holding spell on Foxy Pumpkin's interior, but such a thing was well above my pay grade.

With a full car, I pulled up in front of Zinnia's house.

In the days following Wednesday's coven meeting, some of the other witches had come up with new tactics for ridding Zinnia of her Shadow. I hadn't been told all the details yet, but they'd asked me to pop in and witch-pool.

I let myself into the house. When I hung up my jacket, the hook fell off the wall. Not a great sign. There were no other hanging spots available, so I picked up the hook and affixed it to the wall with a temporary steadfast spell. It wouldn't last forever, but it would keep my jacket off the floor. Zinnia hated it when Zoey and I walked in and tossed our jackets over anything handy.

I found everyone in the living room, sitting on my aunt's tightly upholstered, floral-patterned furniture.

The younger witches, Fatima and Ambrosia, hadn't been invited.

Margaret and Maisy were already there, along with one more person, a gentleman.

Barry Blackstone was dressed in a natty brown suit. He had thick, unruly black hair, and big, brown eyes that roved continuously, always gathering data. He was handsome, with a regally large, humped nose and small, bright teeth with a gap in the middle.

Barry was dating the recently-divorced Margaret Mills. Barry was technically two people, brothers, sharing one body. Their names had been Bill and Harry. Everyone, including the Blackstone brothers themselves, had naturally started calling him Barry.

When it came to pronouns, Barry preferred the pronoun *he* over *they*, because *they* was confusing to people for a variety of reasons. Out of respect for Barry's preferences, I referred to Barry as *he*.

Barry stood when I entered the living room. "Zara! How is the ol' Pumpkin running these days?" He buttoned his natty brown suit jacket, like a late night TV talk show host doing a monologue. He seemed right at home in my aunt's living room, surrounded by witches.

"Better than ever," I said. "Have you been staying away from poisoned peppers?"

He grinned. "I don't even *look* at the peppers at the grocery store."

"You can't be too careful."

"Not in this town."

"What's the deal with the local Realtors, anyway? Is every last one of them corrupt and evil?"

"Now, now." He wagged a finger. "It isn't fair to judge a whole profession based on a few bad apples. People always say that auto mechanics are universally corrupt and evil, but it isn't true."

"Auto mechanics? Barry, I think of that side of you as more of a mad scientist than a mechanic."

"A mad scientist?" One hand went to his chest. "I couldn't be more flattered."

"It's nice to be around someone who appreciates my honesty."

He took my hand and kissed it. "Always a pleasure to be near you, Ms. Riddle. You have all the charm of your father, minus the, uh..."

"Tail," I said with a wink. "Minus the fluffy red tail."

Maisy made a tsk sound and shot a look at Margaret, as if to say *are you going to let Zara flirt with your man like that?* I intercepted the look, and I shot one back: *Mind your own business.*

Zinnia hadn't been in the room when I'd arrived. Now she walked in with a serving tray that contained, much to my surprise, a jar of peanut butter and half a loaf of bread. The bread was moldy. And not just with a bit of surface mold that could be scraped off before toasting. It was green bread.

The other two witches made bewildered, concerned noises.

Barry asked, "Is this a test?"

Maisy shot me a look across the room and mouthed something. She must have used a spell, because I felt her breath on my ear and heard her whisper, "Your aunt is not doing well."

I held out both my hands in the universal signal for DUH.

Zinnia spoke weakly. "This is all I have to serve as refreshments. I'm afraid entropy has taken hold in my kitchen."

We stared at her in shock. Her eyes were red. Both the whites and the eyelids. On the plus side, she was holding steady at a height close to her regular size. On the minus side, the creepy ghost was still trailing her. It was hard to get a good look at the Shadow, but it appeared to be holding a tray as well.

The other two witches weren't helping, so I crossed the room and took the tray from her.

"You told me you were feeling better," I said.

She smiled wanly. "I'm fine, Zara. Honestly. I don't know why everyone's making such a fuss. It's not as though I have a giant boil on my nose."

"No. It's much worse."

She sighed. "I'm fine."

"If you're so fine, what's with all the sighing?"

She frowned. "I don't sigh."

I had my back to the others, but I could hear Maisy, Margaret, and Barry all moving, shifting their bodies on the seating with discomfort. None of them spoke up.

I steered my aunt back into her kitchen, where I threw out the moldy bread. The room smelled as bad as Humphrey the Komodo Dragon's breath. There were stacks of unwashed dishes all over the counter. I heard the hum of flying insects, but couldn't see anything.

"What's that noise?" I asked. "That buzzing. Is it a spell?"

"Invisible bees," she said. "I put out traps." She waved one limp hand half-heartedly.

Behind her, the medium-sized girl entity copied her movements in a mocking way I didn't like one bit.

"Enough is enough," I said. "We are getting rid of that thing today."

Zinnia blinked at me, her red, sunken eyes empty. "There are guests in the living room," she said vacantly. "Zara, when did you get here?"

I was too stunned to answer. Her hippocampus was shutting down. This was so much worse than we'd all thought. Why hadn't I insisted on visiting her at her house before now? I'd been so distracted by Archer Caine, which was understandable. But I'd also been distracted by Halloween, which was unforgivable.

I took my aunt by the shoulders and looked into her sore-looking eyes.

"Hang in there," I said. "We're going to get you back from wherever you've gone. But you've got to keep fighting. Don't give up." My voice cracked, and my throat stung. My tongue felt too large for my mouth. "Hang in there," I repeated, feeling utterly useless. *Hang in there?* Was she a kitten dangling from a tree branch on a motivational poster?

Zinnia blinked in two stages, left eye then right, her eyelids out of sync with each other.

"I ought to put out snacks," she said. "A witch must always be hospitable when friends drop by unannounced."

She pulled her shoulders free of my hands, turned, and opened her refrigerator.

The interior of the appliance buzzed in a way I definitely did not like. There was nothing visible inside the fridge except condiments and jars full of eyeballs in various sizes.

I gently pulled her away from the fridge, then used another steadfast spell to keep it closed for the next hour. I added a magic password. Zinnia tugged at the fridge door. When it wouldn't open, she cursed, which only further scrambled the password, so that even I couldn't have unlocked it.

"Don't worry about the refreshments," I said gently. "I've got heaps of stuff in my car for the Halloween party."

"Party? Oh, right. Your party. Because you're having a party. Is it tonight?"

"Yes," I lied. Why correct her when she was going to forget in a few minutes anyway? "I'll bring in some of the snacks for your friends in the living room."

"I wouldn't want to be any trouble," she said. "Those supplies are for your party."

I steered her out of the buzzing, stinky kitchen, and back into the living room. "It's no trouble. Consider it a preview."

"At least let me go outside and get the food from your car."

"Are you sure you can do that without getting lost?"

A little of the Zinnia fire I was more familiar with lit up in her eyes. "Don't be ridiculous," she said sharply. "I can retrieve items from a vehicle, whether it's sitting still or moving at one hundred miles per hour."

"Be my guest." I handed her the keys to Foxy Pumpkin. Witches didn't need keys, but I had a feeling Zinnia's magic wasn't working as well as she thought it was.

The living room was quiet and unsettling behind me. A room filled with silent human bodies was always more eerily quiet than a room that was simply empty.

With Zinnia out of the room, I turned to Margaret and said, "This is bad."

"I know," Margaret said. "That's why we're here."

Maisy chimed in. "That's why we're here, Zara."

I didn't look at Maisy, because I suspected the look on her face was going to push me over the edge.

In a more cheerful tone, Margaret said, "I brought lots of spells. A Canadian dozen."

Behind me, Maisy said, "That's not a thing, Margaret."

Margaret snorted. "Of course it is." She patted Barry's knee. "A Canadian dozen is fifteen, and I brought fifteen spells to try," she told him.

Since nobody had explained to me why Barry was there, I asked.

Margaret answered. "Barry is here because of his device. It's an invention of his own making. My Barry is a genius, you know."

One of Barry's cheeks flushed pink with embarrassment, but the other did not. "It's just a prototype," he said shyly. "A very promising prototype," he said proudly.

I asked, "Does it work on Shadows?"

"It's a prototype," he said, scratching the back of his neck.

"Can't hurt to try," Margaret said.

"Are you sure about that? Zinnia wasn't this bad until the coven stuck her onto that cactus."

Maisy said, "We needed to do something after you shrunk her, Zara."

Barry looked at Margaret and asked, "Is it always like this? How do you ever get anything done as a team? I have two people inside this body. If we weren't able to sublimate our individual egos so that we could work together, we'd be worse off than you three." He shook his head. "Typical women."

In perfect unison, the three of us witches said, "Shut up, Barry."

The man jerked his head back, then smiled. "There you go," he said. "That's the ticket. You can work together. You just need to unite against a common enemy."

A second time, because it felt so good, we said, "Shut up, Barry."

He chuckled and mimed zipping his lips.

Margaret and Maisy began laying out the supplies for the spells we would be trying, and we got to work.

CHAPTER 25

We were ready for at least fifteen spells. We had plenty of potions and powders, plus we had three witches in good working order, and three witches in good working order could do pretty much anything, even if one of them was Margaret Mills.

Barry clapped his hands. "This is so exciting," he said, beaming. "Just like that time—"

Suddenly, he was on the verge of tears, holding a handkerchief under one eye.

"Excuse me, ladies. Apparently, I'm a big old softie," Barry said. "Forgive me for feeling nostalgic about that special day you performed the soul transfer and saved my life." His face jerked crookedly. "I mean ruined my life. Ha ha. Just kidding." One eye twitched. "Changed my life? Yes. The day you changed my life."

All three of us witches exchanged looks.

Margaret said, "Now you two see what I mean about the rapid mood swings."

Barry turned to gaze at her. "You love it."

"I love *you*," she said. "I do not love the mood swings." To us, she said, "It's like dating Jekyll and Hyde. Or like dating someone who's on a diet." She wrinkled her nose. "Mike used to do this terrible celery juice cleanse."

Barry sniffed. "I don't like it when you talk about your ex."

"He's the father of my children. He's not going away anytime soon. Why? Are you jealous?" She leaned toward him and baby-talked. "Is my Barry-boo-boo jealous?"

"Intensely," he said through clenched teeth. "You're a lot of woman, Margaret Mills, but I could never share you with another."

Maisy, who was next to me on the couch, snickered.

The two lovebirds continued talking their new-love nonsense.

"I'll go see what's keeping Zinnia," I said, getting to my feet.

"Oh, no." Maisy jumped up. "Don't you dare leave me here with those two."

As we walked toward the front door, she said, "Do you hear something buzzing in the kitchen? If I didn't know better, I would guess your aunt's house has been infested with invisible bees."

"Huh," I said, feigning ignorance. I'd learned a lot about invisible insects lately, so I knew the bees were basically harmless. Even so, I didn't want Zinnia to get a reputation for bad housekeeping. The bad housekeeping crown belonged to me.

Outside, we found Zinnia wandering the sidewalk with an armful of red plastic cups. When she spotted us, she turned and made a dash for one of the neighbor's houses.

We called after her.

"I'm not lost," she said defensively. "I know it's this one." She ran up the steps of someone else's house.

"We've got to help her," I said to Maisy.

"It's happening so fast," she said. "We might be too late."

I felt tears coming but fought them back. "I don't know if I can handle this."

Maisy grabbed me by the shoulders, squared me to face her, and looked me in the eyes. Was this our moment? Was she going to start being nice to me?

Maisy shook me, hard, and said, "Suck it up, buttercup."

Then she released me, and ran after my aunt.

* * *

We managed to get Zinnia safely indoors before she could get arrested for breaking and entering.

After I handed out refreshments, including peanut butter cups and red licorice, we began our spellwork.

The first attempt didn't work.

Nor the second.

And the third one wasn't the charm, either.

By the tenth spell, my mouth was sore from all the Witch Tongue casting.

My heart was heavy in my chest. Nothing was working.

Zinnia nodded off. The Shadow nodded sleepily, still standing behind her, but swaying, like a sleeping horse.

We kept going. The room turned orange and then red as the sun set.

Barry kept his mouth shut and took notes on a tiny notepad.

My phone buzzed. Charlize kept sending text messages, demanding updates and good news we didn't have.

It was midnight when we performed spell number fifteen.

For all the good it did, you would have thought we were reciting ancient nursery rhymes backwards for our own amusement.

Fifteen spells, and none of them had worked. Plus there had been three spells on Wednesday, and before that, all the ones I'd tried on my own. Over twenty spells, and the only thing we'd done was blow through magical supplies and eat our weight in peanut butter cups.

With no other options left, we turned to Barry Blackstone.

"Whip it out," I said.

Maisy elbowed me in the ribs and said, more eloquently, "Please, Mr. Blackstone, may we try your prototype device?"

Barry wiped some beads of red fluid from his forehead. He wasn't injured, and it wasn't blood. Spell number thirteen had caused all of us to sweat myoglobin. It wasn't an unforeseen side effect, but part of the protective measures. Margaret had explained it an hour earlier, and it had flown over my head. Something about the binding of oxygen atoms, and the suffocation hazards of unleashing zanziweed smoke while not on a hydrogen-filled dirigible.

"It's all come down to this," Margaret said to her boyfriend. "May we try it?"

"You may." Barry nodded and opened a black suitcase on his lap.

He lifted the lid, turned the suitcase, and revealed the invention that might be our last hope at saving Zinnia.

The object was red, plastic, and surprisingly familiar. It was one of those rechargeable handheld vacuums. The brand name on the side had been altered from Dirt Devil to Devil Duster.

"I'm still working on the name," Barry said.

"Devil Duster is catchy," Margaret said.

Maisy asked, "What does it do?"

"It sucks," he said. "It's a miniature version of another powerful device I designed."

I raised my hand like a kid in class. "Would that be the Sucko Three Thousand?"

Barry beamed. "Why, yes, Zara. Are you familiar with that device?"

"Ruth and her cleaning crew used it at my house."

"Then you must have noticed it's awfully noisy," Barry said. He tapped the Devil Duster lovingly. "This new version is more sophisticated, and includes scream dampeners, among other things."

"Genius," Margaret said proudly.

Zinnia, who was conscious, but just barely, asked, "Shall we plug it in?"

"No need," Barry said. "It's battery operated."

He lifted the device from the suitcase.

I held my breath.

And then...

To my utter shock and delight, the Devil Duster worked.

What? You didn't have faith in the two genius brothers known as Barry Blackstone?

Be honest. Was it because Barry willingly chose to date Margaret Mills?

That's what I thought.

Here's how it went down:

Barry pointed the business end of the vacuum at Zinnia.

The wallflower girl came out from behind the wingback chair where Zinnia was sitting, leaned forward, and examined the red appliance.

"Hold steady," I said to Barry. "Something's happening. The Shadow seems to be curious about the Devil Duster. She's leaning forward, looking at it right now."

He asked, "Am I pointed in the right direction?"

"Yes, but—"

He flicked the switch, and the vacuum turned on.

The girl jerked back, but it was too late. One of her hands was caught in the mouth of the vacuum. As she struggled to get the hand free, she turned and gave me a pleading look.

Zinnia started twitching in her wingback chair like an actress in an exorcism movie.

"It's working," Margaret said excitedly. "You're a genius, Barry!"

Maisy took Zinnia's hand and checked her vitals. "She's fading," Maisy said. "I don't know about this."

Margaret jumped up and began bouncing on the sofa like it was a trampoline. "More power," she urged Barry. "Crank it up!"

Barry was swaying back and forth, like a fisherman trying to reel in a big salmon.

The girl was struggling to get free, but now both of her arms were trapped in the device. She opened her mouth, and seemed to be screaming, but I couldn't hear anything. Was she still mute, or was it the device's scream dampeners?

Margaret paused her frantic bouncing, leaned over Barry's shoulder, and turned a dial on the red device.

The Devil Duster roared at max power, and suddenly the girl was gone.

Zinnia let out a long sigh, then her body went still.

My first horrifying thought was that we'd killed her.

Someone turned off the Devil Duster.

Zinnia was limp. Lifeless. The Shadow was gone.

Trying to keep my panic under control, I asked Barry, "Does that thing have a reverse mode?"

"No," he said. "It's one way only, into the containment unit."

I looked over at Maisy, who was still holding Zinnia's wrist.

Maisy held one finger over her lips. "Shh. Hang on."

We waited for what felt like an eternity.

"She's okay," Maisy finally said. "Her pulse is getting stronger."

Margaret let out a long sigh of relief that echoed how I felt. Then she started jumping up and down on the couch with glee. The springs creaked under her feet. I noticed Margaret had worn striped witch socks for the occasion. She looked hilarious, and I had to laugh. I was overwhelmed with relief. After such a tense day, it felt good to laugh at Margaret, bouncing on my aunt's couch in her silly striped socks.

Maisy zapped me on the butt with a spell, and gave me a hard stare. "Zara, is the entity gone? Pull yourself together. You're the only one who can tell us if we succeeded."

I rubbed my hip and glanced around the room twice. "No guarantees, but I don't see her, or *it*, in the room."

Zinnia cleared her throat and said, "Stop."

Margaret kept bouncing. All of us talked over each other, asking Zinnia what was wrong.

"Stop," Zinnia said again, sounding stronger. "Margaret Mills, stop treating my sofa like a bouncy castle."

Margaret kicked out her striped legs and landed on her bottom. "I was excited," she said. "We fixed you, Zinnia. We fixed you with Barry's wonderful Devil Duster."

"I wasn't broken," Zinnia snapped. "Honestly, I don't understand what all the fuss was about. It's not as though I had a real problem, like a big boil on my nose." She got to her feet, apparently at full strength. Her eyes were no longer red, and she looked as healthy as ever.

Barry let out a low whistle, then said, "Well, that was anticlimactic."

Zinnia started gathering the wrappers from our snacks and the red plastic cups, muttering under her breath about the lack of coasters currently in use.

Barry replaced the Devil Duster in its suitcase and snapped it closed. "Don't worry about the toxic waste in the containment unit," he said, then, "I trust you've all seen the GhostBusters movies?"

We stared at him. Had Barry Blackstone built a device based on a successful movie franchise from the 1980s, or was the movie franchise based on one of his early inventions? The man wasn't that old. He would have been a child when the first movie released.

Barry tapped the suitcase lovingly. "My grandfather, Alvus Blackstone, created the plans for this device not long after developing the formula for turning lead into gold. He filed several patents. For the spirit containment devices, not the gold." He smiled with one side of his mouth and frowned with the other. "He had plans for an incinerator, which converts the spirit energy into, well, it's complicated. But I am working on that part of the process. So, unlike the events of the movie, we won't have a third act problem with this little beast escaping." He patted the suitcase.

"Good," Zinnia said, and she marched off to the kitchen with our wrappers and cups.

From the kitchen she yelled, "Zara! What have you done in here?"

Maisy gave me a knowing look. "No good deed goes unpunished," she said knowingly.

"Thank you," I said. "Thank you for everything."

Maisy shrugged. "I did what I had to do. Barry should get most of the credit."

I took Maisy's hand and looked her in the eyes. "Thank you," I said again.

She looked away.

Margaret and Barry were already headed for the door. Yawning, Maisy stood and joined them.

"Give us an update in the morning," Maisy said, pulling on her jacket by the door.

There was the sound of a struggle in the kitchen, then Zinnia yelled again, "Zara! What have you done to my refrigerator?"

"I'd love to stick around," Margaret said, "but I don't want to."

"You've done plenty," I said. "Thank you all. I don't know what I would do without the coven."

Maisy said, deadpan, "Without us, you'd be dead by now."

I wagged a finger at her. "Joke's on you. I've already been dead once."

She shook her head, then led the others out of the house.

My aunt was banging away in the kitchen.

It was now the wee hours of the morning. I wanted to return home to my own bed, but I dutifully went to the kitchen to help my aunt clean up.

There was no sign of the Shadow.

Whatever it was, for better or worse, it had left with Barry Blackstone.

CHAPTER 26

Zinnia Riddle

Three Years Ago

September

Aiden wouldn't even look at the presents Zinnia brought him. He turned his thin face toward the window. His cheeks were hollow now. The gauntness was such a contrast to his abdomen, hidden under the folds of blankets, distended with fluids. He said he looked like a snake who'd just eaten a Thanksgiving turkey.

He'd said that last week, when he'd still had the strength to make jokes. Before the doctors had revealed to his father and Zinnia that there was no hope. None of the adults involved in Aiden's care wanted to break the news to him, yet he knew. Of course he knew. It was *his* body that was shutting down.

The next step was to stop treatment and move him to hospice, unless he preferred to "be" at home.

The doctors were careful not to say the word *die*. It was always about where Aiden wanted to "be" when "it happened."

Now he was at home, in the beige and gray brownstone, in the only bedroom he'd ever had or ever would have.

"Don't you think it's a bit dreary in here?" Zinnia had asked on the day he'd come home from the last trip to the hospital. "What do you say we redecorate a little?"

"It's okay," Aiden said. "Don't waste money on me. You and Dad can redecorate for the next kid." He looked at her midsection pointedly. "Maybe it will be a girl."

If the boy's father had been in the room, an argument would have started. There would be no replacement for Aiden, so why would he say such a hurtful thing? Mitchell would fume and pout, and Aiden would smile. If his father was upset, then, just for a minute, Aiden didn't have to be.

Zinnia had a different approach.

She patted her stomach, which was as flat as ever, and said, "A little girl would be quite an upgrade for us, but it will take a professional cleaning crew to get the boy stink out of this room." She looked around. "We could make it work, though. We could put a nice dollhouse over there. By the window."

"And wallpaper," Aiden said. "Girls like wallpaper."

"Oh? What kind of wallpaper do you think we should put up for your shiny new replacement?"

"Unicorns," he said, then, "No. Nothing for little kids. She's going to grow up in this house, all the way to adult size. The wallpaper pattern should be something she can grow into."

"Stripes?"

"No."

"Zig zags?"

"I don't think so." He rubbed the bandaged spot on his chest where the port had been. "I feel like I know exactly what she's going to love, but I can't see it inside my mind. When I close my eyes, it's just black. All my pictures are gone."

"I have an idea," Zinnia said. "The decorating stores have these wonderful, big books full of wallpaper samples. I'll bring some home, and you can pick out the perfect one."

"Will you tell her I picked it out just for her?"

"Of course I will." Her eyes stung at the idea. It hurt Zinnia so much to play this game. "I'll tell her all about her big brother who loved her so much."

* * *

That conversation had happened a week ago.

In the days since, Aiden had declined dramatically.

Now, he wouldn't even look at the new things she'd brought him.

"It's school supplies," she said. "You'll be a few months behind your classmates when you go back, but all of their pencils will be worn down, and yours will still be brand-new." She set the items on the bed. "And it's not just pencils. There's a new laptop, and all sorts of things."

He was absolutely still in the bed, facing the window.

"Aiden, you could start using the laptop now, in bed. It's very light and easy to handle. I asked the young man at the store to put all the new games on it."

Aiden coughed weakly. "Did you bring the books? With the wallpaper samples?"

"Your dad thought it was a bad idea." Talk about an understatement. They'd had a terrible fight about it.

Mitchell couldn't understand why Aiden wanted to pick out wallpaper for an imaginary girl that was going to replace him. Mitchell thought it was too cruel. He didn't understand that it wasn't about wallpaper, let alone the people who might someday sleep in Aiden's bedroom. It was a symbolic action. It was about giving the child back some of the control that had been taken from him.

At least the screaming match had taken place outside of the house, so Aiden couldn't have heard.

And yet, somehow, the boy knew. He always knew.

She moved the untouched school supplies over to the dresser, and took a seat on the sunny side of the bed.

"You have to hold on a little longer," she said.

"Why?"

"Do you remember my friend Margaret? She was here last month."

"The witch?"

Zinnia turned and faced the window, letting the autumn sun turn her vision red through her eyelids.

"Yes," she said. "Margaret, the witch."

Aiden said nothing, but she felt his jubilation that she was no longer denying it.

"She might have a spell that could help you," Zinnia said. "As soon as she finishes her research and gets all the ingredients ready, she's coming back to New York, and she's going to do it."

"Why can't you do it?"

"I'm not a witch. Margaret is."

He said nothing.

"I don't know how," Zinnia admitted. "It doesn't matter how strong a person is, they can't do something if they don't know how."

"How long?"

"Another week or two."

"Okay," he said. "Deal."

"Deal," she agreed.

They sat in silence for a while, and when he seemed to have dozed off, she rose to leave.

"Zinnia," he said.

She stopped, her back to him because she didn't want him to see her tears. "Yes, Aiden?"

"We still need to pick out the wallpaper for the baby's room. Just in case your friend's spell doesn't work."

"That's a good idea," she said. "Don't tell your father, but I'm going to get the sample books and sneak them into the house. Just in case."

"Just in case," he agreed.

CHAPTER 27

Zara Riddle

Sunday

1 Day to Halloween

I'd planned to spend the entire morning in bed, reading, but Boa decided to "help" me by rolling around on my open book. She waved her pink toe beans in my face, tempting me to touch her belly.

"You're not helping," I said.

"Ham," she replied.

I gave up on the paperback that was now underneath a pile of white fur, and threw back the covers.

"I guess I might as well get up and finish decorating for the party, since I'll be busy at work tomorrow during the day."

I'd been talking to the cat a lot more since she'd started talking back.

Boa rolled onto her side, gave me a thoughtful look, then said, "Ham."

"And eggs? For breakfast? That's a great idea, Your Highness." I pulled on my slippers. "Race you to the kitchen."

She jumped up and bolted for the door.

I looked at the flattened paperback next to my pillow and considered betraying her trust.

I couldn't do it.

She'd already been through a lot of stress that month, being sequestered to the basement multiple times for her own safety, plus the multi-day presence of the noisy cleaning crew. I would cave in to her demands this morning.

This is my life now, I thought as I walked down the stairs. *My schedule is dictated by ghosts, the coven, my family, a gorgon, and a cat with a limited vocabulary.*

And I wouldn't trade my life for anyone's.

* * *

At two o'clock, Charlize's sister, Chloe Taub, also a blonde gorgon, showed up at my house unexpectedly. She looked tired, and was accompanied by baby Jordan Junior, snoozing in his stroller.

I invited her in and asked what had brought her by.

She stayed on the porch. "Charlize told me to ask you about our grandmother's pendant."

That would be the pendant that had been destroyed by my failed attempt to banish the Shadow.

"I'm confused," I said. "Your sister didn't tell you what happened?"

"Tell me what?" Chloe shifted her weight from one foot to the other impatiently. "She said you borrowed it or something?" The snakes that lived in her short blonde hair twisted into view and eyed me with suspicion.

"I did. For a spell."

"You didn't lose it, did you?"

"Oh, no. I know exactly where the pendant is."

"Where?"

"Nearby," I said. "It's definitely on the property."

She held out her hand. "Then give it back."

"I'd be happy to. Did you bring a forklift?"

"What?"

"It might be better if I show you." I waved for her to follow me through the house to the door that led to the back yard.

"I'll just leave Jordan Junior napping in here," she said, parking the stroller in a dark region of the hallway. "If he wakes up, we'll hear him." She gave me an exasperated look. "Trust me. He's got a set of lungs on him."

"Treasure these days. They grow up fast."

"How's Zoey doing? I hear she's working on a job for the coven. Some sort of fake haunting?" She followed me to the back yard. The air was chilly, but the sky was clear and blue.

"Yes. It's technically a punishment for Ambrosia Abernathy, but they're both having way too much fun."

"Abernathy. Who's that again?"

I gave her a quick update on the town's newest witch.

"I'm so out of touch," Chloe said, shaking her head. "Motherhood is intense. It's so hard to have your body not be your own anymore, or your time." She jerked her head up and quickly added, "But it's the best job in the world, and it's totally worth it."

"Chloe," I said gently. "It's just us here, and I'm not judging you."

She and her hair snakes regarded me with suspicion.

I asked, "Can I give you some advice, mom to mom?"

"I don't know." She bit her lower lip. "Sure."

I felt something flowing through me. Not a typical witch spell, but something just as primal. When Zoey was just a baby, I'd been feeling bad about everything I was doing. Then, one day, a woman, a kind stranger, had come up to me on a bus and told me the exact words I'd needed to hear.

As I stood in my back yard with Chloe, I repeated those words to her.

"It's okay to feel however you feel," I said. "How you feel is not a measure of your worth. Bad feelings might not even be a sign of anything at all. All those fears and doubts about parenting, they come and go. If you don't like how you're feeling about motherhood, give it a minute. It'll change."

"It will?"

"And here's the most important thing: You're doing the best you can."

Her pretty but deadly blue eyes shone, and her lower lip trembled. "I am?"

"You are," I assured her. "You're doing the best you can."

She repeated the words back as though memorizing a spell by rote. "I'm doing the best I can."

"Exactly."

She tilted her head and gave me a thoughtful look. "You're kind of wise, considering your breeding."

"Uh, thanks."

"What you said reminded me of these self-improvement talks I've been listening to, by that wise little troll."

"You mean Thackery Tollster? The guy who's always on TV?"

"That's the one. He's a troll, but he's got some good ideas."

"They prefer to be called sprites."

Chloe rolled her eyes. "Of course they do. And I'd like to be called a supermodel, but it doesn't make me one."

"I don't know," I said. "You're cute. You could model."

"I could model baby spit-up." She looked past me and surveyed the back yard. "Why are we out here? Don't tell me you buried my grandmother's pendant for good luck."

"Far from it. Come with me." I led the way down the steps, and over to an enormous boulder near the back fence. "Here it is." I spread my hands in the gesture for ta-da. "Your grandmother's pebble."

Chloe's jaw dropped. Her short hair snakes popped straight out like those party horns you blow into on New Year's Eve.

"Your little pebble grew up," I said.

"It sure did!"

"My professional cleaning crew used a sling and a pair of oxen to get it out of the dining room."

She seemed to be taking the news well. "It must weigh a ton."

"Half of that. Only a thousand pounds, give or take a few." I walked her over to the boulder. "The setting didn't grow. You can see the clasp and chain embedded here, and here." I pointed out two specks of gold.

She put both hands on the boulder and bowed her head, eyes closed.

Was she laughing, or crying? Or just exhausted? She did have baby spit-up on her shoulder. And down her back. And on one shoe.

"I'm so sorry," I said. "I didn't know this would happen to your family's artifact. I've been searching through my reference books to see if there's a way to reverse the effects without sucking the whole town into a hell dimension. I'm sure I will eventually get the pebble back down to a reasonable size for you. Maybe not wearable on a necklace, but a trim twenty pounds or so. You could use it for biceps curls."

"Don't bother." She opened her eyes and turned to give me a peaceful, satisfied smile. "My sisters and I have been fighting over this stupid pebble for years. Chessa wanted to have it sent to her in London." She patted the boulder. "This is perfect, Zara. I can't thank you enough." She laughed. "This pebble isn't going anywhere. And I can always visit, right?"

"You're welcome any time," I said. "I'd like it if you stopped by."

She shivered and pulled her spit-up-covered jacket tighter. "Well, at least that's settled," she said.

"Do you have time for lunch?" I asked. "It's about that time."

"I wouldn't want to put you out."

"That's not a *no*." I nodded for her to follow me back into the kitchen.

* * *

Over lunch, we talked about the self-improvement talks she'd been listening to—the ones by Thackery Tollster.

He was the person who had introduced to the mainstream the very old concept of a certain kind of cacodemon. Thackery Tollster called it the Pain-Body, which was a term that sounded remarkably similar to its ancient name, only with less guttural horking and sphincter clenching.

"That's a funny coincidence," I said. "The, uh-oh, I can't pronounce it right, so I'll just call it a *Pain-Body*— sounds exactly like what we accidentally summoned that night when I supersized your grandma's pebble."

"You summoned one of the original Old Ones?"

"I *might* have summoned an Old One. It sure didn't look very new. Not with all of its wrinkles, and crooked spikes, and knobby, warty, hemorrhoid-like bits. Plus the bad teeth and liver spots. You don't expect a creature like that to have so much sun damage."

She blinked in astonishment. "You're lucky you're not dead."

"I'll say. Tried that once. Didn't care for it."

"What?"

"Oh, you don't know about that one? Girl, pull up a seat!"

She was already in a seat, but she smiled and told me to go on.

We spent the next two hours trading battle stories. I loaned her some clothes while I put her dirty clothes through the laundry.

When Jordan Junior woke from his nap, Chloe fed him, then we watched as he played with Boa and Ribbons. Both the cat and the wyvern had a surprisingly gentle touch when it came to babies.

Chloe and I continued trading stories and comparing scars until dinner time, when she really had to get going.

"You should come over with Charlize for our next Wicked Wives viewing party," I said.

"I'd love to, but I missed the first episode."

"We can catch you up," I said. "Or you can come early and watch the first one before the new one runs. I wouldn't mind sitting through it again. When it comes to my favorite books or shows, I'm so excited that I usually miss stuff, so I have to read or watch it again anyway."

"Thanks for the offer," she said. Jordan Junior squealed happily in the stroller.

"Come by any time. You don't need a reason."

She thanked me, and we rolled the baby to the front door.

"Take care, sister," she said as she hugged me goodbye.

"You, too, sister," I said back.

I had an actual sister now, thanks to Persephone, but it still meant a lot to me that two out of three gorgon triplets considered me an honorary sister.

You couldn't have too many sisters.

CHAPTER 28

Monday

Halloween

2 Hours Before the Party

"Something is different, Zed."

The wyvern perched on the edge of my bed, rubbing his scaly chin with the finger-like talons of his left wing.

I raised my eyebrows. "You think?"

"Your appearance has been altered," he said.

"I'm wearing a costume. For tonight's party. You know all about this, Mr. Snout-Pout. The first guests will arrive in a couple of hours."

"Now I understand, Zed. This change to your appearance is so that your foe, Maisy Nix, does not recognize you. This disguise will allow you to get close enough to plunge a dagger into her midsection without warning, and rip out her organs. I shall assist you in this very exciting plan. I shall wear a disguise as well."

"I'm not ripping out anyone's organs. Is evisceration all you think about? Talk about a one-track mind. You're worse than that pork-obsessed cat."

"It is vital in a long life to have concrete goals." He switched his chin-rubbing to the other wing and crossed his green scaly legs. "Inform me now of the intended time the home invasion is to end. I shall return to roost once the last vile intruder has been dispatched."

"It's a party, Ribbons. If things go well, it might go until morning. Are you sure you don't want to stick around? Chloe is going to stop by early with Jordan Junior. You enjoyed playing with him yesterday."

"I do not like babies, nor playing."

"That wasn't how it looked to me, when you were down on the floor clapping while he squealed."

The wyvern blew ribbons of fire from both nostrils. "That human blob in an excrement wrapper is a possible future ally. I was testing his reflexes."

"By shaking a rattle and playing peek-a-boo?"

"He passed all of my tests."

And with that, he flitted up into a dark corner of the room and disappeared, seemingly into thin air.

The little food pirate must have used the wyvern flap, I thought.

I finished what I'd been doing, giving my costume the finishing touch: a set of plastic vampire teeth.

Then I admired myself in the full-length mirror. I looked perfect. Sexy, but scary, too.

My costume consisted of tan pants, a white blouse, a black wig, pale makeup covering my freckles, plus the low-quality vampire fangs.

I was dressed as the most upsetting entity I could think of, that still had a human form: my mother, the vampire.

I called in my daughter to reveal my look.

Zoey was surprised. "Gigi? I didn't know you were in town." She ran up and hugged me. "Did you gain weight?"

"Excuse me?"

She stepped back, blinking. "Mom? Is that you?"

"Very funny. I know you didn't actually think I was your grandmother."

She smiled. "You didn't smell like Gigi, but my eyes thought you might be her, just for an instant." She looked me up and down. "I like it. You're going to freak out Mr. Bentley."

"Bentley? No way. He's the last person who's going to be afraid of another vampire." I played with my fake fangs. "Or is it *vampiress*? Is that the culturally sensitive term for the lady ones?" I waved a hand. "Oh, who cares. I'm so sick of everyone being offended all the time."

She was staring at me.

"What?" I patted myself. "Am I missing some key detail? What have I forgotten?"

"You look perfect," she said. "Exactly like Gigi. But don't you think it's weird, dressing like Mr. Bentley's ex?"

I groaned and fell backward on my bed. "Zirconia Cristata Riddle was *my* terrifying mother *long*before she was his ex. I have every right to dress like this, at my own party."

Zoey came over and sat next to me on the bed. "I know, but you wouldn't dress up like his other ex, Larissa Lang."

"Of course not. She's too normal. And too pretty." I fluttered my eyelashes.

Zoey frowned at me.

I poked her in the arm. "This is where you tell me I'm pretty enough to be anyone."

"Of course you are," she said. "But I'm not so sure Larissa Lang is, you know, *normal*."

"Why? What did you hear?"

"Nobody that young makes it that far in Hollywood without the help of demonic forces. She's not just an actress. She's an executive producer on the show." Zoey gave me a deadly serious look.

"Oh, well that settles it," I said. "All executive producers are demons, therefore she is a demon."

Zoey grabbed a pillow and settled in next to me. I resisted the urge to reach out and touch her face or pull her in for a motherly hug. It felt good to be talking like this. It seemed like we hadn't had a good gossip session in a thousand years.

"Tell me what you heard," I said. "We've got some time before the first guests arrive."

"Francie and Jade have a theory that she's not just one person. She's a team. A dozen duplicates, cloned from a reincarnated Illuminati priestess."

"That sounds like Francie and Jade, all right. You've been talking to your old friends from back home?"

"There's a group text. One of the two Tanyas looped me in." She wrinkled her nose. "Brianna is on there, but she mostly lurks. You forget she's there until she jumps in with the most absurd non sequitur comment, out of nowhere. Ambrosia thinks Brianna is hilarious. The three of us also have a private chain to make fun of the other chain."

"Ambrosia is on there, too? Is that what she's always reading on her phone?"

"Mom, don't make that face."

I pulled out the vampire teeth. "What face? This is what my face looks like."

"You always make that face whenever we talk about Ambrosia. Like you're trying to remember a really bad smell."

"Why would anyone try to remember a bad smell?"

She stared into my eyes a moment before saying, "Mom, Ambrosia isn't replacing you."

"I never said she was."

"I know about the coven calling her New Zara."

I played with my plastic fangs. "They're just trying to make her feel welcome. It's kind of a huge compliment, if you think about it."

"Why do you think she has the same specialty as you? Spirit Charmed?"

"We're not even sure she does. There are other specialties that come with the ability to see ghosts." I shrugged. "But even if she does, it doesn't have to mean anything. It's life. Random stuff happens. It doesn't mean you deserve it, or that you don't."

She stared at me. "Then why bother trying to be good?"

"What?"

Her eyes glistened. "If bad stuff just happens, and it doesn't matter if you deserve it or not, then why bother trying to be good?"

"Because it's what a person does. You try to be good. Why wouldn't you?"

She looked up at the ceiling and blinked hard. "Maybe because there's no point?"

The room was very still and quiet.

It was happening. My daughter was finally opening up, talking to me about her father dying. She just wasn't saying it in those words.

"What I meant about the randomness of life is that a *portion* of it is random," I said carefully, weighing my words before they came out. "You can't control everything. You'll drive yourself crazy. But a person can always do things that might lead to positive outcomes. You can plant good seeds in a garden, and you can..." I trailed off and stared at the ceiling for a long moment.

With every fiber of my being, I wanted to protect my daughter. I wanted to shield her from the truth, about how harsh and unfair life could be. She was my baby. But my baby was sixteen, and she was her own person, with her own life—a life that was becoming less and less embedded in mine.

I wanted her to hold onto her youthful optimism, and to believe that doing good was always the right choice, but it was also my duty as a mother to prepare her for life.

Sometimes the most cynical sayings were true. Good deeds did not go unpunished. The road to Hell was paved with good intentions. And terrible things happened to sweet, lovable kids.

I thought of the little boy Zinnia had cared for. He had died before reaching the age my daughter was. The loss had probably changed Zinnia forever. I would never know who my aunt might have been as a person, if her heart hadn't been scarred by such terrible heartbreak.

My daughter elbowed me to continue. "You can what? Something about a garden, and seeds?"

"You got me," I said. "I am all out of analogies. Does it suck that Archer Caine is going away? That your father is dying? Your father, who just came into your life? Your father, who is kind of a jerk but also not that bad? Yes. It sucks."

"Thank you for admitting it," she said. "It sucks so bad!"

"So bad," I agreed. "Ugh, life!" I shook my hand at the ceiling. "Why do you have to suck?"

She wiped her eyes and tried to smile. "It sucks harder than the Sucko Three Thousand."

"Good one," I said. "Very topical."

I offered her a high five.

She took it.

* * *

After our heart-to-heart, and a good rest, I offered to help Zoey with her costume. The decorations were all in place, and our first guests would be there soon.

There were some strange sounds coming from the lower floor. Zoo sounds. I chalked it up to squeaky wheels on the catering trays that Vijay and his family were rolling in.

I went with Zoey to her bedroom, where she pulled her costume from the closet and revealed it to me.

"Surprise," she said. "It's the most upsetting thing I could think of."

"Marzipants!" I jumped up and down with delight. "Oh, Zoey. It's perfect!"

For Halloween, Zoey would be dressed as her former tormentor, a budgie named Marzipants.

She ruffled the white feathers to reveal silver fabric underneath. "Charlize gave me the base. It's one of her old jumpsuits, a hooded one. The front has a bunch of weird acid burns, so she decommissioned it. You can't even tell with all the feathers."

"It looks perfect. How did you stick the feathers on?"

"Hot glue gun," she said. "Ambrosia helped. Boa did not help. She kept stealing the feathers."

"Don't tell Kathy about the hot glue gun," I said. "She's got a thing about it. People get snobby about the strangest things." I gestured for her to put on the suit.

Zoey stripped down to an undershirt and stepped into the feathered jumpsuit.

"This feels so wrong," she said. "I'm a shifter, and I'm putting on a bird suit. Do you think the other shifters will be offended?" She paused, pinching the skin on the front of her neck nervously. "Frank is coming tonight. I think I'd better change."

"Don't you dare," I said. "Frank has a wonderful sense of humor. The only thing that would please him more than seeing you dressed as a budgie would be seeing you dressed as a flamingo."

"I know, but..." She winced. "At school, we had an assembly to talk about cultural sensitivity."

"Did anyone tell you it was wrong to dress up as a budgie?"

"No, but..."

"If you get in any trouble tonight, I'll take the blame," I said. "I'll tell everyone I sanctioned your costume."

She narrowed her eyes at me. "Sanction is an auto antonym. It could mean you imposed a punishment for budgie costumes, or that you specifically allowed them."

"Exactly. A little wiggle room in interpretation makes life more interesting." I snapped my fingers, sending hurry-up sparkles through the air. The spell worked like a shot of espresso. "Zip it up. I want to see the hoodie."

She pulled on the crowning glory and looked at herself in the mirror. Her shoulders slouched and she made a disappointed sound.

"Floopy doop," she said. "I look more like a cockatiel than a budgie."

"It's these feathers on top," I said. "Ambrosia must have glued them on wrong. Here. Let your mother fix you, little hatchling." I plucked out the feathers that were giving my budgie a cockatiel appearance. "That's better."

She patted the exposed silver ridge on top of her head. "Now I have male pattern baldness."

"Perfect. You'll be extra upsetting for all the men in attendance."

She groaned.

"Hang on," I said. "Speaking of baldness, I actually know a spell. It's got terrible side effects if you use it on a human to regrow hair, but I think it's perfect for this situation."

I took a moment to retrieve the spell from memory and mentally rehearse it. I was taking longer than usual because all of the recent failures had shaken my confidence. But they say you need to get right back on the broomstick and start casting again, lest you become an OCW.

I took a calming breath, then cast the spell, carefully limiting it to the costume. My daughter wouldn't be thrilled if she suddenly sported thick red hair all over her body.

The spell worked as warranted. For every hot-glue-gunned feather on the costume, the spell sprouted a dozen more, thick and lush. The top of her head filled in first, and then cascaded down. The feathers looked natural, the black and gray striations lining up beautifully.

Zoey's jaw dropped. She lifted her arms, and the feathers spread as though organic, forming realistic-looking wings.

"I think I could actually fly," she said, giving the wings a test flap.

"Not without your beak." I twirled my finger.

She yelped and took a step back, covering her nose with the tips of her wings. "Mom! Don't!"

"The look on your face! I was only joking, my little duckie." I handed her the rubbery orange thing that was still on the costume's hanger.

She took the beak and put it on. "How do I look? We made this out of one of Charlize's old yoga mats."

"You look adorable."

She frowned, which only made her look more adorable.

"You look horrifying," I quickly amended. "You'll be wearing the most upsetting costume at the whole party."

The doorbell rang.

Our first guests had arrived. The unfashionably early ones.

"Doorbell," Zoey said.

"Doorbell," I replied.

"Doorbell!" She flapped her wings and bolted past me toward the stairs. She whooped as she caught some air— very briefly—on her way down.

"I'm flying," she whooped. "I'm flying!"

CHAPTER 29

Zinnia Riddle

Three Years Ago

Halloween (Morning)

Zinnia was in the brownstone's beige and gray kitchen with the maid who now answered to Fiona, even though it was not her name.

The boys were yelling at each other in the living room. Mitchell threatened a year-long grounding, and Aiden pitched a tantrum so loud and powerful, the breakfast dishes on the serving cart clattered.

"Listen to that," Fiona said, smiling.

"I know," Zinnia replied. "I never thought I'd be so happy to hear those two at it."

"Is this real?" Fiona's expression grew serious. "My grandfather was better for three days, and then he died."

"His scans are clear. It's real."

"But how? No offense, Ma'am, but I don't understand how someone could be so sick and then..." She waved in the direction of the loud yelling. Aiden and his father were equally matched.

"Terminally ill patients are sometimes allowed access to experimental treatments that aren't yet approved," Zinnia said. "An old friend of mine, Dr. Mills, was able to treat Aiden."

"He must be very smart, this Dr. Mills."

"Oh, *she* thinks she is." Zinnia waved a spray of sparkling magic at the maid. "Everything has worked out in a perfectly logical fashion. There's nothing odd going on. People get sick, and sometimes they get better. That's what happened for Aiden. We are all very happy."

"Sometimes they get better," the maid agreed. "We are all very happy."

There was a crash in the living room.

The two women smiled at each other.

"That poor lamp," Zinnia said.

"It sounded like a vase to me."

There was more shouting, and then a gleeful squeal, followed by another crash.

"That was the vase," Zinnia said.

"It's going to be a very long day," Fiona said. "Disasters come in threes."

"Well, I'm taking Aiden out Trick or Treating, so you'll have a break between six o'clock and eight, or whenever he's collected more candy than he can carry on his own." She smiled. "Whichever comes first."

"I thought Mr. Harrington said Aiden was too old for that."

"That's why we're not *telling* Mr. Harrington." Zinnia winked. "If anyone asks, we're out for a carriage ride with Mimi, and Kiki, and their children." By *children*, she meant dogs, who would be in costume.

"Are you sure it will be all right? He still gets tired so quickly."

"I'll bring the wheelchair, just in case."

"Are you sure, Ma'am?"

Zinnia refreshed the spell. "I have the situation under control. Everything will be fine."

The maid nodded. "Everything will be fine."

The yelling out in the living room had morphed into laughter. It sounded like a pillow fight might be happening. There was squealing, playful taunting, and the sounds of pillows being tossed.

"They stopped fighting," the maid said. "It's a Halloween miracle."

"See? Everything's working out. It's going to be a long and wonderful day."

CHAPTER 30

Zara Riddle

Halloween

I was not surprised that my self-renovating house had prepared itself to accommodate a large crowd for a Halloween party.

But I was a wee bit surprised by the massive scale of the magical changes.

For starters, the house had shifted around so the entry porch was now a good-sized cloak room, complete with an attendant. The attendant was a Capuchin monkey in a red vest. It was an actual Capuchin monkey, not a tiny person in a convincing costume.

"Hi there," I said to the monkey.

The monkey saluted me.

My daughter, the budgie, opened the front door and then flew off to make some last-minute adjustments to her costume.

The first guests were my coworkers from the library, Frank and Kathy.

The little monkey snatched their coats and bags. The monkey handed Frank and Kathy a pair of tokens with coat check numbers, then disappeared into the murky depths of an absurdly large cloak room.

"You really pulled out all the stops," Kathy said. She hadn't come as an owl, as she'd been hinting at for weeks. She was dressed as a Popsicle. A bright pink one.

I leaned in and sniffed. "Maybe it's my mind playing tricks on me, but I swear you smell like strawberries."

She smiled, her orange-brown eyes crinkling behind her round glasses. "I *do* smell like strawberries. It's intentional."

"Crafty!" I exclaimed. "I never considered scent as an aspect of costume-wearing. You have broken into another dimension, Kathy."

"Thank you." She looked very pleased with herself.

I wiped my chin. "Now my mouth is watering. I kinda want to nibble on your shoulder."

She held up one hand, palm facing me. "I'm not edible," she warned.

Ribbons, who must have been lurking nearby, sent a telepathic cackle into my head. "Oh, she is edible," Ribbons said. "Anything that has a mouth with which to claim itself inedible is, as a rule, always edible."

I kept a straight face and didn't talk back, since the others couldn't hear the wyvern.

Frank, who was craning his neck looking around, said, "Winona would be so proud of what you've done with the place."

"Maybe she'll drop in," I said. "It is All Hallows' Eve, after all. People around here keep telling me there's nothing special about the date, but I don't believe it. There are so many stories in popular culture about monsters rising up this one night of the year, and we all know that even the strangest stories have a grain of truth."

Kathy, who, unlike us, had been through many Halloweens in Wisteria as a supernatural, shook her head inside her Popsicle shroud. "Newbies," Kathy said.

"Except for some houses getting egged and some trees getting toilet-papered, it's just a regular night."

"Not exactly," Frank said. "I mean, that is what the Department wants you to think, so go ahead and believe that if you prefer."

Kathy gave him a skeptical look. "What do you mean?"

"I'll tell you tomorrow," he said. "Not right now. I wouldn't want to tempt fate by talking about the history of incursions that have happened on Halloweens past."

She stamped one Popsicle stick leg. "I can't believe you've been keeping this from me."

"Don't be mad," he said. "I only just found out myself."

"When?"

The two continued bickering about who knew what when, and who was holding out on whom.

While they argued, I looked over Frank's costume, trying to figure out what he was supposed to be. The children's librarian wore a puffy, pale-green tube of fabric that covered him from head to toe. His sole accessory was a pair of round glasses that looked an awful lot like Kathy's.

When I sensed a break in their argument, I prodded Frank with one finger and asked, "What are you supposed to be? A moldy french fry?"

"Kiss me and find out." He puckered and leaned toward me. "I'll give you a hint. Kissing me can be a real shocker."

I didn't have to kiss him to figure it out. "You're a bookwyrm," I said. "I should have known. But why the glasses?"

"I'm a bookworm bookwyrm. A bookwyrm who loves books."

"I see it now. Do you know what I am?"

He gestured for me to twirl around. "Show me the whole look."

I twirled for him, even though my white blouse and tan pants didn't swirl out at all. "Well? What do you think of my terrifying ensemble?"

He looked me up and down thoughtfully before pronouncing, "Why, Miss Zara Riddle, you are the spitting image of your mother."

Kathy gasped. "Oh, dear. She is!"

Frank said, "When your brooding beau sets his eyes on you, he is going to turn into a bat."

"Why does everyone keep saying that?"

Frank exchanged a look with Kathy, then asked, "Isn't your mother his ex?"

"They weren't *really* dating. She was grooming him to be my big, strong protector." I looked down at my hands. They were extra pale from my costume makeup, and I kept thinking bone-crawlers were coming to get me.

"*Of course* she was only grooming him," Frank said. He wriggled one arm free of his bookwyrm costume and patted me on my shoulder. "Of course she was," he repeated. "Right, Kathy?"

Kathy waved one pink-gloved, strawberry-scented hand. "It's none of my business," she said, which was quite the lie. Like most nosy people, Kathy was in complete denial of her nosiness. "Is your mother coming tonight?" Kathy asked. "Ooooh! Ooooh! Is she dressed as you?"

I wrinkled my nose at the suggestion. "My mother could never pull off my look," I said. "Last I heard, she was in Paris, shacked up with the real-life inspiration for the Phantom of the Opera." I glanced up at the hallway ceiling. "Or was it Andrew Lloyd Webber? Which one of those guys has a castle?"

Frank and Kathy laughed, because they thought I was joking.

The doorbell rang again.

A giant budgie flapped past us, crying out, "Doorbell!"

The next to arrive was a couple dressed in shades of blue: Archer Caine and Carrot Greyson.

Archer was dressed as a genie, as imagined by the cartoon artists at Walt Disney.

Archer's white hair—assuming he hadn't gone bald in the three days since I'd last seen him—was covered in a blue bald cap, and his face had been painted blue to match. His cheeks were even more gaunt, and his green eyes were cloudy, but he looked healthy at a glance, thanks to the padded blue costume on his upper body. The blue suit was bulky, with rippling chest muscles, broad shoulders, and an eight-pack of abs. I didn't want to think about how gaunt his body might be under the padding.

"Nice muscles," I said.

Archer, the real genie wearing a blue genie costume, held up an antique oil lantern. "Care to rub my lantern, young lady?"

"Not tonight," I said.

His date giggled. "I'll rub your lantern."

"And I will grant you three wishes, my princess." He gazed at her with adoration.

Carrot Greyson, the rune mage tattoo artist, was dressed in a blue gown suitable for royalty. There was a beautiful tiara sparkling on her head. Her makeup was impeccable. Her dyed-orange hair—usually scruffy and on the verge of dreadlocks—was swept up in an elegant chignon. Like Archer, you'd think she'd stepped out of a Disney film... if it wasn't for all the tattoos of flowers and jungle cats across her chest and arms.

"You look gorgeous," I told her. "I see you finally settled on the blue." The gown was one of several she had tried on the day we'd shared a changing room. "Are you a specific historical princess?"

"I'm Cinderella," she said.

"Disney version, or Brothers Grimm?"

"Neither," she said, and turned to her date.

"The costume is based on a real person," Archer explained. "Zara, what do you know about Cinderella?"

"I know there are many variations on the story, and that the Aarne-Thompson-Uther system classifies Cinderella as Tale Type 510A, Persecuted Heroine."

"Then you know the gist of it," Archer said. "But what you may not know is that the real Cinderella preferred the company of cats and mice to the company of men, so I'm afraid the marriage to the prince didn't last."

"She preferred the company of cats and mice to men?" I fake-laughed, channeling my mother uncannily. "Who doesn't?"

Archer stepped back and gave me a wary look.

Carrot said, "Zara, I know the idea was to come dressed as something that scares you, but I hope you don't mind that I went a different way. I've always loved Cinderella stories. I suppose that makes me a bad feminist, but I like what I like."

"Tonight's party is for everyone, even the so-called bad feminists," I said. "Whatever that means."

"Are you sure?" She adjusted her glittery tiara. "I brought a backup costume in my car, just in case."

"No need! Your costume is welcome here, and so are you. Rules are for other people's parties."

"I'm so glad you feel that way," Carrot said. "Being Cinderella is like a dream come true. When I was growing up, we weren't allowed to watch animated movies. My parents said that Mr. Walt Disney and his associates were part of a secret cabal that is still in power today. They're the ones behind Agenda Twenty-Two. They want to normalize monsters in America, and everywhere else, to prepare for the monster takeover and extinction of humans. Most modern holidays are all pro-monster because of their doing."

I was just curious enough to take the bait.

"Carrot, what other holidays besides Halloween are pro-monster?"

"For starters, there's the one where mutated giant herbivores trick children into eating their waste by disguising it as chocolate." Carrot was not joking.

"I have never heard the Easter Bunny described quite so colorfully. Dinners around the Greyson household must have been entertaining."

"Oh, they were." Her blue eyes bugged out and her face lit up. "My cousins Jeremiah and Jebediah used sock puppets to deliver helpful life lessons."

Just then, the Capuchin monkey who'd been checking coats climbed up the hooped skirt of Carrot's dress. The monkey took the shawl from her hand with a gleeful chitter, then jumped onto the shoulder of her date.

Archer Caine didn't even react to the coat check monkey chittering next to his ear.

He said to me, "It was wise of you to hire servants for the evening. The large parking attendant you have outside, seeing to your guests' carriages, was a nice touch."

"Parking attendant?" I had not hired one, but then again, I hadn't hired a coat check monkey, either.

"The man in the Wookie costume," Archer said.

"Hmm." I gave him a thoughtful look. "Are you sure about what you think you saw?"

Archer said, "Now that I think about it, I do not believe the servant who took the keys for Carrot's carriage was a human in a Wookie costume."

Carrot tugged on his padded blue arm. "She wasn't a Wookie, Archer. She was Forest Folk."

Archer asked, "That was a *she*?"

She swatted his pumped-up blue chest playfully.

He pushed back with a single finger on her tattooed bare shoulder, making her wobble on her shoes, which were not glass slippers, but elegant heels studded in opalescent beads.

The two quibbled over what type of creature had parked Carrot's 1991 Cadillac Brougham.

They really were a cute couple.

When they were done, Archer said to me, "You look regal, Zara."

Carrot agreed.

Archer said, "You make an attractive... What do you call it? Grave-digging, brain-munching zombie?"

"Oh, I would *never* call them that." I winked. "When they're around."

Carrot looked confused. Carrot frequently looked confused. "Aren't you dating a vampire?"

"That is the rumor," I said.

Archer sniffed and said, "I don't sense him nearby. Is Theodore Bentley fulfilling the duties of town detective?"

"Sort of," I said. "It's a political thing. He had to drive up the coast to *that other party*, the boring corporate one at Castle Wyvern. Just to put in an appearance, officially. He's going to sneak out after it gets busy, when people won't notice." I leaned to the side and looked behind the dressed-in-blue couple, through the open doorway, at the high volume of vehicles driving up the usually quiet Beacon Street. "Then again, the castle ballroom might stay empty. It looks like the real party is happening here."

"It sure is," Carrot said. "I'm glad to be here, Zara. Thank you so much for inviting us." She took my hand and squeezed it, her eyes glistening and her lower lip trembling. "I don't care what other people say. You are a genuinely good person."

I was taken aback, but before I could demand the names of the people who claimed I wasn't a good person, Archer whisked his date deeper into the house.

"Let me give you a tour," he said. "That is, if I can find my way around. I see the house has been redecorating."

There was movement on my front lawn.

Six child-sized figures in rustling, store-bought costumes ran up the porch steps and yelled together,

"Trick or Treat!" They held up plastic pumpkins and pillowcases.

I was confused for an instant, then I remembered my original excuse for staying home that night. It was a shame I hadn't remembered when I was near the store, where they supplied Halloween candy. What to do now? These kids didn't look like the type who'd appreciate a stranger handing them hot samosas, no matter how good they were.

"Floopy doop," I said. "Sorry, kids. I'm having a party tonight, and between all the planning and costume shopping, I forgot about trick-or-treaters. I don't have any candy."

There was a chorus of outrage and confusion.

"I did buy lots of peanut butter cups and red licorice," I said. "But then a bunch of witches ate them all up when they were casting spells last week."

The children tittered with laughter. They thought I was joking.

"Witches get hungry when they're casting spells." I felt bad about the lack of candy, but I was enjoying the truth telling.

Something tapped me on the shoulder. It was a creature the size and shape of a Douglas Fir tree, but hairy. I let out a surprised sound, and the six trick-or-treaters on my porch absolutely howled with laughter.

There was a throaty rumble within the giant thing's shaggy coat, then an enormous bowl of packaged candy was thrust at me.

"Thanks." I turned and started tossing treats into the children's bags.

Satisfied with their haul, the costumed kids ran off to the next house, their plastic pants swishing. One little girl in a pixie costume didn't leave with the rest.

She gave me a bratty look and said, "You're not a real vampire."

"You're not a real pixie." I tilted my head back and showed her my plastic fangs as I hissed.

She shrieked and scampered away, nearly knocking over a woman in a witch costume.

The woman in the witch costume was either dressed as my aunt, or she was my aunt.

"Scaring small children, I see," she said with a sniff. "This day of the year certainly brings out a person's true nature."

It was Zinnia, all right.

I did what anyone in my pointy shoes would do.

I hissed and tried to bite her on the neck with my plastic teeth.

To her credit, Zinnia was a good sport about the play biting. She squealed and called for the next group of trick-or-treaters to rescue her from her scary vampire sister. The kids went wild.

Zinnia was in high spirits, which I was glad to see.

Given the way the evening was about to go for her, and everyone else at the party, it was nice that things had started out happy.

CHAPTER 31

A few hours later, the hordes of trick-or-treaters stopped demanding candy at my door. All the kids returned home to organize their loot and secure the retirement plans of our local dentists.

I'd grown up without siblings, but I did have fond memories of bartering treats with Nash Partridge. He'd lived with his father in the rental portion of my house, and was like a big brother to me. He'd always wanted the yucky candies I didn't care for, so negotiations were easy. In hindsight, I realized he must have pretended to like candy corn to make me happy. Nobody liked candy corn.

My latest Halloween was going well. My house party was in full swing. Everyone looked happy to be there. Nobody had been offended by anyone else's costume, which was saying a lot. There was plenty to potentially be offended by. I'd never seen so many witches outside of a coven meeting. Many of them were painted green, with big boils on their noses. What an unflattering stereotype.

Should I have been insulted?

Someone dressed as the Grim Reaper had sung "Witch Doctor" directly at me during karaoke hour. And people kept saying "walla walla bing bang" whenever I walked by, which I had never considered offensive before, but the constant repetition did make me wonder. Was the song actually about a man drugging a woman who didn't want to date him? And wasn't the chorus just a wee bit racist?

Oh, well. I would probably go to Hell eventually for letting people play the cheerful '50s tune at my party, but Halloween was just one night.

I stood near a wall in the living room with Charlize Wakeful. We were taking a breather, looking over the crowd as they hooted and danced to "Monster Mash" playing on the stereo. I was a little sweaty from the "Chicken Dance," which my daughter had led moments earlier. The budgie and her best friend had since disappeared to explore the house.

My gorgon friend was dressed as Perseus from Greek Mythology. She was using her mirrored shield as a plate for her party food.

"These samosas are dee-lish," she said to me. "Not too spicy, but not too mild. Vijay and his wife really pulled through."

"And they're quite the ballroom dancers," I said. "People keep clearing the floor and cheering for the couple to dance another song."

"Oh?" She scanned the crowd of people bobbing their heads in time to the music playing in the living room. "Where? I don't see them."

"They're in another wing of the house."

Charlize raised an eyebrow and put another samosa in her mouth. Whole. I'd never noticed before that night, or perhaps she'd never done it in front of me, but the pretty blonde gorgon could unhinge her jaw, like a snake.

"Yes, there's another wing," I said.

"Where?"

"You know how people always crowd into the kitchen at a house party? I was in the kitchen near the start of the party, and right when party flow was starting to bottleneck in there, a doorway leading to a new corridor suddenly opened up. And then another, and another. The kitchen has twelve exits now." I held up both of my hands. "More exits than I have fingers!"

"Wouldn't that make the kitchen bottleneck worse?"

"It would, except for the powerful vacuum that transports people from one side to the other. The twelve openings are randomly paired up, like six speed tunnels. If anyone who isn't involved in catering sets foot in there, they immediately get sucked to a new location."

Charlize swallowed another samosa whole. "And Vijay and his wife are dancing somewhere off the kitchen?"

"A bunch of people are. There's a big room that looks like a ballet studio, plus more rooms and hallways. I went in myself to check it out. I counted up about five thousand square feet before I got the heebie jeebies and turned around." I leaned in and whispered, in case the house was listening, "I've come to trust my house, but I can't say I'm comfortable hanging out in those eerie rooms that poke through dimensions."

"What are you afraid of? Opening a window, and getting sucked into the vacuum of space?"

"Not until you just said it." I shuddered and rubbed my forearms.

"Where's Bentley? He'd better not stand us up." She snickered, or at least her snakes did. "I mean *you*. Bat Boy had better not stand *you* up."

Bentley couldn't turn into a bat, but that didn't prevent people from talking about him as though he did so regularly.

"He had to put in an appearance at Castle Wyvern," I explained, for the two hundredth time that night. "Politics. Blah blah. Sneaking out. Not as a bat. Coming here. In a car. Not flying as a bat."

"What is he dressed as?"

"A Vulcan tax auditor."

"How is that different from his usual look?"

"Pointy ears."

She nodded. "Spooky."

"I wouldn't know. I haven't seen him in his costume. He's like a nervous groom on his wedding day. He thought seeing each other would be bad luck."

"He's so corny." She quickly added, "But also the best."

"Speaking of which, I'm going to give him a call to find out how much longer he's going to be."

I was too impatient to text, so I dialed his number, like an old-fashioned person. It rang for a while, then went to voicemail.

"I'll try Persephone," I said to Charlize, who couldn't look less interested in my phone business.

My sister's line rang three times, then connected.

Persephone whispered hoarsely, "Zara? Is that you?"

"Yes, but if you're busy there, you can tell Bentley to call me back. It's no—"

"Don't hang up!"

My witch senses tingled. "Persephone? Is something wrong?"

"Oh, Zara, it's so horrible! We're all blocked in here, and our phones aren't working to call out!" She paused, breathing heavily. There was screaming in the background, and the sound of something ripping. "Zara, please don't hang up!"

"I'm not going to—" The phone went pop, and the call disconnected.

I tried redialing, with and without telephone spells, but only got a recorded message that the party I was calling could not be reached. Then I got the more disturbing message that all available circuits were busy.

Meanwhile, people were dancing in my living room as though nothing horrible was happening to all of our friends at another location.

I grabbed Charlize's arm so roughly, she coughed and spat out a whole samosa.

"Something's happening at Castle Wyvern," I said. "Something bad. We have to go there immediately. Round up everyone who has a weapon, or *is* a weapon."

"That covers about ninety percent of the people here."

"We'll need transportation. Did you bring Bugsy?"

"I did, but..." She breathed rapidly, nostrils flaring. "The castle's all the way up in Westwyrd. If there's traffic, it could take us an hour to get there."

"Then we'll fly." I flung out one hand and caught the broomstick I'd summoned. Hey, a witch could be dramatic sometimes if she deemed it necessary.

Charlize touched her hand to the wall, and everything from her fingertips to the stereo turned to white marble. The music stopped. A gorgon could be dramatic, too.

All eyes turned our way.

Charlize started yelling instructions to the crowd, urging them to gather as many people as they could into cars with sober drivers, and form a caravan.

Someone asked, "Is this the Big One?"

Someone else yelled, "What has your latest computer program done now, Wakeful?"

People laughed.

The gorgon turned a few folks into statues, and the laughing stopped.

I let her run the show, since she knew all the DWM protocols. I told her I would be on the porch, waiting for her with my broomstick.

Just one problem.

I couldn't find the porch, because I couldn't even find the door.

The front of my house was entirely coat closet, and full of monkeys in red vests. They seemed agitated, but I couldn't understand what they were saying.

Fatima Nix was there, communicating with them. "Something bad is happening," the Whisper Graced witch said.

"Are the Capuchins telling you anything specific?"

"They're unhappy about the lack of cash tips," she reported. Fatima was dressed as a dog catcher. "Also, all the doors and windows in the house have disappeared."

A tiny monkey jumped out of the coats and screamed at her.

Fatima said, "He wants you to know their union is not responsible for the house being sealed, but they did protest working conditions by leaving surprises in a few coat pockets."

I thanked her, promised the monkeys I'd set things right once this was over, and raced around the reconfigured house.

The monkeys weren't bluffing.

Not only was the front door missing, but I couldn't find a single door or window that led outside.

I was trapped.

We were all trapped.

Inside my house.

CHAPTER 32

At first, the party attendees didn't take the threat seriously. But then, when person after person couldn't get in contact with a friend or family member who was at Castle Wyvern, panic set in.

It doesn't matter how big a house is. When three hundred people are desperate to get outside, and there are no working exits, that house starts feeling claustrophobic.

Everyone expected me to know the way out. So, while I searched for an exit, yelling at everyone to stop following me because I was lost, too, they all ignored what I was saying and formed a congo line behind me.

Me and my giant centipede of costumed partygoers rounded a corner and nearly ran over a giant budgie and her friend. Zoey's best friend, Ambrosia Abernathy, was dressed in what I'm sure everyone thought was a hilarious costume. She wore a cheap red wig, and a classic librarian outfit: pretty white blouse and black pencil skirt. Her outfit was so familiar, in fact, it must have come directly from my own closet. I would have a few words with my closet about this when all was said and done.

Zoey looked at the crowd piled up behind me and asked, "What's going on?"

The partygoers all started talking at once, yelling about the emergency at Castle Wyvern, their loved ones in terrible danger, and the lack of exit from the house.

Normally, this sort of chaos would only confuse a person and slow down the action, but Zoey had very keen fox hearing. She was able to separate out different voices, parse the stories, and immediately comprehend what was going on.

Ambrosia, not the sharpest eyeliner in the makeup box, blinked uncomprehendingly.

Zoey said to me, "Why don't you use the wyvern flap?"

The people behind me buzzed and murmured excitedly. Why *didn't* I use the wyvern flap?

I waved to shush them. "There's no such thing," I explained. "It's a family in-joke. We use it to explain how Ribbons gets in and out of the house without..." I paused for a dramatic gasp of mid-speech understanding, then yelled, "Ribbons!"

He replied directly into my head with a weary-sounding, "You may use my tunnel, Zed."

There was a rushing of air, and the wyvern came flying into the hallway. "This way, Zed."

"Follow that wyvern," I told my crew. "He's taking us to a tunnel."

There were a variety of reactions from the partygoers:

"Never trust a wyvern!"

"What good is another tunnel that's just going to lead us back to the kitchen like all the others?"

"Get going, or get out of my way!"

"We're running low on ice!"

After a bit of confusion, the crew got going, their costumed feet rumbling as they barreled—stampeded, really—down a twisting corridor after the wyvern.

I held back to make sure Zoey was safe and not too scared.

"I'm sure everything will work out," I said soothingly. "Go upstairs, find your bedroom, lock the door, and wait this out."

My daughter the budgie was wide-eyed and grinning. "Are you kidding? I always miss out on the adventures. No way am I missing this one." She grabbed Ambrosia by the hand, and the two ran off after the others.

Ribbons touched my mind to say, "The others are crossing the threshold, Zed."

The threshold? What did he mean? Didn't the tunnel simply lead outside?

I ran after the group.

There was a thundering sound up ahead, then screaming. The people who had been in the lead had apparently done a U-turn. Now they were stampeding toward me, more panicked than ever.

I hugged the wall to keep from being trampled. Once the herd passed, I kept running in the direction from which they'd come. I found Zoey and Ambrosia standing off to the side, looking apprehensive.

I put on my Mom voice and said to Zoey, "Go to your room, lock the door, and stay safe. No arguing. If you don't do exactly as I say, you'll be grounded until Christmas."

She flapped one feathered arm half-heartedly. "I want to help. I can change into a fox and bite people."

I pointed down the tunnel behind me. "Room."

She ducked her head and pulled up her budgie hood. "You're probably right. I'll go to my room, if I can find it."

"Good girl," I said.

She started to slink off, sticking to the wall so that any stragglers from the stampede wouldn't knock her over. Ambrosia tried to follow along, but I grabbed her by the hand and tugged her back to me.

"I could use another witch," I said to the girl. "Even if that witch is a novice."

"She gets to go?" Zoey rushed back, and gave me a petulant look, but didn't argue further. Foxes had their place, but they were not witches.

The teen girls said goodbye to each other, and Zoey went off in search of her bedroom.

I cast some hurry-up sparkles her way.

Soon the hallway was empty, except for two witches.

We weren't alone for long.

A giant white snake slithered up to us. Ambrosia grabbed my hand and squeezed it, ready to cast a tandem spell.

"It's just Charlize," I assured her.

The snaked shifted back into her human form. She was still dressed as Perseus, in a white toga and decorative armor.

"I talked to Zoey on the way here," Charlize said. "Did you really banish her to her room?"

I wrung my hands. "I did. Why? Don't tell me I sent her directly into danger."

"Probably not. The upper floor is virtually unchanged," she said. "You did the right thing. You're a good parent." She looked around. "Where's Archer Caine?"

A door suddenly appeared in the stone wall next to us. The door opened, and out came Archer and Carrot, running. The door closed behind them, and the surrounding stone wall grew, sealing up the area.

"Zara, we have to get out and drive to the castle," Carrot said, breathing heavily. "Dawna is there at the ball, and Gavin, and so many others." She bit her lower lip. "We have to do something."

Archer, who'd lost his blue bald cap and was sporting wildly tousled white hair, said, "Let me at it. I don't care what it is. Send me in. I've got nothing to lose."

"Whatever it is, be assured I will gladly toss you directly into its gaping maw," I said to the deteriorating genie. "But we have to get there first."

Carrot asked, "What's the plan?"

I looked at Ambrosia, who was still holding my hand. She pulled her hand away and shrugged.

I held up one finger. "Just a minute." I cupped my hand around my mouth and yelled, "Ribbons?"

He answered calmly. "The threshold is still open, Zed."

Ambrosia, who must have been part of his telepathic broadcast, asked, "What is this threshold he's talking about?"

Carrot whipped her head back and forth, staring at us witches. "Threshold? What's going on? I'm so confused."

Charlize put her hand over Carrot's mouth and said, "Hold your tongue, mage, before I turn it to stone."

I kicked Charlize in her sandal-clad ankle. "Be nice," I said. "Do you see any more doors opening?"

"No," she said.

I pointed at each of us in turn. "It's just me, Ambrosia, you, Carrot, and Archer. I don't know what's about to happen, but clearly the five of us are going to pass through a threshold. Together. It's what the house wants, and the house is always right."

Charlize didn't look impressed. Nor did the others.

"Guys," I said. "We don't get to pick who stands beside us in battle."

"Of course we do," Charlize said. "It's always our friends. The ones who stand with us in battle are our friends."

"No," Archer said. "It is our former enemies, the ones we have defeated, who must fight at our sides. You know how it goes. You hate them, you fight them, most of them die, then the survivors see the error of their ways and join your side." He waved a blue hand casually, as though explaining something that should have been painfully simple to us, something we should have learned in the first grade. "Everyone wants to be on the winning team."

"Not everyone," Carrot said, "I always root for the underdog."

"Of course you do," Charlize said.

"Don't speak to her in that tone," Archer said.

The three began arguing over levels of power and mutual respect.

I looked around at the group. Were they my friends, or my former enemies, or both?

My gaze landed on Ambrosia. The young witch reached up and removed her red wig. She offered me a weak smile as she ruffled her wispy, bleached-blonde hair.

Both, I thought. Did it really matter? No relationship was ever completely static.

There was a flapping sound as Ribbons winged his way back to us. He hooked his feet on a wrought iron wall light, and swung lazily. "Why are you standing around, Zed?"

"Ribbons, tell me exactly what you meant by *the threshold*."

"The threshold for the castle, Zed." He made a throaty squawk for the others, then explained the rest of it to both of us witches. The threshold was a portal that would take us directly to Westwyrd, the site of Castle Wyvern. He really did use a wyvern flap, of sorts, to get around. We didn't need an exit from the house. We could use the house itself to travel to where we needed to be.

I turned to Charlize and explained it all. "Ribbons says that around that corner is the ballroom for Castle Wyvern. We don't need to get outside and pile into cars. We're already there."

She shook her finger at Ribbons. "I knew you were up to something! Portals? Really? Has your kind not created enough messes in this world?"

I grabbed her hand and lowered the finger. "He's helping us," I said.

"We'll discuss this later," she said to the wyvern.

Archer asked, "What are we waiting for?" He glanced back the way we'd come. "Should we wait for backup?"

"What backup?" Charlize asked. "The people here all ran off. The tough ones who like to fight are all up at the castle, which is apparently straight ahead."

The four of us, plus Ribbons, agreed that she had a good point.

Charlize turned back into a giant snake, and led the way.

The four of us walked down the hall after her. Ribbons flew for a bit, then landed on my shoulder.

After a few minutes, we passed over a floor tile that was transparent, like a window, but hazy. I looked down through it to see Boa, curled up in my basement on top of an open book. I looked up, hoping to see a similar viewing tunnel going to my daughter's room, but there was none.

We kept going.

The rock walls changed color and texture, from shades of brown to shades of gray.

The air, which had been warm and dry, turned cool and moist. The light fixtures were no longer conventional bulbs, but flickering flames.

Carrot said, "My stomach feels weird, like I'm in an elevator that goes sideways."

Archer said, "My sense of location is going haywire. Either I'm about to implode, or we are crossing an entire mile with every step we take."

Carrot took three long strides, then stopped. "It's not happening anymore." She patted her stomach.

"We're inside the castle now," Archer said. "I know this corridor." He pointed ahead. "The ballroom is through that door."

Nobody had to ask which door he meant. The tunnel was ending, and there was only one exit.

Charlize slithered ahead, then shifted back to human form as she stepped up to the door.

"There's no handle," Charlize said. "How can I open a door that has no handle?"

Carrot asked, "Is that a riddle? *What kind of door had no handle?*"

"It's no riddle that I know of," Archer said.

"That's weird," Charlize said. She was touching the door. "What kind of material is this? The surface is scaly."

Carrot asked, "Who would fill in a doorway with a scaly wall?"

The scaly wall rippled, then lifted, like a drawbridge. And then it came back down again, but further from the door, so we could see its shape.

It wasn't a door, or a wall. It was an enormous foot.

Carrot called it: "Godzilla."

"Not Godzilla," Charlize said, then she pronounced its true name. "Also known as a Pain-Body Demon."

Ambrosia grabbed my arm and hid behind me, whimpering. "Not again," she said.

It was the same type of beast that had destroyed my dining room eight days earlier. Except bigger. Way, way, way bigger.

I turned to Archer. "Well? You're the genie. How do we vanquish such an enormous Pain-Body? I got rid of one recently, but I'm a little short handed on supplies and witches at the moment, but even if I had the whole coven, I don't think we could handle one this big."

Archer gaped at me. "You know this entity?"

"One of them came through a hand mirror when we were casting a banishment spell. With Ambrosia's help, we battled it back through the portal, but only just barely. Also, if I'm being totally honest, it was mostly dumb luck. Our pebble turned into a boulder, which blocked its path, so it couldn't quite get its body all the way through to our dimension. We can give it a try with the same spell, but this one's really big. Like, ten times bigger."

Slowly, Archer said, "Zara, there is only one. You are at a disadvantage, because now it knows you. It knows your powers, and your limitations."

Ambrosia whimpered, "We're all going to die."

"I have an idea," Carrot said, waving her hands to get everyone's attention. She got mine, Archer's, and Ambrosia's, but not Charlize's.

The gorgon was standing just inside the ballroom, trying her best to turn the beast to stone. It wasn't working. Her powers were intense, but she was outmatched. The demon turned to see what was tickling its scales, knocking over a dozen screaming people with its enormous spiked tail.

"Go ahead," I told Carrot. "Charlize has her hands full. If you've got an idea, spill it."

"Everybody wants something," she said. "It's the basic rule of the universe."

"That's my girl," Archer said, smiling. "She really gets humans," he said to us.

Ambrosia asked, "What do you mean?"

Carrot said, "This Godzilla thing must be here because it wants something. Why don't we give it what it wants?"

"We could try," I said. "What do you figure a beast that big and ugly wants? Besides utter destruction and annihilation?"

Charlize came running back through the doorway as a scaly hand swiped the air behind her. The hand was too big to fit through the door.

Panting, she slid to a stop next to us. "What did I miss?"

Ambrosia said, "They're talking about rolling over and giving in to its demands." She looked at me. "It's too bad Fatima wasn't here. Maybe she could talk to it."

I looked down the hallway. "Where did you last see her?"

"She was in the coat check room, talking to the monkeys." Ambrosia frowned and looked at me. "You and I could try communicating with it. We could ask what it wants."

"Just like a couple of witches," Charlize said, rolling her eyes. "Typical of your type, wanting to get cuddly with cacodemons. I hear that's how all the interbreeding got started in the first place."

Archer snickered. "I have several interesting woodcut illustrations of such acts."

Carrot said, "My family has some of those, too."

"Hey!" I shot dirty looks all around. "Enough with the gossip. And enough with the slagging of whole groups of people. Haven't you ever heard of creative problem solving? Brainstorming?" I pointed to my temple. "A smart witch's magic starts up here."

"Ooh," said Ambrosia. "That's very wise."

"I can't take full credit," I said. "I learned that lesson from..." I drew a blank. "I learned it from my mentor. She's a redheaded woman, related to me. Why can't I think of her name?" I rubbed my head. "It feels blocked."

Charlize said, "I know exactly who you mean. She's exactly like you, but older. She has the best herbal teas in town. She can hold her tequila better than you—no offense. Her name is..."

"This is no time to joke around," Carrot said. "Don't you mean...?" She frowned and scratched her head, freeing sprigs of orange hair from her updo. "Why can't I say her name? I worked with her at City Hall. We worked side by side."

Ambrosia croaked, coughed, and said, "I can't say her name, either. Must be a spell. Dark magic."

"This is not a coincidence," I said.

Carrot clapped her hands. "That's it. We figured out what Godzilla wants. It must want that which we cannot name. It must want..."

Archer asked, "Are my ears imploding, or do you hear a new source of screaming?"

We stared at each other, all five of us waiting for something to happen. The inevitable. It was coming.

My black wig hair fluttered across my face. There was a breeze inside the tunnel. And Archer was right about the new scream. We'd been hearing a constant cacophony of howling and shrieking from the ballroom, but this one was different. It was coming from behind us.

We turned and looked.

A dark shape appeared in the distance. It grew closer.

It was a witch, dressed in stereotypical witch gear-pointy hat and everything, flying toward us. She was on a broomstick. Was that my broomstick?

Her face came into view.

The anti-naming spell broke. All together, the group of us said, "Zinnia Riddle."

It was her, all right. Red hair flying. Teeth bared. Battle face on.

She didn't slow down. She flew through us, knocking us down like bowling pins. She kept flying, ducking to get through the doorway, then soaring straight into the ballroom.

As I scrambled to my feet, I noted that Zinnia wasn't alone on the broomstick.

Hanging on tightly behind her were two others. They'd whizzed by quickly, so I couldn't be certain about the person seated in the middle, but by the look of the nearly-white hair, it might have been Mayor Paula Paladini. What was she doing here?

Riding on the back of the broom was the inventor of the Sucko Three Thousand, Mr. Barry Blackstone. He was the one who'd been screaming.

CHAPTER 33

Our motley crew of adventurers didn't have much of a plan, let alone a surplus of magic. Ambrosia and I were still at full power, but Charlize was already waning, thanks to her charge-in-blasting solo battle with the monster. And what was Carrot supposed to do as a rune mage? Give the demon bad tattoos until it agreed to go away?

Our odds didn't look great, and then Archer admitted to the group that he wouldn't be able to perform any of his genie magic.

"No time bending stuff?" I asked. "No freezing? Because that would be really helpful, right about now."

"I can barely start a fire with a box of matches," he said.

"You're plenty strong, and you can inspire us," Carrot said, taking his hand. "You always inspire me. You make me want to be a better mage."

He looked into her eyes adoringly. "That's impossible. You are already the *best* mage."

"Oh, Archer."

Charlize cleared her throat. "Are you two going to embarrass yourselves all night, or are you going to help the rest of us tag-team that thing in there and teach it some manners?"

Archer squared up his padded blue torso. "I'm ready. If I falter, remember what I told you."

"We know, brave soldier." I pushed him to go in first. "You're volunteer cannon fodder. When things get dicey, we'll throw your blue body into its mouth. Got it."

"Only if necessary," he called back over his shoulder. "Only if there's no other way!"

With our padded genie leading the charge, we entered the ballroom.

Funny how, after a month of lead-up, I wound up at the exact place I'd sworn I wouldn't go.

Just inside the doorway, Ambrosia helped me cast shielding magic around our adventure party. The spell wouldn't protect us from everything, but it could buy us some time.

We looked around.

The castle ballroom must have been breathtaking at the start of the party. The bloodied shreds of Halloween decorations that were still standing were very nice. And, when it came to either ballroom dancing or bloody supernatural carnage, you really couldn't beat a checkerboard dance floor.

The demon had its back to us—if you could call the rows of sharp-looking spiky things a "back."

The town's mayor, Paula Paladini, ran up to us, breathless. "It's about time you dragged yourself the rest of the way here," she wheezed. But was it really the mayor? This woman had the mayor's icy blonde and white hair, wore lipstick the color of dried blood, and was dressed in an impeccable black and white pinstriped pantsuit. But the mayor was taller than most men, and the woman before us was shorter than most women. Had something happened to the powerful time paladin?

Carrot stepped forward. "At your service, Mayor Paladini," she said bravely.

"Carrot, you ding-dong, it's me," the woman said impatiently. "I just flew past you, with Zinnia." She pushed off the wig to reveal her frizzy gray hair. It was Margaret Mills. I'd never noticed how much she resembled a squashed version of the mayor. Or that the mayor was a stretched-out version of Margaret.

Most of our group gasped.

Margaret tossed the ice-blonde wig aside. "I enjoyed being a blonde, but that thing was sweatier than a Hairy Spider Snatcher on a hot tin roof."

"Who is this?" Archer asked, sounding annoyed. "Am I supposed to know who this is?"

"It's Margaret Mills," Carrot said to her date. "You've met her at least three times."

I had been busy with other guests when Margaret and Barry had arrived at the party, so I didn't know she'd come dressed as what scared her the most. I also hadn't realized that the town's mayor was beating Cruella De Vil for that title.

Margaret looked from me to Ambrosia, then back again. "I see the loose cannon brought the other loose cannon," she said.

Ambrosia sniffed. "Nice to see you too, *Margaret*." She pronounced the witch's name in a way that made it sound even more old and unfashionable. Ambrosia often mocked people's names, which was ironic, considering Ambrosia's name was synonymous with that Cool Whip and marshmallow salad that non-classy people like me brought to potlucks.

Ignoring the young witch, Margaret said to me and Charlize, "Stay here. Keep a low profile, and be quiet until it's over. Zinnia and Barry have it handled."

Carrot asked, "Have what handled?"

"The PAKK-AKK-AKK-HER-BAUZH-OHH-SHISHCK—" Margaret thumped her chest with one fist and cleared her throat. "The Pain-Body Demon," she said, substituting the modern words.

So, it was the Pain-Body Demon. We'd already figured as much, but it was good to get confirmation.

Ambrosia asked, "Did you find out what it wants?"

"Of course," Margaret said. "Isn't it obvious?"

Behind her, people screamed as the monster rampaged through an abandoned band stand. Cymbals crashed. Microphone feedback squealed through an amplifier before the sound equipment was crushed under an enormous, Godzilla-like foot. Zinnia and Barry zipped around its car-sized head on the broomstick, magic flying everywhere.

"It's not obvious to all of us," I said to Margaret. "How about you explain it to us like we're all ding-dongs?" *Like how you explain everything.*

Margaret shrugged. "It wants the Shadow. That's what it was after the first time it showed up at your house, Zara. Thanks for not inviting me, by the way." She sniffed. "We think the Shadow came here in the first place to hide from it. Now we're going to get rid of both of them. Two for one."

Ambrosia, whose idea it had been, moments earlier, to give the demon what it wanted, gasped. "Not the little girl!"

Margaret ignored Ambrosia and continued telling us what was going on.

Barry, Margaret's genius inventor boyfriend, had determined, using various scientific instruments, that the entity he'd captured in the Devil Duster was acting as a magnet, attracting an interdimensional force. After consulting with Margaret and Zinnia, the three of them had whipped up a plan.

The ballroom at Castle Wyvern had the largest mirror around, so they had all visited the castle earlier that afternoon to prepare. They'd opened a portal, just a crack, and left several beacons running with a soul signature similar to that of the captured Shadow. They expected the Pain-Body to appear at midnight, and planned to safely evacuate the guests to another area of the castle well ahead of time, for safety.

What went wrong?

They forgot to account for the time change between dimensions, and the monster showed up early.

"Three hours early," Margaret said ruefully.

"Unfashionably early," I agreed. "But right on time, as far as it was concerned."

"Apparently," Margaret said. "And it caught us with our pants down, because the three of us had to drive all the way back into town to put in an appearance at *your* party, so you wouldn't get your nose out of joint like you always do."

"Are you saying this is my fault?" I waved in the direction of the screaming. "You're the ones who didn't account for interdimensional time changes."

"This wouldn't have happened if you'd been able to tone down your specialness and go to the Monster Mash like everyone else." She waved her pudgy hands. "This was the first year the witches were invited! The first year! You fed your invitation to your pets, and now this!"

Behind her, the Pain-Body Demon had stopped moving. Its enormous nostrils flared, and it sniffed in our direction. Margaret's sweaty, frizzy curls fluttered in the breeze, but she didn't seem to notice.

Ribbons, who'd been missing in action for several minutes—probably because he was so caught up in the violence—landed on my shoulder and touched my mind with his words. "Look, Zed. You have its attention now. It feeds on negative energy. Step back so it doesn't eat you when it devours the foul creature known as Margaret."

I thanked him psychically, then said to Margaret, "You might want to dial your witch down, honey. Word has it Godzilla over there eats up bad juju. Plus you don't want to jinx yourself and get your spells inverted."

She glanced over her shoulder, then back at me. "It's nice to have you here," she said through gritted teeth, almost smiling. "Tell me, Zara, do you have any of your usual keen insights... as regards our plan, as outlined previously?" She was trying so hard, she sounded like a lawyer.

The beast lost interest in us, and went back to nipping at the end of the flying broomstick.

"My keen insight?" I patted the side of my cheek and made bubble sounds. It helped me think, and it was a good warm-up for casting with the Witch Tongue. "I guess I'm wondering when this whole plan was hatched, and why I wasn't involved."

"It all happened today," Margaret said. "Barry stopped by City Hall right around lunch time. His machines had just given him the readings. You were probably working at the library." She looked at Carrot. "And you would have known, if you hadn't quit the Permits Department to doodle pictures on people."

Carrot pointed to the beast and said, "Be nice."

"The plan is simple," the frizzy-haired witch said, still smiling. "We open a portal all the way, using the big mirror, then we toss the Devil Duster through. That Godzilla thing will follow, chasing the Shadow. Then we seal the portal again."

"That could work," Archer said.

"It's going to work," Margaret said.

"But the Shadow," Ambrosia said, sounding vexed. "She's just a harmless little girl."

"That 'harmless little girl' was killing Zinnia," Margaret said. "Don't be such an OCW." She rolled her eyes, then said to me, "New witches can be so soft."

"Speaking of soft," I said. "Have you seen Detective Bentley? I'm not saying he's soft, but I guess I might be getting soft, since..." I trailed off, feeling like an OCW.

"He's dead," Margaret said.

Carrot gasped.

"Oops," Archer said. "Oh, well."

Margaret cackled, then said, "But he's no more dead than he was before, what with him being a creature of the grave."

"Not funny," I said. "You don't ever, ever tell another witch her boyfriend is dead. Not unless he is."

Margaret shrugged. "Join the club. We're both grave groupies. My boyfriend's dead, too. Well, half of him."

We all looked up at the two figures on the broomstick that was whizzing around the enormous beast.

I didn't say what we were all thinking. The rest of Barry Blackstone might be dead in a few minutes, if Zinnia didn't get the portal open soon.

I surveyed the chaos in the ballroom. There was a lot of blood. The red kind, and the black kind, and some colors I'd never seen before. There were DWM agents limping around, and all sorts of debris, but no dead bodies that I could see. Groups of people were huddled along the walls, building makeshift shields out of tables and chairs. I spotted Agent Knox, in his burly human form, moving furniture. Agent Rob was in bird form, flying alongside Zinnia and Barry.

"What about Persephone?" I asked Margaret. "Have you seen her? She might have shifted into a black fox."

"There's a black fox tending the wounded underneath the buffet table." Margaret took another look at the doorway behind us. "Hey, is that tunnel we all came through still open?"

It was.

Margaret asked Charlize, "Does the portal work both ways? Can we evacuate people from here, into Zara's house?"

"It should work," Charlize said. She looked at me. "Zara?"

"They might not be able to get out of my place right away, but there should be room."

Mindful of the monster's giant feet, we all started moving toward the huddled survivors, keeping to the walls where it was theoretically safer.

Archer called after us, "Someone should stay here, keeping the portal open." He was leaning against the doorway. "I volunteer."

I thought of a quip about him making a nice doorstop, but I bit my tongue. The poor guy could barely hold himself upright. He needed a door frame, or a wheelchair. He was fading fast, and all this stress couldn't be helping.

With Archer in the doorway, the rest of us started the task of evacuating people into the tunnel and back toward my house. They were a frightened and hysterical mess. While the DWM employed many tough agents, like Knox and Rob, the majority of their employees were clerical. These folks had never experienced battle, outside of typing up the reports.

A woman dressed as what I guessed was a cloud, grabbed my arm and thanked us for saving her life. She had purple goo spattered on her cheek, and a patch of something green in her teeth.

"You're welcome," I said. "When you get over there, try the samosas."

"Samosas?" She gave me a stunned, wide-eyed look, then shuffled, sheep-like, along with the group.

Charlize leaned over and said, "You need to work on your melee-side manner. Get it? Like how doctors have a bedside manner. Your *melee-side manner* could be better."

"Better how? Should I be more irreverent, or less?"

"One or the other. The middle ground is weird," she said. "Pick an extreme and stick to it."

"Maybe it's the word *samosas*. You don't hear it every day."

"Now I'm hungry," she said.

"You get hungry during a melee? I don't get hungry until a few hours after."

"It's the smell of blood," she said.

I gagged a little.

"Don't judge," she said.

"It's a reflex. I can't help it."

"You look like you're coughing up a hairball."

I gagged a second time as I remembered accidentally touching one of Boa's hairballs. With my bare finger. In the dark.

Charlize turned away and got back to directing people through the tunnel.

We had succeeded in getting most of the bystanders through the exit when some serious magic started happening in the ballroom. The air crackled with energy.

"She's doing it," Margaret said, then, "Go, Zinnia!" The short witch closed her eyes and held up both hands, palms facing the flying witch.

"It's happening," Carrot said, standing beside me. She looked up in awe, and removed her tiara for some reason.

Days later, I would still be thinking of what I'd seen: the image of Carrot Greyson removing her tiara. But I would have a difficult time picturing the rune mage with her tattoos.

Soon, everything would change.

CHAPTER 34

The showdown in the ballroom was happening, and my rag-tag crew and I had front row seats.

The portal that the monster had traveled in through seemed to be reopening.

Folks, for those of you playing along at home while doing laundry and kidding yourself that you can actually multitask, let's make a note that it was *not* the same portal that I'd traveled through from my house, but one leading to another dimension. Not a dimension I ever wanted to visit, not even if they offered cheap flights, non-stop margaritas, and white, sandy beaches. If I had to hazard a guess, I'd say the name of that dimension started with the letter H and rhymed with spell. And if they did have margaritas, they would be on fire, as would be the waiters, the beach chairs, and the white, sandy beaches bordering the pools of bubbling lava.

My aunt was still flying on her broomstick, and streaks of lightning passed from her fingertips, into the giant mirror at the end of the ballroom. As the spell took hold, the mirror sparkled, then rippled like the water on a lake.

The Pain-Demon turned to face the mirror, raising several of its spiky eyebrow ridges.

From his seat on the back of the broomstick, Barry Blackstone removed the dust cartridge from the Devil Duster, and heroically tossed the small metallic box at the mirror.

Unfortunately, Barry's arms were not nearly as strong as his heart was heroic.

The silver box fell short of the mirror. And not by a small distance. It fell short by approximately two-thirds of the length of the ballroom.

Everyone groaned.

The giant beast roared and began shuffling toward the box, the marble floors cracking under its enormous feet.

Ambrosia elbowed me. "The box is just sitting there," she hissed. "That's not part of the plan, is it?"

No. It was not part of the plan. We had a problem, but we also had an opportunity. Seeing Barry's heroism had inspired me. I wanted to pass it along, and inspire the plucky young witch.

"Now's your chance," I told Ambrosia. "Zinnia has her hands full. You can use your levitation to throw the cartridge through the mirror."

"Me?"

"Sure. I could do it myself, but it's about time someone else got to be the hero."

Carrot, who'd been listening, said, "Aww. You're a good mentor, Zara."

Archer hadn't heard, due to the thick white hair that was now growing from his ears, so Carrot explained to the ailing genie what was happening.

"No time like the present," Archer said to Ambrosia in a fatherly way that made my heart skip a little. He was a good dad. "What are you waiting for?"

We all turned to watch Ambrosia, who was breathing hard and sweating profusely.

The box couldn't have weighed more than a pound, but she was nervous, like a novice witch taking a major exam—which she sort of was. Margaret had stopped witch-pooling her powers with Zinnia, and was watching as well.

Ambrosia wiggled her nose, and got the box to rise up from the marble floor. It lifted a split second before the Pain-Body's enormous maw snapped the space where it had been.

Ambrosia levitated the box perfectly, weaving and bobbing it left and right, up and down, keeping it from the beast's enormous swinging paws. All five of them. Five paws? What kind of hideous monstrosity wasn't even symmetrical? This one, apparently.

Then, still wiggling her nose nervously, Ambrosia sailed the container through the rippling mirror.

The beast howled, then dove after the box. It was too large for the enormous mirror, so it had to compress itself to squeeze through. It got stuck halfway, its enormous butt dangling out. Or was that the butt? The whole thing looked like butt.

I held my breath.

It seemed way too large to fit through the ornately-framed portal, but then, just like me getting into a pair of Spanx, it managed to squeeze the flesh up, like its hindquarters were the last dollop of toothpaste in the tube.

There was a pop as it disappeared, and then a whoosh.

The mirror was going away too, being sucked through a vortex in the wall, along with the ornate mirror frame, three wall tapestries, and, finally, its wheels squealing in protest, one dessert cart.

Then all was quiet.

I heard the crunch of Zinnia's and Barry's shoes contacting the grit-covered floor as they stuck the landing.

My adventure party, along with a few of the braver guests who had stayed behind, cheered in victory.

Charlize ran over to the bare castle wall. She placed her hands on the stones and inspected the spot where everything had disappeared. Agents Rob and Knox joined her, along with Barry, who took readings with a small gadget.

Now that the action had toned down, I noticed Barry was wearing two different suits, joined along the center. *Cute costume*, I thought. *This is exactly why we need Halloween.*

Archer mumbled about staying where he was in the door frame to keep the domestic portal open, just in case.

Ribbons was hanging upside down high above us, swinging from the busted chandelier.

"Good job, Zed. Now get everyone out of the house so we can return home and roost."

I told him I'd do what I could, but first I had to check on my aunt.

Carrot was holding my hand, which was funny, because I didn't remember her grabbing it. I reached over and grabbed Margaret's hand, and the three of us ran toward Zinnia.

Zinnia was standing with her back to us, swaying. I couldn't have put my finger on anything specific, but something—no, everything—about her energy was wrong.

She's just tired from flying and opening the portal, I told myself.

"Uh-oh," Margaret said. "Zinnia, listen to me. Stiff knees! You are not a fainter!"

We reached Zinnia just in time to catch her as she collapsed.

Margaret tried to convince my aunt that she had not fainted. It did nothing to revive her.

Carrot cradled Zinnia's head with both hands as we eased her to the floor.

People were gathering around. I recognized a few faces, but not many. Most of my friends, including Frank and Kathy, had been at my house party, and were trapped back at my place.

Margaret blasted out a shockwave of magic with a wave of her arm. "Step back! Give her room to breathe!"

Step back, I thought distantly. *Give her room to breathe.*

How often had I heard that in a movie or TV show? Countless times. Zoey and I had a running joke, about how oxygen behaved differently in the event of an emergency. It was of utmost importance to get the crowd to step back whenever someone had suffered a life-threatening injury. And then, after the commercial break, when the camera was zoomed in close, the person would always gasp and recover, brought back from the brink of death by having room to breathe.

But this was my aunt who had fainted. My aunt, who, according to Margaret, did not faint.

This was happening, and there was no commercial break.

Zinnia wasn't just passed out. She had stopped breathing.

Precious seconds passed, and though the crowd backed up and gave her space, she didn't open her eyes and gasp for air.

I screamed for Ambrosia to get over there, or maybe I just screamed.

I placed my hands on Zinnia's waist, since Margaret had her head. The other witch and I made eye contact as we pooled our energy and began sending pulses of healing into our fallen friend.

After a moment, Carrot wailed, "It's not working. And something's happening to me."

I broke focus and looked at Carrot. She was right on both counts. Our healing energy wasn't flowing into Zinnia, and something was happening to Carrot.

All across the rune mage's chest and shoulders, where she'd once had tattoos of wild creatures and swirling flowers, there was nothing but pale, bare skin. Her tattoos were gone.

And then, faintly, there was a new tattoo.

An image of a redheaded woman.

"It's Zinnia," Margaret said.

The tattooed woman on Carrot's blank skin was moving. She walked from one shoulder to the other. She was pacing.

More details came into focus, manifesting as crisp lines on the tattoo artist's skin. Zinnia, the tattooed version, was in a hospital room.

Margaret started to pull away from Zinnia, but I barked at her to hang on. In my peripheral vision, I noticed that Ambrosia had come over, but she was standing by, unsure what to do. Then a fuzz passed over my surroundings.

I felt the deep resonance of powerful soul magic taking hold.

Something similar had happened to me once before, while I was also inside the castle. I'd been holding a dead girl, trying to heal her, but she was too far gone. What I *had* done was dive into her memories.

It was happening again.

I could have tried to explain it to Margaret and Carrot, but it would be simpler to show them. Keeping one of my hands in contact with Zinnia's limp body, I used the other to grab Carrot's arm. I slapped her hand down on my aunt's leg. With my eyes, I told Carrot to hold on and not let go. Her eyes told me she understood. We were in sync.

The redheaded woman on Carrot's skin continued to pace.

I inhaled the magic, and now it was breathing me.

Everything shifted onto its side, rolled, went upside down, and righted again.

The three of us—me, Carrot, and Margaret—had been holding Zinnia Riddle's limp body, and now we were not.

We were in a hospital room, standing by the wall, watching her as she paced. She didn't know we were there. She kept scratching the same spot on her neck, and the skin was raw and red.

A little boy lay in the hospital bed. "He's such a D to the B," the boy said.

"Language," Zinnia said.

"What?" He grinned impishly. "I didn't say the actual word."

"But I knew exactly what you meant."

"Only because he *is* one. You wouldn't know what I meant if he wasn't such a D to the B."

The two fell into an argument that must have been a regular one, given how easily the words came.

I watched, and I listened, and I even smelled the hospital perfume of decay and antiseptic.

I knew without being told that this was a memory, and it was Zinnia's. This scene in the hospital had taken place just over two years ago. The little boy was Aiden.

The three of us were witnesses, seeing the secret that Zinnia wouldn't talk about. The secret pain she was willing to die for.

The same one you already know about. Most of it, anyway.

CHAPTER 35

Zinnia Riddle

Three Years Ago

Halloween (Evening)

Aiden could have gone as anything he wanted for Halloween. He could have had his heart's desire custom sewn by a top tailor. Instead, he chose a cheap superhero costume from a dollar store.

It wasn't even a well-known hero from the DC or Marvel universe. The suit was made of thin, inexpensive fabric. There were red leggings, a purple shirt, and an orange cape. Instead of the standard mask, there was a single black eyepatch. Zinnia insisted on punching a viewing hole in the middle of the patch, for safety.

"Only pirates have solid eyepatches," she told Aiden, and he agreed. They were going Trick or Treating, and he couldn't have been happier.

Zinnia had offered to bring along a few of Aiden's friends from school, but he'd declined.

"Let's keep it simple this time," he said. "Just the two of us."

Zinnia and Aiden hiked several streets over to a neighborhood famous for its lit-up Halloween displays and high-quality treats. The residents gave out full-sized chocolate bars, along with toothbrushes, sample tubes of toothpaste, and miniature spools of dental floss. A number of dentists lived in the area.

The kids actually loved getting the dental stuff. Anything given freely from a front door was a treat, and all treats were good treats.

Aiden ran from house to house, and then he walked from house to house. Then, when his bag grew heavy and he began stumbling from exhaustion, he sat in the wheelchair and allowed himself to be rolled from house to house.

"Should we go home now?" Zinnia would ask.

"Not yet," he would say.

The lights on the houses began flicking off, and a few apologetic dentists explained that, sadly, they had run out of toothbrushes.

"We should head home now," Zinnia said. "Your father has probably dozed off in the den by now. I can sneak you in without him seeing all that candy."

"Not yet," Aiden said, craning his neck to peer up at her from the wheelchair. "One more house."

He had a dark circle under his non-eyepatched eye, and his voice was weak. Firecrackers went off nearby, and a dog barked.

"You're tired," she said.

"Please? Just one more."

"Just one more," she said, and began wheeling him to the corner.

"Zinnia?"

"Yes, Aiden?"

"Do you think I'm hard to love?"

"Not at all," she said, without hesitation.

He let out a long sigh, as if he'd been waiting to hear that for a long time.

She rolled him up to the last house, leaned over the wheelchair and rang the doorbell.

The door opened, and an elderly woman dressed as a fairy opened the door.

"Oh, my," she said. "And who are you supposed to be?"

Aiden didn't answer. He'd been giving a variety of responses to that question. The one that had elicited the best response had been Captain Obvious.

Zinnia rested her hand on his shoulder and said to the woman, "He's Captain Obvious."

"Never heard of him." The lady dropped a full-sized chocolate bar into the bag on Aiden's lap, then said to Zinnia, in a whisper, "Captain Obvious seems to have fallen asleep."

Aiden's head was slumped to the side.

"He's had a long day," Zinnia said. "I'll take him straight home to his secret hideaway."

The old woman frowned and stepped back into her home, crossing her heart with one hand before closing the door.

Zinnia wheeled Aiden all the way home in silence. The walk should have taken forty minutes, but later, when she tried to think back, she wouldn't be able to remember one minute, or a single thing she'd seen.

When they reached the brownstone, she circled around to the front of the wheelchair and kneeled.

"I'm not carrying you in on my shoulder," she said. "Come on. Wake up and walk yourself in."

He didn't stir. His expression was very relaxed.

"Aiden?"

She held his face in her hands. His cheeks were cool. His breath was gone. His pulse was gone. He was entirely gone, except for one thing: the small piece of herself she had given him.

It was a portion of her soul, and it was still there, still burning within him.

With Margaret's help earlier that month, she had ripped it from herself and given it to the boy, to bind him to her, and to life.

Zinnia's soul had been cleaved, and cleaved again.

The spell had worked. It had!

As she knelt before him, a tiny spark of light left his chest and floated toward her, heading home.

She grabbed the spark and pressed it against the boy's heart.

"No," she said. "I don't accept this. No."

Time stood still.

And then time shifted into a blur.

Zinnia Riddle was spared, this time, the slow unfurling of the memory.

She distantly viewed the attempt at CPR.

Screaming for help.

Mitchell running down the steps of the brownstone.

The paramedics.

The ambulances.

The long, awful, inevitable sequence of everything that happened next.

But she did walk more slowly through the memory when it was time to enter Aiden's empty bedroom.

She moved at half speed as she reached out, grasping for the note he had left for her, tucked into the book of wallpaper samples.

This one is my favorite, he had written.

Except Mitchell had been two steps ahead of Zinnia. He was always two steps ahead, no matter how many times she relived the night.

And Mitchell had ripped the note from the book in his grief, or his anger, or his desperation.

With the bookmark removed, Zinnia would never know which sample Aiden had chosen—only that it had been from somewhere in the middle, with the floral patterns.

From here, the memory shifted forward at high speed, like a montage.

Zinnia continued to live in the brownstone—if you could call it that—for ten sad months. She split her grief with Mitchell, and he split his with her, and together they doubled their grief. This wasn't how it was supposed to work.

She remembered moving out, and standing in front with her suitcase.

The time folded, like origami, and she was back where she had started. Moving in with Mitchell and his son.

Time folded forward, to another point, and it wasn't clear where she was.

Zinnia saw the familiar front door, but everything was so still and quiet, like a movie set.

She couldn't have been in the city. New York was never quiet.

Zinnia realized she wasn't alone.

Three people stood on the street. They were watching everything, witnessing.

It was her niece, Zara, and her friends, Carrot and Margaret. Zara had tears in her eyes. A cloud was swirling around Carrot, and the rune mage didn't have any tattoos. Margaret was looking down.

Zinnia still didn't know where she was, or when, but she found that she could speak.

"I shouldn't have taken him out that night," Zinnia said. "He wasn't fully recovered yet."

Margaret spoke first. "It wasn't your fault. I told you the spell was a long shot. He wasn't one of us, Zinnia. It was never meant to work. I only did the spell because you were right that we had to try."

"You did have to try," Zara chimed in. "I've seen everything, and I understand. As a mother, you had to try."

"But I'm not the boy's mother," Zinnia protested. "I'm not. I wasn't even his stepmother. I had no right."

The three witnesses exchanged looks.

"I could have tried more things," Zinnia said. "Other potions. Other rituals. I should have given him a larger piece of my soul."

"You gave enough," Margaret said. "You gave everything you could."

"But it didn't work." Zinnia's face screwed up with bitterness and anger. "Look."

Zinnia put her hands together, summoned her pain, and stretched it out as she pulled her hands apart.

The wheelchair was there, on the sidewalk, and the boy was in it, his head slumped to the side. The eyepatch was flipped up, on his forehead. Both of his eyes were closed.

Zinnia knelt before the boy and shook him. "Wake up, Aiden. It's not funny anymore!"

The three women walked over to Zinnia and gently pulled her away. She was too weak to stand, so they lowered her to the cold concrete, and knelt beside her.

She wished she could melt, like a witch in a storybook. She wished she could drain off the sidewalk and down into the gutter, and then trickle away.

Zara waved one hand, and the wheelchair and the boy turned to mist and evaporated.

"You've got to stop torturing yourself," Zara said.

Weakly, Zinnia said, "I don't have to do anything."

"This won't bring him back," Zara said. "None of this is doing you any good."

Carrot held Zinnia's face in her hands. "Bad things happen, Zinnia, but it's over now," she said. "You have to carry on living. You're not the one who died."

"That's not how it feels," Zinnia said. "I am the one who died. Part of me died."

"That's nonsense," Margaret said. "Stop feeling sorry for yourself. Not everything you plan in life works out. Sometimes you take a detour. I know this isn't where you wanted to wind up, but you did the best you could."

"You did the best you could," Zara agreed.

Carrot, who was still holding Zinnia's face, looked into her eyes and whispered, "You did the best you could." The white skin of Carrot's chest and shoulders blossomed with roses.

By the power of three, the spell was cast.

The sidewalk, and the brownstone, and all of New York dissolved.

CHAPTER 36

We came out of Zinnia's memories to the sound of sweeping—stiff bristles on a hard floor, and broken dishes tinkling.

Some of the castle's more dedicated staff had returned from my house, or wherever they'd been hiding, and were doing their best to clean up.

One man was asking another, "Have you seen Glen? Or Frances?"

"No. And we're still missing Norm and Kathleen."

"They probably ran off at the first sign of trouble. They're the smart ones. Not like us."

The two men laughed ruefully and continued sweeping.

I was distracted from their conversation by the giant red squid that was coming at me.

I completely forgot about Zinnia, who was still on the floor.

The squid was a woman in a costume, Dr. Aliyah Ankh. I knew her from the DWM. She'd patched up my father at least once, and was responsible for my undead mother's continued reign of terror.

Dr. Ankh pulled one of her long-fingered hands from the costume and offered me a vial of red liquid.

"Zirconia," she said, apparently mistaking me for my mother. The doctor with the lavender eyes, large mouth, and smooth face spoke with her lilting, sing-song voice. "I did not know you would be in attendance. I brought you some serum. Take it now, and you can help me revive the weak." She did a double take and gave me an astonished look. "You are not Zirconia."

"I am getting so much mileage out of this costume," I said. "I should dress as my mother every year from now on." I finally pulled off the black wig, letting my scalp breathe. "It's me. Zara Riddle. And this is Zirconia's younger sister, Zinnia."

Dr. Ankh looked down at my aunt, who was still limp on the floor.

"She is dying," Dr. Ankh said.

"Not anymore," I said. "We used soul magic to go into her memories. We gave her a classic pep talk, and now she's fine."

"She is dying," Dr. Ankh said again.

Margaret wailed, "Zinnia! Don't you dare die on me. Zinnia Riddle does not faint, and she does not *die*."

Carrot, whose exposed shoulders and arms were now blank, began to cry. Her tears splashed down on my aunt, who seemed to be breathing, but shallowly.

Dr. Ankh unzipped her squid costume and stepped out, wearing only her underwear. She lay the rubbery material on the floor and calmly instructed us to transfer Zinnia onto it, to keep her body warm and protect her from the cold marble tile.

We did so, and the doctor knelt to check my aunt's vitals.

"She will be dead within minutes," Dr. Ankh said. "There is very little time for me to save her. Which of you speaks for this woman?"

We glanced around. Did I speak for her? Did anyone? Zinnia was the sort of woman who spoke for herself.

Dr. Ankh still had the vial in her hands. She brought it to my aunt's lips and paused, looking around at our faces for an answer.

"I'll speak for Zinnia," Margaret said. "I'm her best friend. What's that potion?"

Dr. Ankh looked at me, and I understood that she wanted me to break the news to the others.

"It's the serum that vampires drink," I told them. "The elixir, or whatever."

Margaret said, "So, it's like a Red Bull for the undead?"

Nobody answered.

Dr. Ankh's smooth face remained expressionless, but I sensed the distaste in her silence.

Margaret asked, "If you give it to a witch, does it just give her energy, or does it turn her into one of them?"

"It could go either way," Dr. Ankh said. "If I administer the elixir now, she may live as she once was. If we wait, she... will live, but not as she was."

"She'll be a vampire," I said. "Like her sister."

We all looked down at Zinnia, then at each other.

"Decide now," Dr. Ankh said to Margaret. "Once the light of the soul is extinguished, ATP production halts, and everything changes." She cast her otherworldly lavender eyes down. "It may already be too late."

Zinnia had all but stopped breathing.

Carrot said, "Zinnia wouldn't like being a vampire."

Margaret scoffed at Carrot. "You think she'd prefer being dead?" Margaret turned to the doctor. "Do it," she said. "If Zinnia gets mad when she comes to, I'll take the heat. She always blames me for everything, anyway."

Dr. Ankh popped the cork off the vial and brought it closer to my aunt's lips, which were turning gray.

I grabbed the doctor's arm. "Wait."

A droplet spilled and landed on Zinnia's cheek.

The doctor hissed at me, like a cat. "You are wassssting it."

My head was buzzing, like it was full of invisible bees.

"Wait," I said again. "You said that she dies when the light of her soul goes out, right?"

The doctor blinked at me. "It is an oversimplification, but yes."

I reached over and grabbed Margaret's hand. "We need to reopen that portal," I said.

"You're crazy," she said.

I gave her a serious look. "It's what we need to do."

Carrot said, "But then that monster is going to come back! We just got rid of it!"

"That's a risk we need to take," I said. "We have to get the rest of Zinnia's soul back. She's dying because we sliced her soul in two when Ambrosia tossed the box through that portal."

I glanced up to see Ambrosia's expression turn from confusion to horror, then back to confusion, then briefly joyful, then horrified again.

She locked eyes with me, and I was certain that she knew what was happening. It was possible she understood it even better than I did. I still had the buzzing in my head, and my heart was pounding with terror over losing my aunt. I thought I finally understood the Shadow, but I'd guessed at the puzzle multiple times already, and I'd been wrong. Was I finally right, or had I lost all perspective?

I nodded for her to go ahead and explain it to the others.

Speaking carefully, Ambrosia said, "The little wallflower girl who was following Zinnia everywhere wasn't a ghost, or a ghoul, or anything from another world." Ambrosia paused, making sure we were all paying attention and not talking over each other.

We were listening. Even the sweeping and cleanup had stopped. All was still. You could have heard a spider walking.

Ambrosia said, "The Shadow was a part of Zinnia's soul. The part she gave to the little boy, to bind him. It

302

was the piece of herself that she refused to accept back after he..." Her eyes were shining.

Margaret and Carrot said, in chorus, "Ahh. That explains everything." Then, still in tandem, "Thank you, Ambrosia."

I felt a smidge of relief. Her theory matched mine. We might both be wrong, but this time the answer felt more right than ever. Everything fit: Dorian Dabrowski describing the little girl as lost, trying to find her way home; the entity's blurred identity but familiar expressions; how she grew when Zinnia shrank; the name, Aiden, being written on the mirror; the fact it seemed to be triggered by Halloween; and how Zinnia's unwillingness to be whole again was attracting dark forces that ate negativity.

What didn't make sense was my aunt choosing to harm herself, day in and day out. But, then again, regular people who weren't witches did that all the time. They took poisons that hurt them, in order to not feel emotions they couldn't live with. Being supernatural hadn't saved my aunt from being human.

Everyone was still quiet around our circle.

I pulled myself from my buzzing thoughts and gave Ambrosia a wary look. "How did you know, anyway? You weren't in Zinnia's memories with us."

The teen witch ruffled her bleached-blonde hair and gave us a wild-eyed, bewildered, almost guilty look. "I was there, standing right behind you three," she said. "I was dressed as a nurse at the hospital, and then—"

Dr. Ankh interrupted. "She is nearly dead. Whatever you wish to do, do it quickly."

There were more questions.

Hadn't the Pain-Body presumably eaten the canister containing the portion of Zinnia's soul?

Would Zinnia actually mind being a vampire, if it came down to it?

How were we supposed to open a portal when the mirror had disappeared with the last one?

We got to work. Quickly.

It turned out the lack of a mirror was the least of our problems.

We found a silver serving platter, and affixed it to the wall where the mirror had been, using a steadfast spell.

Margaret, Ambrosia, and I joined hands, and we cast the spell to open the portal. We rolled the spell over to reverse its previous actions. It was a complicated bit of magic, what with all the inverting of entropy, but there was more than enough bad juju floating around from the melee to make it work.

We got the first sign the portal was functional. The shimmering surface of the platter rippled, and then a spray of pastries came flying out.

Next was the dessert cart. It couldn't come through in one piece, because it was larger than the platter, so it dismantled itself and came through in pieces, like an IKEA purchase.

Next came three tapestries, rolled.

And then a stunned-looking waiter, whom I hadn't noticed going through the first time. He had narrow shoulders and a slim build, luckily for him.

Next came one enormous monster foot. Then the portal plugged with flesh.

We three witches cackled. "It's too narrow for you," we said, taunting it.

The lumpy beast struggled to push through anyway.

We cackled again, which seemed to be a side effect of sharing a psychic connection and working as one.

Our unspoken plan was to make the demon cough up the cube on the other side, yank it through, then shut down the connection. We'd smash open the box, put Zinnia's soul back into Zinnia, and then hugs and hot cocoa would be shared all around.

Easy peasy, lemon squeezy.

Except the monster was not having any of this.

The big pile of rotten carcass finally shoved its foot through the platter, and the rest followed.

I felt Ambrosia falter. Her energy wavered, and her fear rose up until I could taste it in the back of my throat.

Margaret sensed it, and growled in frustration.

I went the exact opposite direction, like what Zinnia had done with Aiden when the boy antagonized his father.

I wrapped Ambrosia in love.

Her fear dissipated. As the love spread around, even Margaret's energy changed, becoming more malleable.

The demon roared toward us, but we didn't even bat an eyelash.

We had no potions or powders, but we had three witches in good working order, and three witches in good working order could do pretty much anything, even if one of them was Margaret Mills.

The rest went better than anyone could have hoped. Perhaps it was because the time was exactly midnight on All Hallow's Eve. I'm not saying that was it, because that would make me a superstitious ninny, but I'm not saying it *wasn't* the date and time.

For our opening gambit, we cast an inebriation spell—Ambrosia's specialty—on the beast.

It drunkenly stumbled around.

Then we cast Silvester Syroppe's Ipecaccus spell. It worked on Boa's furballs, but would it work on a Pain-Body?

The beast heaved forward, bending what might have been the knees or elbows of its many paws.

It made the HERK-HERK sound, like a cat bringing up a hairball, only a million times worse.

Then it released the metal cartridge, along with five more Castle Wyvern staff, miraculously still alive.

The staff, in their panic, began clumsily stumbling around, kicking the slime-covered metal box.

Someone—it was hard to say which of us witches did which spell when we were joined like this—cast an invisible umbrella inside the box, then opened the umbrella.

The box popped open, and a spark of light emerged.

The light turned into a little girl, who ran toward us, then slid into Zinnia like a baseball player taking home base.

Meanwhile, over by the platter portal, the beast drunkenly stumbled around, still vomiting. Its belly was empty, and all it brought up was more slimy ectoplasm.

We cackled quietly and waited for our opportunity. When it staggered toward the portal, we hit it with a triple dose of the spell for reducing the size of a boil on a witch's nose.

It shrunk, exactly as we'd hoped it would.

Then we hit it with our favorite spell, the one that mimicked being nipped by a toothy animal.

The smaller Pain-Body yelped, and jumped through the mirror. Swish. It didn't even touch the sides.

Our trio broke contact.

Sweating and breathing heavily, we raised our fists in the air triumphantly.

The portal closed, and the platter clattered to the floor.

There was no applause this time. The castle's doors had opened, and all the staff, including the slimy ones, had wisely left, abandoning their brooms and dustpans.

The first to speak was Dr. Ankh. "Oh, well," she said, sounding disappointed. She stuffed the cork back into her vial of vampire elixir.

Zinnia, who was lying on a rubbery red squid costume, dressed in a cheap witch costume, moaned. Her eyes fluttered open. We helped her to sit up.

She gestured to her throat, like someone asking for a glass of water.

Dr. Ankh handed her the vial, looking hopeful.

Zinnia, who was smarter than the average witch even at her worst, waved the vial away.

Someone dashing and handsome gave her a plastic bottle of water. It was my vampire boyfriend, Bentley. He gave me a knowing wink, then backed away two steps before becoming a blur.

Zinnia sipped the water.

All of us exchanged cautious looks. I snuck a questioning look at Margaret. I thought I understood what had just happened, but magic could be so complicated. If Aiden had died two years ago, and Zinnia had refused to take back that portion of her soul the whole time, why had things only gotten so bad now?

Margaret seemed to understand exactly what I was asking. She glanced up meaningfully at a tattered shred of Halloween banner. Zinnia must have been triggered by the time of year. She might have squeezed through the month of October last year, but this year it could have hit her harder for other reasons. Maybe Zoey and I were part of those reasons.

Margaret blinked calmly, and I had a thought that might have come from her: *Some poisons are slow acting.*

Meanwhile, Zinnia continued to sip her water, and calmly looked around at all of us.

"Thank you," she said, nodding in turn at Margaret, Dr. Ankh, Carrot, and Ambrosia.

Then she looked at me, and said nothing.

I felt the pain in her silence. The two of us had grown so close, yet she'd kept her past hidden from me. And it had put all of our lives at risk.

What was a person supposed to say? How could you get past a buried secret like that? Did you just box it up and leave it in a corner, about as settled as it was going to get?

I didn't know if she should apologize for not telling me about her past, or if I should apologize for barging into her memories without permission just now. I felt guilty for how I'd been the past few months, and for apparently not giving her enough support for her to open up and talk to me about it. Did she have rigid boundaries, or was I not a sympathetic soul?

I was angry that she hadn't even tried.

And then I felt lousy for being angry. She had lost a child. She might not have given birth to Aiden, but he had belonged to her as much as she belonged to me.

Where would we go next? What could I say?

Zara tries to be a good witch, but it's hard to know what good is.

The moment stretched out, and Zinnia didn't speak, but her expression softened, and, finally, she exhaled, as though she'd been waiting for this moment a long time.

I spoke, because someone had to.

"Good to have you back," I said.

The others murmured in agreement.

"Your wig," she said, worry lines creasing her forehead. "Why did you take it off? You looked so perfect, Zara, and I didn't even get one picture."

"It's around here somewhere." I cast my object retrieval spell, and the black wig came flying to my hand.

Carrot must not have realized what was happening with my spell, and the wig. All she saw was a hairy black thing coming at her. She screamed and threw her tiara at it.

It was the perfect end to the night.

Did we laugh at Carrot? Did we mock our dear friend who'd just risked her life and her sanity, not to mention all her tattoos, to help save one of us? Of course we did.

CHAPTER 37

Tuesday

The Day after Halloween

Carrot Greyson opened the door of her apartment, which was an attic space above her tattoo studio.

She looked nervous and hopeful, her cheeks flushing as she tugged at the collar of her cream-colored turtleneck sweater.

"Carrot," I said. "I barely recognized you without your tattoos." She still had her bright orange hair and cute but buggy blue eyes, so I'd had zero problem recognizing her, but it seemed like the nice thing to say.

"Still a blank slate," she said. "I feel so naked." She pinched the thick, cable-knit fabric at her throat.

"You don't look naked."

"Thanks, Zara. You always know what to say. You and Zinnia are too good to me." Tears gathered at the edges of her eyes.

I placed a comforting hand on her shoulder. "No crying. This plan of ours is going to work."

She blinked away the tears, lifted her chin bravely, then helped me bring in the bags of supplies I'd brought.

Some of the bags contained snacks that hadn't been opened at the previous night's Halloween party. The other bags contained the supplies for the soul cleaving I was there to perform.

Carrot and I set up everything I would need in the living room, then she went to get Archer, who'd been resting in bed.

When she brought him out, my heart dropped. He looked terrible. Were we too late?

What good would it do, ripping off a piece of my soul to weave Archer Caine and his cloned body into this world, if he had to live as a walking skeleton?

Archer seemed to read my thoughts. "If it goes wrong, promise you'll put me out of my misery quickly." He mimed cutting his scrawny neck.

"It's going to work," I said, sounding braver than I felt. "I could have been here earlier, but the ingredients are deceptively complicated, like when you buy a box of cake mix and think you have everything for a cake, but then you need all sorts of extra things like oil, and eggs, and butter, which means the cake mix isn't much of a mix, right? Just flour and sugar, plus a cardboard box you have to recycle."

Archer and Carrot stared at me blankly. Had they never made a cake from a mix? It was a perfect analogy, wasted on them.

"Once you have the ingredients, the soul cleaving spell is easy," I said. "I already did it once with Barry, back when he was still Bill and Harry. I didn't know how hard it was to source the combustibles, since Margaret took care of it at the time."

More blank stares. They looked like a broke couple of twenty-somethings trying to get a mortgage. Or like me, when I'd tried to get a mortgage, before my father pulled the right strings.

"The spell itself is simple," I said. "A novice could do it, once she knew how."

"We trust you," Carrot said.

"I've got nothing left to lose," Archer said. "Which is the same."

"It's not," Carrot said to him. To me, she said, "I trust you, even if he doesn't."

Archer waved one skeletal, liver-spotted hand. "Sure. Me, too."

"And here is the last item," I said as I pulled a jar of eyeballs from my purse, and placed them on the coffee table. "The hardest part was picking the magical lock on my aunt's fridge so I could get these."

Carrot asked, "Those are for the spell?"

"Or for snacking," I said.

Archer laughed weakly.

Carrot pressed her lips together and turned a little green.

"They're for the spell," I assured her. "There are a lot of clauses in the spell about eyewitnesses, and this, my friends, is a jar of eyewitnesses."

"I've got to admire your kind," Archer said. "You really know how to bend the rules to get things done."

"Thank you."

We lit the candles.

I cast the spell, reaching inside myself to pull out a piece of soul, which I then transferred, before the eyewitnesses, into Archer's frail body. Thanks to my previous experience, putting brother into brother to make Barry, it was a snap, even without assistance.

I could tell by their expressions that I was making it look easy.

What Carrot and Archer didn't know was that I'd been sitting in my car in front of the house for the last half hour, trying to talk myself out of this. Giving up a piece of one's soul was strongly warned against in every book that begrudgingly admitted the act was possible.

I'd seen first-hand the potential pitfalls. Barry had been a success, but Barry wasn't Bill, and he wasn't Harry. My aunt had nearly died.

Hardly any time passed after the casting before I could tell the spell had worked.

Carrot squealed with joy, and Archer Caine's body filled out before our eyes. He gained volume and mass quickly, until he resembled his Halloween costume, minus the blue paint and the bald cap.

I leaned back on Carrot's red leather sofa, and let the feelings wash over me and settle. A new reality took shape. A new future opened before us, like a portal tunnel that hadn't been there before. Archer would live. He would not outlive me, but he would be around a while, and he would be a father to our daughter.

A trace of fear lingered in my heart, unspoken.

Giving part of myself to another made me vulnerable, because it gave power to the other. As Archer got stronger, I might become weaker—at least according to some texts.

That made sense. A person could donate a kidney and still live, but they didn't grow a replacement kidney.

On the other hand, some books said the soul donor could recover.

That made sense, too. A person could donate life-saving blood, or part of a liver, and those things would regenerate.

The tie-breaker for me had been one obscure reference in an even more obscure magical tome: *The cleaving of the soul is both the poison and the cure, the darkness and the light; the gift is selfless, and thus can do no harm.*

I chose to believe that text.

I chose to have faith.

I chose to give Archer a piece of my soul, to do with as he wished. Together, he and I had once created a new soul from ours, and she had turned out great.

Plus saving Archer seemed like the right thing to do, and I did always try to be a good witch.

CHAPTER 38

Saturday

5 Days after Halloween

"Chin up, chin up," said the hot-yoga instructor. "I want to see your hearts shining up, and your radiant souls glowing!"

I blew air at Charlize to get her attention, then whispered, "Does she always talk this much about souls?" I'd heard Riverflow, the rubber-limbed yoga instructor, drop the word *souls* into her patter a half dozen times. She may have been referring to s-o-l-e-s, as in the soles of our feet, a few times, but even so, the constant use of the word, or its homophone, was bothering me.

Charlize replied, "Why? Are you feeling sensitive about something, you soulless redhead?"

We moved into the next pose. I was getting to know the routine and the sequence of the asanas, and I could do the triangle one without my sweaty foot slipping out from under me. Charlize always did an extra Cobra pose in between the other poses. Show-off.

"Do you think she knows?" I nodded in the direction of our instructor. "People in this community gossip a lot."

I wasn't just making chit chat to take my mind off the heat or the poses. I really did wonder if Riverflow kept using the word *soul* because she was looking at my shiny silver butt, and thinking about how I'd given up a chunk of my soul to keep a genie alive.

"There's a simple explanation," Charlize said. "Animal minds run on pattern recognition software." Sweat trickled down the bridge of her nose and dripped onto the yoga mat.

"Are you saying I'm doing things that give away my lack of a full soul? That she's spotted me, somehow?"

"I'm saying you're seeing connections that aren't real. You know what this reminds me of? When I bought my car, I thought I was the only person in town with a Beetle. I thought I was *so* unique. But then, I started seeing them everywhere. Even people I knew were driving Beetles. The seamstress who does my alterations drives the same color and model as Bugsy. I never even noticed. And do you know what she named her car?"

"Bugsy?"

"No. She named it George." Charlize stuck out her tongue at me while her hair snakes snickered. "I may be a clueless blonde, but I'm not *that* clueless."

"You're anything but clueless." I blinked rapidly to clear my eyes of stinging sweat. "But I know exactly what you mean. It's the Baader-Meinhof phenomenon. It's a frequency illusion, or recency illusion. I like to call it the Red Car Phenomenon."

"But my car is white." She faked a silent laugh.

Riverflow walked up to our mats. "Ladies," she said. "If you have time to chat and giggle, you're not working hard enough. Can't you be more like my star students?"

She waved at the couple near the front of the class, Carrot and Archer.

Carrot—her pale skin still a blank slate—was wobbly in her pose, but had a look of serene commitment on her face.

Archer looked even more serene. After receiving part of my soul, the genie's recovery had been rapid, but not instant, or complete. His dark hair was streaked with white, and the healthy periorbital fat hadn't returned to his eyes, but it had only been four days since the transfer. He seemed to be in good spirits. Who wouldn't be, with a little bit of me inside them?

Over on his blue yoga mat, Archer was doing yoga like he'd invented it.

For all I knew, he had.

* * *

After yoga, and the cold dip in the creek, then a bit of hot tub time, Charlize drove us back into town. Archer and Carrot were traveling in Carrot's car, so the gorgon and I were alone.

"What's next on the agenda?" I asked.

Charlize didn't answer. We'd entered town, and she was distracted by a person walking on the sidewalk. She slowed the car and followed the person.

"That's Karen," she said. Her snakes began seething and snapping at each other.

"Uh oh," I said. "Karen, as in, the sheep shifter who works in payroll? The one who always has salad in her teeth?"

"That's the one."

"Karen who kept objecting to all your costumes by going to NHR? Allegedly?"

"It was her, obviously. I ran it through an algorithm, and hers was the only name that kept popping up."

On the sidewalk, Karen the sheep shifter noticed a vehicle was following her, and sped up her pace.

Charlize increased our speed.

"So, we're stalking Karen now?" I asked. "Is that how you want to spend your afternoon?"

Charlize hit the horn. The beep, cute as it was coming from the Beetle, made Karen startle, and then break out in a run.

"All right. That's enough," I said. Using magic, I killed Bugsy's engine, brought the car safely to a halt, and affixed the gorgon's hands to the steering wheel.

While Charlize howled in protest and threatened to turn me into petrified witch jerky, I jumped out of the car and ran to catch up with Karen.

"I come in peace," I called out. "My word is my bond!"

Karen came to a stop and turned around. She clutched her purse to her side and slowly reached into it.

"I just want to talk to you for a minute," I said. Her face jogged my memory. "Hey, didn't I see you at Castle Wyvern? During the evacuation? I told you to enjoy the samosas, and you looked at me like—"

I didn't get to finish.

She shot me with the DWM cocoon blaster.

I fell to the sidewalk, my arms trapped against my sides by the white webbing. It really was an effective immobilizer! I was relieved to note that the Research and Development people at the DWM had improved on the weapon. The cocoon I was in had breathing holes. The holes didn't match up perfectly with my nose and mouth, but the accuracy wasn't bad.

It wasn't designed to hold witches, though. Getting free was simple enough. I could have used any number of spells, but I settled on the veggie-slicing technique. It worked perfectly. I cut the cocoon in a spiral fashion, because I had a plan for it.

I stepped out of the white threads, summoned a blue bird made of light, and flung it at the woman.

She shrieked, and then she bleated. Karen had shifted into her sheep form, thanks to the blue bird, which had been a spell.

Next, I caught Karen the Sheep, cowgirl style, by tossing a lasso fashioned from the spiralized cocoon.

"Sorry," I said, running up to the hog-tied sheep. "I know it's extremely rude to force a shift, let alone hog-tie someone, but you did shoot first."

"Baaah," she said.

"Karen, I just want to talk to you for a minute. Change back."

"Baah."

I untied her legs. She got to her hooves and stared at me with her big sheep eyes. I remembered the costume she'd been wearing at the Monster Mash. I'd thought it was supposed to be a cloud, but she must have been a sheep. Simple, but inoffensive.

"What's wrong?" I asked. "You can't change back when you're nervous?"

"Baah." She shook her head.

"I totally understand. I have a family member who's the same way. Do your clothes sometimes come back on inside out?"

"Baah." The sheep nodded

Charlize ran up and joined us. She was holding a steering wheel.

"Zara," she gasped, eyes wide. "What did you do to Karen from Payroll?"

"Me? You started it."

Charlize pointed at the sheep. "She started it. She's the one who kept blocking all my costumes with NHR."

"Baah." The sheep scraped the sidewalk with one cloven hoof. She seemed to be angry.

"Don't you play dumb with me," Charlize said. "I know it was you. Who else would object to Little Bo Peep?"

"BAAAH!" The sheep began stamping angrily. She was noisier than Margaret Mills.

Charlize started yelling, and the sheep kept making sheep sounds.

"Calm down, both of you," I said, stepping between them. We were still on a town sidewalk, in broad daylight.

They dialed it down to dirty looks.

"Enough is enough," I said. "Unless either of you has anywhere you need to be right this minute, we're going to sort this out. We're going to have a civilized conversation about our issues. Like mature adults."

"I will if she will," Charlize said.

"Baah."

Charlize crossed her arms. "I don't have anywhere I need to be."

"Baah."

"Then it's settled." I checked that nobody was looking, summoned my purse from the car, then began removing the strap.

* * *

It took three walks around the nearby park before Karen was relaxed enough to shift back into human form.

Karen had straight, brown hair, and she looked like someone who you'd trust to pick up your mail and look after your cat if you went out of town.

She removed the pink leather strap of my purse from around her neck. We'd been using it as a collar, so people walking their dogs wouldn't object to our pet being off leash.

She handed me the strap and said, "Thank you."

She had something green in her teeth.

"Karen." I bared my teeth and scratched them with my fingernail.

Karen sighed. "Did it happen again?" She picked out the bit of green. "I was eating a spinach salad the first time I changed, and now *that* happens all the time, whether I've shifted or not." She flicked the green onto the grass. "I understand that magic has a mind of its own, and that we have to accept these things without questioning them, but what I can't understand is why anyone would complain to NHR about me dressing up as a spinach salad for the costume ball."

Charlize said, "Maybe they only objected to your salad costume to get back at you for objecting to *their* costume."

"But I never objected to anyone's," Karen said.

"Me, neither," Charlize said. "Not even to yours. I swear."

"It's so strange," Karen said. "Out of all the people at work that I'm friendly with, not a single one of them said they'd objected to anyone else's costumes."

"None of my friends did, either."

"So strange," Karen said.

"So strange," Charlize agreed.

"Ladies," I said. "How big is your NHR department?"

"Just one person," Charlize said.

"One very uptight person," Karen said. "One time I held the elevator door for that person, and I didn't hear the end of it for days. You can't win with some people."

"You think that's bad?" Charlize's hair snakes spat and hissed. "One time that person and I wore the same belt, and I mentioned, in a casual and friendly way, that they wore it better. Can you believe I got an official letter of warning for my misconduct?"

"You don't think..." Karen covered her mouth with her hand.

"Oh, I *do* think," Charlize said.

I cut in. "Are you two saying that this whole ordeal with the costumes, and the sensitivity issues, was the work of one person? The one person who's supposed to be fostering harmony in the workplace?"

Charlize snorted. "Except for the harmony part, you may be onto something."

Karen explained, "Harmony is not part of our corporate culture."

I dusted imaginary dust from my hands. "Well, my job here is done. I'm glad we got to the bottom of another mystery."

"It was NHR all along," Karen mused. "The Pinkwyrm Proxy Mimic is out of the bag now."

"Let the beheadings commence," Charlize said. "You know, we could see justice as early as Monday."

Karen smiled. "There's nothing quite like a public beheading to get the work week started."

Charlize turned to me and explained, "Where we work, dismemberment tends to boost morale."

The two looked at each other and giggled.

I decided they were joking, and that I was in on the joke.

Then Karen's spinach spontaneously reappeared on her teeth, which only made them laugh more.

CHAPTER 39

Sunday

6 Days After Halloween

The first Sunday in November, we would not be hosting our largest dinner party ever, but Zoey and I put the extender leaf in the table anyway. There were a few reasons.

Firstly, it gave everyone a little more elbow room, paw room, and wing room.

Secondly, I'd restocked the house with candles, and the larger table would allow me to put out samples of each kind.

Thirdly, we'd never had a table that was so long, and were excited to try it. Back before the accidental demon summoning that destroyed the table we had, we'd used pop-up card tables as mismatched extensions. The old table only fit seven people comfortably, even with the leaf. People used to complain about sitting at "the kids' table," even though the card tables were only an inch shorter.

Our new-to-us table came from Mia's Kit and Kaboodle. It was labeled in the store as being "possibly very old, maybe teak?" The price was right. I bought the table, booked a delivery, and promised Mia I would let her know if I happened to find out anything about the table's composition or history.

Once we had our new-to-us, possibly-very-old, maybe-teak table set for our guests, Zoey reminded me I'd been planning to do a spell on it.

I retrieved what appeared to be a tube of lipstick from the bathroom. The lipstick itself, a ravishing shade of red, had been eaten by invisible spiders, but I'd kept the tube, because it contained a magic powder.

With Zoey watching, I pulled up a corner of the tablecloth and sprinkled the powder on the table. She'd seen me do this once before, on a knife with a curved blade.

I didn't need to cast a spell, as it was already "baked in," so to speak. The powder's magic had weakened with the passage of time, but it seemed to be working, as it gave off the scent of ozone.

Zoey asked excitedly, "Do you think it's from an old castle?"

"Or an old tavern," I said. "Look at all the dents and scratches. These must be from years of being banged by heavy pewter cups full of ale."

"I wonder if Archer would recognize it from the old days." Zoey referred to her father as Archer most of the time, or even Mr. Caine. She only referred to him as Dad when she was trying to play us off each other.

"Hang on," I said. The ozone smell became stronger. "Here comes the answer."

The results came as words spoken softly in my head.

Without parsing the words, I relayed them to Zoey. "One table with extension. Composition: distressed hardwood, poplar veneers, and medium-density fiber board. Common name: Benchwright Extending Dining Table, Rustic Mahogany. Origin: Pottery Barn."

Zoey looked down at the table, then underneath it at the metal support rods, then back at me.

"*We* are a couple of ding-dongs," she said.

"The lighting in the furniture section at Mia's is terrible," I said. "We could barely see it."

"Pottery Barn," she said, rubbing her chin. "How old do you think it is, really?"

I sniffed the residue of the powder. "It rolled off the assembly line two years ago."

"We tell *nobody*," she said, waving both hands emphatically. "Nobody can know."

She was right. Nobody could know we were a couple of ding-dongs who actually thought a thrift shop table might be a priceless antique from a castle or a tavern.

In a normal city, I never would have jumped to that conclusion. But, in fairness to us, Wisteria was a unique town. Ancient artifacts did show up, all the time. The DWM had an entire department that regularly checked local garage sales—what a great job! Even so, Zoey was entirely correct. Nobody needed to know.

* * *

The first to arrive for dinner was Ambrosia Abernathy. She came in her usual vehicle, an old hearse. She always parked around the corner instead of in front of the house, but everyone in the neighborhood assumed she was connected to the legendary Red Witch House anyway.

People had been talking about my house more than ever, thanks to all the mysterious traffic I'd had coming and going on Halloween.

The local kids raved about the Trick or Treat candy, which was delicious, and made by a company nobody had ever heard of. I didn't know the origins of the candy. A Forest Folk person had provided it to me, free of charge—unlike the services of the coat check monkeys. When asked, I told people that a family member had brought the candy back with them "from Europe." Passing things off as being "from Europe" worked almost as well as a bluffing spell.

Inside my doorway, the teen witch stamped her feet, as though kicking off snow.

"Brr," she said. "It's cold out there."

"You must have walked through my invisible snow," I said.

"Did I?" She leaned down to inspect her boots.

Zoey punched me on the arm. "Mom!"

"What? She needs to be less gullible," I said to my daughter. "Think of how naive you would be if I didn't pull your leg constantly."

Zoey looked at her best friend and said, "My *mother* thought a secondhand Pottery Barn table was a precious antique from an old castle in Europe."

My jaw dropped. "So did you," I said.

We both looked at Ambrosia.

She raised her hands. "I don't want to get caught in the middle of... whatever this is. It seems like a family matter."

"Too late," I said. "You're family now."

"What?" She'd been hanging up her jacket, and dropped it.

"You stood by my side in battle, and you hardly even flinched," I said. "Ambrosia Abernathy, you are not just a member of the coven. You are a part of my family."

Zoey grabbed her friend by the shoulders and said, gruffly, "Whether you like it or not."

I hung up Ambrosia's jacket for her. "Now go wash your hands for dinner. You smell like you've been petting monkeys."

She looked dismayed. "But I haven't been. I swear."

Zoey led her friend away. "Just ignore her. There's a lingering Capuchin smell at the front of the house, and Mom's blaming it on everyone."

"I paid them in full!" I yelled after the girls. "Plus a generous tip! They said the smell would go away on its own, but it hasn't. I might get Ruth's crew in here with the Sucko Three Thousand."

The girls weren't listening.

Next to arrive were the town's detectives, Theodore Bentley and Persephone Rose.

Bentley was dressed in his formal gray work suit, as opposed to his casual gray suit, so I knew they'd come directly from work.

"Keeping the town safe on a Sunday?" I asked.

"You don't want to know," my sister said wearily.

I put my hands on my hips. "We need to spend more time together. If you think that I don't want to know what you've been up to, you do not know me very well."

"Got it," she said, smiling as she hung up her jacket. "We've been doing paperwork related to the ongoing cleanup and decontamination at Castle Wyvern. I've been filling out 401D37 reports for days. Let me tell you all about it over dinner, since you asked!"

"She's very good at reports," Bentley said.

He stood by the door in all his layers of dark-gray wool, plus a scarf.

Persephone went ahead, joining Zoey and Ambrosia in the kitchen.

Bentley kept standing there, staring at me like he wanted something.

We hadn't seen each other much since our fight about Zoey, her father, the teen drinking, and my questionable parenting skills. Tension hulked between us, like the invisible version of something that might come through a portal and feed on pain.

"I heard about what you did for Archer," he said.

"I'd do the same for anyone who needed it," I replied with a half shrug.

"No. You wouldn't."

"Okay," I said, enunciating carefully. "I wouldn't. You're right. You got me. Happy now?"

His silver eyes burned into me. "Zara."

ANGELA PEPPER

"Don't say my name like that. Why don't you call me something cutesy? Like honey, or baby, or schmoopie? Hang around Carrot and Archer for a few hours and you'll pick up plenty of ideas."

A moment passed.

"I don't know what to do," he said.

"About what?"

"Something happened between us. I believe it may have been my fault. Regardless of how it happened, I don't like how things are right now." He paused to swallow. "I don't know how to fix it."

Something changed. I felt the invisible beast between us reduce in size.

"You can't fix me," I said.

He tilted his head. "What do you mean?"

"How should I know?" I almost laughed. "Words come out of my mouth sometimes. When I don't keep an eye on them, that's usually when things get, you know, real." I looked down and fixed my outfit, straightening my belt buckle so it was front and center. "I guess what I'm saying is you can't fix me, so maybe you should stop trying so hard."

"Do you still want me here tonight?"

I jerked my head up. "Of course I do. Why would you say that?"

"Because..." He trailed off, and the edges of his eyes crinkled. Sometimes, like now, he looked so much older than me.

I finished for him. "Because sometimes I give off the vibe I don't need you, and a man like you needs to feel needed, as opposed to simply appreciated."

"It's not just a vibe," he said. "At Castle Wyvern, you told me to take a hike at least three times."

"Only because other people needed you more. There were all sorts of injuries, and castle staff who needed to be rounded up for the mind wiping. You were needed elsewhere more than you were needed by me."

He gave me a sidelong look. "Are you sure about that?"

"No," I said, speaking quickly, so the words tumbled out without a filter. "I guess I shooed you away because I knew if you gave me so much as a hug, I was going to wimp out and turn into a quivering OCW right in front of my friends, and Ambrosia."

"What about in private?"

"What?"

He took off his wool overcoat and scarf, hung them up, then faced me with open arms.

In a low, gravelly tone, he asked, "How about now?"

"I don't need you to rescue me," I said.

He nodded.

"And I don't need your advice about Zoey as a coparent. But... I guess I don't mind if you give me the occasional intel about whatever she's up to. And I should probably consult you more, because you're a sensible adult, and I do trust your insight. I probably could use your help, now that I think about it."

He nodded again.

"That was a nice touch when you brought my aunt the bottle of water," I said.

"See? I can be handy at times," he said. "I'm not always in the way, telling you what to do. I'm not so bad."

I shook my head. "You're not bad at all."

"Thank you." His arms were still open.

"Are we making up right now? Is this happening?" I passed one hand through the air between us. No monster. No bad juju.

I looked at my handsome vampire boyfriend.

He said nothing with his mouth, and everything with his eyes.

Finally, when I couldn't hold back a second longer, I threw myself into his embrace. Then I showered him with kisses and apologies.

After a few minutes, Persephone came by to see what was taking so long. She scoffed and told us to "get a room." We would have, except the house hadn't provided one we could sneak off to without being seen.

There was a knock on the front door, and then Zinnia let herself in.

She was back to her regular size, and looked healthier than ever.

My aunt hung up her coat, took one look at us making out in the corner, wrinkled her nose, and asked, "Do you smell monkeys?"

* * *

For a full list of books in this
series and other titles by
Angela Pepper, visit

www.angelapepper.com

CPSIA information can be obtained
at www.ICGtesting.com
Printed in the USA
BVHW042005120721
611759BV00016B/289